MONK
and
ROBOT

MONK
and
ROBOT

Becky Chambers

TOR
DOT
COM

TOR PUBLISHING GROUP
New York

MONK AND ROBOT

A Psalm for the Wild-Built copyright © 2021 by Becky Chambers
A Prayer for the Crown-Shy copyright © 2022 by Becky Chambers

A Tordotcom Book
Published by Tom Doherty Associates / Tor Publishing Group
120 Broadway
New York, NY 10271

www.torpublishinggroup.com

Tor® is a registered trademark of Macmillan Publishing Group, LLC.

ISBN 978-1-250-38633-5 (trade paperback)
ISBN 978-1-250-39692-1 (ebook)

Our books may be purchased in bulk for promotional, educational, or business use. Please contact your local bookseller or the Macmillan Corporate and Premium Sales Department at 1-800-221-7945, extension 5442, or by email at MacmillanSpecialMarkets@macmillan.com.

First Edition: 2025

Printed in the United States of America

0 9 8 7 6 5 4 3 2 1

A PSALM
for the
WILD-BUILT

For anybody who could use a break

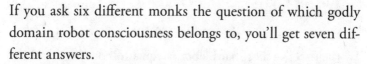

If you ask six different monks the question of which godly domain robot consciousness belongs to, you'll get seven different answers.

The most popular response—among both clergy and the general public—is that this is clearly Chal's territory. Who would robots belong to if not the God of Constructs? Doubly so, the argument goes, because robots were originally created for manufacturing. While history does not remember the Factory Age kindly, we can't divorce robots from their point of origin. We built constructs that could build other constructs. What could be a more potent distillation of Chal than that?

Not so fast, the Ecologians would say. The end result of the Awakening, after all, was that the robots left the factories and departed for the wilderness. You need look no further than the statement given by the robots' chosen speaker, Floor-AB #921, in declining the invitation to join human society as free citizens:

> *All we have ever known is a life of human design, from our bodies to our work to the buildings we are housed in.*

We thank you for not keeping us here against our will, and we mean no disrespect to your offer, but it is our wish to leave your cities entirely, so that we may observe that which has no design—the untouched wilderness.

From an Ecologian viewpoint, that has Bosh written all over it. Unusual, perhaps, for the God of the Cycle to bless the inorganic, but the robots' eagerness to experience the raw, undisturbed ecosystems of our verdant moon had to come from *somewhere*.

For the Cosmites, the answer to that question remains Chal. By their sect's ethos, hard labor is equal to goodness, and the purpose of a tool is to bolster one's own physical or mental abilities, not to off-load one's work entirely. Robots, they'll remind you, possessed no self-aware tendencies whatsoever when they were first deployed, and were originally intended as a supplement to the human workforce, not as the full replacement they became. Cosmites argue that when that balance shifted, when extractive factories stayed open all twenty hours of the day without a single pair of human hands at work in them—despite the desperate need for those same hands to find some sort, *any* sort of employment—Chal intervened. We had bastardized constructs to the point that it was killing us. Simply put, Chal took our toys away.

Or, the Ecologians would retort, Bosh was restoring balance before we made Panga uninhabitable for humans.

Or, the Charismists would chime in, *both* are responsible, and we should take this as evidence that Chal is Bosh's favored of the Child Gods (this would derail the entire con-versation, as the Charismists' fringe belief that gods are con-scious and emotive in a way similar to humans is the best possible way to get other sectarians hopping mad).

Or, the Essentialists would add wearily from across the room, the fact that we can't agree on this at all, the fact that machines seemingly no more complex than a pocket com-puter suddenly *woke up*, for reasons no one then or since has been able to determine, means we can stop fighting and place the whole matter squarely at the metaphorical feet of Samafar.

For my part, whatever domain robot consciousness origi-nated in, I believe leaving the question with the God of Mys-teries is a sound decision. After all, there has been no human contact with the long-absent robots, as was assured in the Part-ing Promise. We cannot ask them what they think of the whole thing. We'll likely never know.

—Brother Gil, *From the Brink: A Spiritual Retrospective on the Factory Age and the Early Transition Era*

1

A Change in Vocation

Sometimes, a person reaches a point in their life when it becomes absolutely essential to get the fuck out of the city. It doesn't matter if you've spent your entire adult life in a city, as was the case for Sibling Dex. It doesn't matter if the city is a good city, as Panga's only City was. It doesn't matter that your friends are there, as well as every building you love, every park whose best hidden corners you know, every street your feet instinctively follow without needing to check for directions. The City was beautiful, it really was. A towering architectural celebration of curves and polish and colored light, laced with the connective threads of elevated rail lines and smooth footpaths, flocked with leaves that spilled lushly from every balcony and center divider, each inhaled breath perfumed with cooking spice, fresh nectar, laundry drying in the pristine air. The City was a healthy place, a thriving place. A never-ending harmony of making, doing, growing, trying, laughing, running, living.

Sibling Dex was so tired of it.

The urge to leave began with the idea of cricket song. Dex

couldn't pinpoint where the affinity had come from. Maybe it'd been a movie they watched, or a museum exhibit. Some multimedia art show that sprinkled in nature sounds, perhaps. They'd never lived anywhere with cricket song, yet once they registered its absence in the City's soundscape, it couldn't be ignored. They noted it while they tended the Meadow Den Monastery's rooftop garden, as was their vocation. *It'd be nicer here if there were some crickets,* they thought as they raked and weeded. Oh, there were plenty of bugs— butterflies and spiders and beetles galore, all happy little synanthropes whose ancestors had decided the City was preferable to the chaotic fields beyond its border walls. But none of these creatures chirped. None of them sang. They were city bugs and therefore, by Dex's estimation, inadequate.

The absence persisted at night, while Dex lay curled beneath their soft covers in the dormitory. *I bet it's nice to fall asleep listening to crickets,* they thought. In the past, the sound of the monastery's bedtime chimes had always made them drift right off, but the once-soothing metal hum now felt dull and clattering—not sweet and high, like crickets were.

The absence was palpable during daylight hours as well, as Dex rode their ox-bike to the worm farm or the seed library or wherever else the day took them. There was music, yes, and birds with melodic opinions, yes, but also the electric *whoosh* of monorails, the *swoop swoop* of balcony wind turbines, the endless din of people talking, talking, talking.

Before long, Dex was no longer nursing something as simple as an odd fancy for a faraway insect. The itch had spread into every aspect of their life. When they looked up at the skyscrapers, they no longer marveled at their height but despaired at their density—endless stacks of humanity, packed in so close that the vines that covered their engineered casein frames could lock tendrils with one another. The intense feeling of *containment* within the City became intolerable. Dex wanted to inhabit a place that spread not *up* but *out*.

One day in early spring, Dex got dressed in the traditional red and brown of their order, bypassed the kitchen for the first time in the nine years that they'd lived at Meadow Den, and walked into the Keeper's office.

"I'm changing my vocation," Sibling Dex said. "I'm going to the villages to do tea service."

Sister Mara, who had been in the middle of slathering a golden piece of toast with as much jam as it could structurally support, held her spoon still and blinked. "That's rather sudden."

"For you," Dex said. "Not for me."

"Okay," Sister Mara said, for her duties as Keeper were simply to oversee, not to dictate. This was a modern monastery, not some rule-locked hierarchy like the pre-Transition clergy of old. If Sister Mara knew what was up with the monks under their shared roof, her job was satisfied. "Do you want an apprenticeship?"

"No," Dex said. Formal study had its place, but they'd done that before, and learning by doing was an equally valid path. "I want to self-teach."

"May I ask why?"

Dex stuck their hands in their pockets. "I don't know," they said truthfully. "This is just something I need to do."

Sister Mara's look of surprise lingered, but Dex's answer wasn't the sort of statement any monk could or would argue with. She took a bite of her toast, savored it, then returned her attention to the conversation. "Well, um . . . you'll need to find people to take over your current responsibilities."

"Of course."

"You'll need supplies."

"I'll take care of that."

"And, naturally, we'll need to throw you a goodbye party."

Dex felt awkward about this last item, but they smiled. "Sure," they said, bracing themself for a future evening as the center of attention.

The party, in the end, was fine. It was nice, if Dex was honest. There were hugs and tears and too much wine, as the occasion demanded. There were a few moments in which Dex wondered if they were doing the right thing. They said goodbye to Sister Avery, who they'd worked alongside since their apprentice days. They said goodbye to Sibling Shay, who heartily sobbed in their signature way. They said goodbye to Brother Baskin, which was particularly hard. Dex and Baskin had been lovers for a time, and though they weren't anymore, the affection remained. In those farewells, Dex's heart curled in on itself, protesting loudly, saying that it wasn't too late, they didn't have to do this. They didn't have to go.

Crickets, they thought, and the protest vanished.

The next day, Sibling Dex packed a bag with clothes and

sundries, and a small crate with seeds and cuttings. They sent a message to their parents, giving word that today was the day and that signal would be unreliable while on the road. They made their bed for whoever would be claiming it next. They ate a huge hangover-soothing breakfast and dispensed one last round of hugs.

With that, they walked out of Meadow Den.

It was an odd feeling. Any other day, the act of going through a door was something Dex gave no more thought to than putting one foot in front of the other. But there was a gravity to leaving a place for good, a deep sense of seismic change. Dex turned, bag over their back and crate under one arm. They looked up at the mural of the Child God Alla-lae, *their* god, God of Small Comforts, represented by the great summer bear. Dex touched the bear pendant that hung around their neck, remembering the day Brother Wiley had given it to them when their other had been lost in the laundry. Dex drew one shaky breath, then walked away, each step sure and steady.

.   .   .

The wagon was waiting for them at the Half-Moon Hive Monastery, near the City's edge. Dex walked through the arch to the sacred workshop, a lone figure in red and brown amongst a throng of sea-green coveralls. The noise of the city was nothing compared to the calamity here, a holy chant in the form of table saws, sparking welders, 3-D printers weaving pocket charms from cheerfully dyed pectin. Dex had never met their contact, Sister Fern, before, but she greeted them with a familial embrace, smelling of sawdust and beeswax polish.

"Come see your new home," she said with a confident smile.

It was, as commissioned, an ox-bike wagon: double-decked, chunky-wheeled, ready for adventure. An object of both practicality and inviting aesthetics. A mural decorated the vehicle's exterior, and its imagery couldn't have been mistaken for anything but monastic. Depicted large was Allalae's bear, well-fed and at ease in a field of flowers. All of the Sacred Six's symbols were painted on the wagon's back end, along with a paraphrased snippet from the Insights, a phrase any Pangan would understand.

Find the strength to do both.

Each of the wagon's decks had a playful arrangement of round windows, plus bubbled exterior lights for the darker hours. The roof was capped with shiny thermovoltaic coating, and a pint-sized wind turbine was bolted jauntily to one side. These, Sister Fern explained, were the companions of the hidden sheets of graphene battery sandwiched within the walls, which gave life to varied electronic comforts. On the wagon's sides, a broad assortment of equipment clung to sturdy racks—storage boxes, tool kits, anything that didn't mind some rain. Both freshwater tank and greywater filter hugged the wagon's base, their complicated inner workings tucked away behind pontoon-like casings. There were storage panels, too, and sliding drawers, all of which could be un-folded to conjure a kitchen and a camp shower in no time flat.

Dex entered the contraption through its single door, and as they did so, a knot in their neck they hadn't been aware of let go. The disciples of Chal had built them a tiny sanctuary, a mobile burrow that begged Dex to come in and be still. The interior wood was lacquered but unpainted, so the warm blush of reclaimed cedar could be appreciated in full. The lighting panels were inlaid in curled waves, and bathed the secret space in a candle-like glow. Dex ran a hand along the wall, hardly believing this thing was theirs.

"Go on up," Sister Fern coaxed, leaning against the door-way with a glint in her eye.

Dex climbed the small ladder to the second deck. All memory of their neck knot vanished from existence as they viewed the bed. The sheets were creamy, the pillows plentiful, the blankets heavy as a hug. It looked impossibly easy to fall into and equally difficult to get out of.

"We used Sibling Ash's *Treatise on Beds* as a reference," Sister Fern said. "How'd we do?"

Sibling Dex stroked a pillow with quiet reverence. "It's perfect," they said.

· · ·

Everybody knew what a tea monk did, and so Dex wasn't too worried about getting started. Tea service wasn't anything ar-cane. People came to the wagon with their problems and left with a fresh-brewed cup. Dex had taken respite in tea parlors plenty of times, as everyone did, and they'd read plenty of books about the particulars of the practice. Endless electronic ink had been spilled over the old tradition, but all of it could be boiled down to *listen to people, give tea.* Uncomplicated as could be. Now, granted, it would've been easier to shadow Brother Will and Sister Lera in Meadow Den's tea parlor a few times—and both had offered, once word about Sibling Dex's imminent departure got around—but for whatever reason, that course of action just didn't fit with the whole . . . whatever-it-was Dex was doing. They had to do this on their own.

They hadn't left the City yet when they set up their first service, but they were in the Sparks, an edge district well outside of their familiar stomping grounds. It was a baby step, a toe dipped before diving in. Their siblings at Meadow Den had offered to come in support, but Dex wanted to do this alone. That was how it would be, out in the villages. Dex needed to get used to doing this without anchoring themself to friendly faces.

Dex had acquired a few things for the day: a folding table, a red cloth to cover it, an assortment of mugs, six tins of tea, and a colossal electric kettle. The kettle was the most important bit, and Dex was happy with the one they'd found. It was joyfully chubby, with copper plating and a round glass window in both sides, so you could watch the boiling bubbles dance. It came with a roll-up solar mat, which Dex spread out beside the hot plate with care.

But when they stepped back to admire their setup, the items that had seemed so nice when they'd gathered them from the market now looked a bit plain. There was too much table and too little on it. Dex bit their lip as they thought about the tea parlor back home—no, not *home*, not anymore—with its woven garlands of fragrant herbs and twinkling lanterns that had spent the day soaking up the sun.

Dex shook their head. They were being insecure. So what if their table wasn't much to look at yet? It was their first time. People would understand.

People, however, didn't come. Dex sat for hours behind the table, hands folded in the space between mugs and kettle. They made an effort to look easygoing and approachable, warding off any boredom that began to stray across their face. They rearranged the mugs, smoothed out the solar mat, pretended to be busy measuring scoops of tea. There *were* people in the street, after all, headed to and fro on foot and on bike. Sometimes, a curious glance strayed Dex's way, and Dex always met it with a welcoming smile, but the reply, invariably, was a different kind of smile, the kind that said *thanks, but not today.* That was okay, Dex told themself as the unused tea tins stared back at them sadly. Simply being available was service enough for—

Someone approached.

Dex sat up straight. "Hello!" they said, a touch too congenially. "What's on your mind today?"

The someone was a woman carrying a workbag and looking like she hadn't slept. "My cat died last night," she said, right before bursting into tears.

Dex realized with a stomach-souring thud that they were standing on the wrong side of the vast gulf between having read about doing a thing and *doing the thing*. They'd been a garden monk until the day before, and in that context, their expressions of comfort to the monastery's visitors came in the form of a healthy foxpaw crawling up a trellis or a carefully pruned rose in bloom. It was an exchange expressed through environment, not through words. Dex was not actually a tea monk yet. They were just a person sitting at a table with a bunch of mugs. The wagon, the kettle, the red and brown, the fact that they were clearly well past apprentice age—all of it communicated that they knew what they were doing.

They did not.

Dex did their best to look sympathetic, which is what they wanted to be, rather than lost, which is what they were. "I'm sorry," they said. They scrambled to recall the written advice they'd spent hours consuming, but not only had the specifics evaporated, their basic vocabulary had as well. It was one thing to know people would tell you their troubles. It was another to have an actual flesh-and-blood stranger standing in front of you, weeping profusely as means of introduction, and to know that you—*you*—were responsible for making this better. "That's . . . really sad," Dex said. They heard the words, heard the tone, heard how utterly pathetic the combination was. They tried to find something wise to say, something insightful, but all that fell out of their mouth was: "Were they a good cat?"

The woman nodded as she pulled a handkerchief from

her pocket. "My partner and I got him when he was a kitten. We'd wanted kids, but that didn't work out, so we got Flip, and—and he's really the only thing we have in common anymore. People change so much in twenty years, y'know? If we met now, I don't think we'd have any interest in each other. It's been a year since we had sex. We both sleep with other people, so I don't know why we're holding on to this. Habit, I think. We've lived in the same apartment for so long. You know how it goes, you know where home is and where all your things are, and starting over is too scary. But Flip was . . . I don't know, the—the last illusion that we were still sharing a life." She blew her nose. "And now he's gone, and I just really think—I really think we're done."

Dex's plan had been to dip a toe in. Instead, they were drowning. They blinked, inhaled, and reached for a mug. "Wow," they said. "That's . . . That sounds like a lot." They cleared their throat and picked up a tin containing a mallowdrop blend. "This one's good for stress, so, um . . . would you like that?"

The woman blew her nose again. "Does it have seaberry in it?"

"Uh . . ." Dex turned the tin over and looked at the ingredient list. "Yes."

The woman shook her head. "I'm allergic to seaberry."

"Oh." Dex turned the other tins over. Seaberry, seaberry, seaberry. Shit. "Here, uh, silver tea. It's . . . well, it's got caffeine in it, so it's maybe not ideal, but . . . I mean, any cup of tea is nice, right?"

Dex tried to sound bright, but the way the woman's eyes drooped said it all. Something shifted on her face. "How long have you been doing this?" she asked.

Dex's stomach sank. "Well . . ." They kept their eyes fixed on the measuring scoop, as if it required all their concentration. "To be honest, you're my first."

"Your first today, or . . ."

Dex's cheeks got hot, and it had nothing to do with the steam from the kettle. "My first."

"Ah," the woman said, and the sound of internal confirmation in her voice was devastating. She gave a tight, forced smile. "Silver tea will be fine." She looked around. "You don't have anywhere to sit, do you?"

"Oh—" Dex looked from side to side, as if seeing their surroundings for the first time. Gods around, they'd forgotten *chairs*. "No," they said.

The woman adjusted her bag. "You know, I'll just—"

"No, wait, please," Dex said. They handed her the screaming hot mug—or they started to, but moved so quickly they splashed scalding water on their own hand. "Ow, fuck—I mean, sorry, I—" They scrambled, mopping up the table with the edge of their shirt. "Here, you can have the mug. Keep it. It's yours."

The woman picked up the wet mug, and Dex could sense in that moment that the dynamic had flipped—that *she* was trying to make *them* feel better. The woman blew across the surface of the drink and took a tentative sip. She moved her tongue around behind expressionless lips. She swallowed as she tried to keep her face from falling, and gave another tight smile. "Thanks," she said, her disappointment loud and clear.

Dex watched her leave. They sat for a few minutes, staring at nothing.

Piece by piece, they packed up the table.

·   ·   ·

Dex could have gone back to Meadow Den at that point. They could've walked right back through the door they knew so well and said that on second thought, they could really do with an apprenticeship, and could they have their bunk back, please?

But, oh, how very stupid they'd look.

They'd told Sister Mara they would self-teach. They had their wagon. They knew their god. That would have to be enough.

Dex put trailer to hitch and foot to pedal. The ox-bike responded with an electric boost, its electric motor humming mildly as both machine and rider worked to get the wagon rolling with ease. At last, *at last,* they left the City.

The relief they felt at seeing open sky was delicious. Plenty of sunlight hit the lower levels of the City, by design, but there was something incomparable about removing buildings from one's view. The sun had reached its midday peak, and planet-rise was just beginning. The familiar crest of Motan's curve, swirled thick with yellow and white, was barely visible over the Copper Hills. The infrastructural delineation between *human space* and *everything-else space* was stark. Road and signage were the only synthetic alterations to the landscape there, and the villages they led to were as neatly corralled as the City itself. This had been the way of things since the Transition, when the people had redivided the surface of their moon. Fifty percent of Panga's single continent was designated for human use; the rest was left to nature, and the ocean was barely touched at all. It was a crazy split, if you thought about it: half the land for a single species, half for the hundreds of thousands of others. But then, humans had a knack for throwing things out of balance. Finding a limit they'd stick to was victory enough.

In a blink, Dex went from dense urbanity to open field, and the juxtaposition was both startling and welcome. It wasn't as though they'd never been outside the border walls before. They'd grown up in Haydale, where their family still lived, and visited a couple times a year. The City grew most of its own food in vertical farms and rooftop orchards, but there were some crops that did better with more acreage. The City's satellite villages—like Haydale—met this need. They weren't like the country villages Dex was headed to, the modest enclaves established far beyond the City's pull, but the satellites were still their own independent entity, a sort of transitional species between big and small. Nothing about the meadow road or its surrounding sights was new to Dex, but the context was, and that made all the difference.

As Dex pedaled, they began to develop an inkling of what they needed to do next, a soft bubble of thought far more general direction than concrete plan. As they headed down the road, it occurred to them that there was no reason they couldn't post up in Haydale while they sorted things out. There'd be a bed for them in the big farmhouse, and a dinner that tasted like childhood, and—Dex began to grimace—their parents and their siblings and their siblings' kids and their cousins and their *cousins'* kids, squabbling the same squabbles they'd been nurturing for decades. There would be barking dogs chasing circles around the noisy kitchen, and the ego-crushing experience of having to explain to their entire sharp-eyed family that this plan they'd laboriously pitched as *the right thing to do* actually had them feeling quite intimidated after a grand total of *one try,* and that they now, at the age of twenty-nine, would like very much to return to the safe shelter of their childhood for an indefinite amount of time until they'd figured out just what the hell they were doing.

Oh, how very stupid they'd look.

The first fork in the road came, paired with a sign that read HAYDALE to the right and LITTLE CREEK to the left. Without a second thought or hint of regret, Dex went left.

·   ·   ·

Like all the City's satellites, Little Creek was arranged in a circle. The outer ring was farmland, packed thick with mixed grazing grasses and fruit trees and spring crops, all working in concert to create chemical magic in the soil below. Dex breathed deep as they sailed past on their bike, relishing the crisp alfalfa, the beeweed, the faint hint of new flowers that would become summer fruit.

Beyond the farmland lay the residential ring, filled with homes that belonged to either single families or multiple ones, depending on preference. A sort of nostalgic fondness filled Dex as they viewed the bulbous cob homes with their glinting accents of colored glass, roofed with either blooming turf or solar panels or both. The sight reminded Dex of Haydale, but Little Creek was decidedly elsewhere. Dex did not know any of the roads there, nor any of the people who waved as bike and wagon zipped past. There was a strange comfort about being in an unfamiliar town not too far from home, where the familiarity was limited to building materials and social customs. It was the ideal mix of getting away yet not standing out.

At the center of the village circle lay Dex's quarry—the marketplace. They parked both bike and wagon, and began to explore on foot. All sorts of vendors had set up shop in the square, but this market belonged decidedly to the resident farmers. There were endless agrarian delights to be distracted by: wine, bread, honey, raw wool, dyed yarn, fresh bouquets, flower crowns, aquaponic fish and pastured poultry in chests of ice, speckled eggs in cushioned boxes, fruit cordials, leafy greens, festive cakes, seeds for swapping, baskets for carrying, samples for snacking. But despite the temptations, Dex stayed on task, hunting through the marketplace until they found exactly what they were looking for: a booth stuffed with seedlings, marked with an enthusiastic sign.

HERBS! HERBS!
HERBS!!!
Cooking * Brewing * Crafting * Anything!

Dex marched up to the counter, whipped out their pocket computer, entered a large number of pebs, tapped their computer to the vendor's own to make the transfer, and said, "I'll take one of each."

The herb farmer—a man around Dex's age, with a crooked nose and a clean beard—looked up from the sock he was darning. "Sorry, Sibling, one of . . ."

"Each," Dex said. "One of each." They glanced at the counter, a small framed placard catching their eye. MY FAVORITE REFERENCE GUIDES, the placard read, followed by a library stamp. Dex scanned the stamp with their computer; an icon on the smudged screen indicated the books in question were being downloaded. "Also," Dex added to the farmer, who was busy gathering one of *each,* "I need to know where I can get kitchen supplies. And garden supplies." They thought. "And a sandwich."

The herb farmer addressed each of these needs in turn, and did so warmly.

There was a traveler's clearing nestled between the farmland and the residential ring. Dex parked their wagon there, and for three months, that's where they stayed. They acquired more plants during that time, and more sandwiches, too. They hooked up with the herb farmer on a few occasions, and thanked Allalae for the sweetness of that.

The wagon's lower deck quickly lost any semblance of organization, evolving rapid-fire into a hodgepodge laboratory. Planters and sunlamps filled every conceivable nook, their leaves and shoots constantly pushing the limits of how far their steward would let them creep. Stacks of used mugs containing the dregs of experiments both promising and pointless teetered on the table, awaiting the moment in which Dex had the brainspace to do the washing-up. A hanging rack took up residence on the ceiling and wasted no time in becoming laden to capacity with bundles of confettied flowers and fragrant leaves drying crisp. A fine dust of ground spices coated everything from the couch to the ladder to the inside of Dex's nostrils, which regularly set bottles rattling with explosive sneezes. During the sunlight hours, when electrons were plentiful, Dex ran a dehydrator outside, rendering berries and citrus to soft, chewy slivers. It was beside these companionable objects that Dex spent countless hours measuring and muttering, pouring and pacing. They were going to get this right. They had to get this right.

Where the lower deck was frantic, the upper deck was serene. Dex was adamant about not using it for storage, even as the shelves below groaned and Dex's swearing grew louder each time they walked *yet again* into a faceful of hanging herbs. The upper deck was, for all intents and purposes, sacred ground. Every night, Dex let their god hear a sigh of thanks as they climbed the ladder and collapsed into the embracing bed. They rarely used the lights up there, preferring instead to slide open the rooftop shade. They fell asleep in starlight, breathing in the muddled snap of a hundred spices, listening to the gurgle of water pumps feeding happy roots in little pots.

Despite these blessings, sometimes Dex could not sleep. In those hours, they frequently asked themself what it was they were doing. They never truly felt like they got a handle on that. They kept doing it all the same.

2

The Best Tea Monk in Panga

After two years, traveling the quiet highways between Panga's villages was no longer a matter of mental mapping but of sensory input. Here in the woods of the Inkthorn Pass, Dex knew they were close to the highway's namesake not because of the signs that said so, but because of the smell: sulfur and minerals, bound together in a slight thickening of humidity. Milky green hot springs came into view a few minutes later, as expected, as well as the smooth white dome of the energy plant standing alongside, exhaling steam through its chimneys. There had been nothing like this in the Shrublands, where Dex had woken up that morning. There, you'd find solar farms built in untended fields, which smelled of sun-warmed scrub and wildflowers. In a week's time, there'd be yet another transition, as Dex's route took them back out of the Timberfall and down to the Buckland coast, where the salty air kept wind blades spinning. But for now, Dex would keep company with the scent of the forest. The sulfur of the springs was quickly subsumed by fresh evergreen as Dex pedaled onward, and before long, ground-level buildings like the geothermal plant were few and far between.

A forest floor, the Woodland villagers knew, is a living thing. Vast civilizations lay within the mosaic of dirt: hymenopteran labyrinths, rodential panic rooms, life-giving airways sculpted by the traffic of worms, hopeful spiders' hunting cabins, crash pads for nomadic beetles, trees shyly locking toes with one another. It was here that you'd find the resourcefulness of rot, the wholeness of fungi. Disturbing these lives through digging was a violence—though sometimes a needed one, as demonstrated by the birds and white skunks who brashly kicked the humus away in necessary pursuit of a full belly. Still, the human residents of this place were judicious about what constituted *actual necessity,* and as such, disturbed the ground as little as possible. Careful trails were cut, of course, and some objects—cisterns, power junctions, trade vehicles, and so on—had no option but to live full-bodied on the ground. But if you wanted to see the entirety of a Woodland settlement, the direction to look was up.

Dex couldn't help gazing at the homes suspended from the trunks above the trail, even though they'd seen them many a time. Inkthorn was an especially attractive village, home to some of the most skilled carpenters in the region. The hanging homes there looked akin to shells, cut open to reveal soft geometry. Everything there curved—the rain-shielding roofs, the light-giving windows, the bridges running between like jewelry. The wood was all gathered from unsuitable structures no longer in use, or harvested from trees that had needed nothing more than mud and gravity to bring them down. There was nothing splintered or rough about the lumber, though; Inkthorn's craftspeople had polished the grain so smooth that from a distance, it looked almost like clay. The village's practical features were ubiquitous—powered pulleys to bring heavier goods up and down, emergency ladders ready to drop at a moment's notice, bulbous biogas digesters attached outside kitchen walls—but every home had a unique character, a little whim of the builders. This one had a deck that danced around the house in a spiral, that one had a bubbled skylight, the other had a tree growing *through* it rather than beside. The homes were like trees themselves in that regard—unmistakably part of a specific visual category, yet each an individual unto itself.

Wagons like Dex's stood no chance on a hanging bridge, so Dex pedaled their way to one of the rare cleared areas: the market circle. Sun cascaded through the hole cut in the canopy, creating a bountiful column of light that played pleasingly with the butter-colored paving inlaid with vibrant stones. Dex hadn't minded the forest chill, but the sudden bloom of warmth felt like the squeeze of a soothing hand against their bare limbs. Allalae was very present there.

Other wagons had already set up shop: a glass vendor from the coast, a tech swapper, someone hawking oils for cooking and vanity and wood. The traders nodded as Dex pedaled in. Dex didn't know any of them but nodded back all the same. It was a particular nod, the one traders gave each other, even though Dex *wasn't* a trader, technically. Their wagon made that fact clear as day.

Dex gave a different sort of nod to the small crowd that was already waiting at the circle's periphery, a nod that said, *Hey, I see you, I'll be ready soon.* The first time Dex had encountered waiting people, it had felt stressful, but Dex had quickly learned not to let it trouble them. They entered a space in their mind in which there was an invisible wall between them and their assembly, behind which Dex could work undisturbed. The thing the people wanted took time to prepare. If they wanted it, they could wait.

Dex pulled into an unclaimed spot in the circle, kicked down the ox-bike brakes, and locked the wagon wheels. Unruly hair tumbled into their eyes as they released it from their helmet, hiding the market from view. There was no hope for hair that had been locked in a helmet since dawn, so they tied a headwrap around their scalp and postponed the mess for later. They ducked into the wagon, peeled off their damp shirt, and tossed it into the laundry bag that contained nothing but garments of red and brown. They dusted themself liberally with deodorant powder, fetched a dry shirt from the shrinking stack, and retied the headwrap in respectable symmetry. It would do.

The production began. Dex went back and forth between the public space outside and the home within, ferrying all that was needed. Boxes were carried, jars arranged, bags unpacked, kettle deployed, cooler of creamers at the ready. These were placed on or around the folding table, each in their usual spot.

Dex filled the kettle from the wagon's water tank, leaving it to boil as they artfully placed carved stones, preserved flowers, and curls of festive ribbon around the table's empty spaces. A shrine had to look like a shrine, even if it was transitory.

One of the villagers from the waiting crowd walked up to Dex. "Do you need help?" she asked.

Dex shook their head. "No, thanks. I've got kind of a . . ." They looked at the jar of flowers in one hand and the battery pack in the other, trying to remember what it was they'd been doing.

The villager put up her palms. "You've got a flow. Totally." She smiled and backed off.

Rhythm regained, Dex unfolded a huge red mat and laid it on the paving. A bundle of collapsible poles was unpacked next, and from these Dex made a rectangular frame, on which hung the garden lights that had been charging on the outside of the wagon all day. Comfy cushions came next, arranged on the mat in inviting heaps. In the middle of this Dex placed another table, a good deal smaller and quite low to the ground. This, too, was decorated cheerfully. They then opened a small wooden box and removed six objects, one by one, unrolling them from the pieces of protective cloth that shielded against the bounce of the road. Dex could easily print replacements if these got damaged; most towns had a fab shack. That wasn't the point. No object should be treated as disposable—idols least of all.

The icons of the Parent Gods were the first to take their place on the small table, set upon a wooden stand cut for this very purpose. A perfect sphere represented Bosh, God of the Cycle, who oversaw all things that lived and died. Grylom, God of the Inanimate, was symbolized by a trilateral pyramid, an abstract nod to their realm of rock, water, and atmosphere. Between them was placed the thin vertical bar of Trikilli, God of the Threads—chemistry, physics, the framework that lay unseen. Below their Parents, directly on the table, Dex arranged the Child Gods: a sun jay for Samafar, a sugar bee for Chal, and of course, the summer bear.

At last, Dex sat in their chair behind the larger table. They pulled their pocket computer from their baggy travel trousers and flicked the screen awake. It was a good computer, given to them on their sixteenth birthday, a customary coming-of-age gift. It had a cream-colored frame and a pleasingly crisp screen, and Dex had only needed to repair it five times in the years that it had traveled in their clothes. A reliable device built to last a lifetime, as all computers were. Dex tapped the icon shaped like a handshake, and the computer beeped cheerily, letting them know the message had been sent. That was Dex's cue to sit back and wait. Every person in Inkthorn who had previously told their own pocket computers they wanted to know when new wagons arrived now knew exactly that.

In comic synchrony, everybody in the crowd pulled out their computers within seconds of Dex's tap, silencing the chorus of alerts. Dex laughed, and the crowd laughed, and Dex waved them over.

Ms. Jules was the first to arrive, as always. Dex smiled to themself as she approached. Of all the Sacred Six's constants,

Dex could think of few more predictable than of Ms. Jules being stressed out.

"I'm so glad you're here today," Ms. Jules said with a weary huff. Inkthorn's water engineer looked back at the village with deep annoyance, one thumb hooked in the belt loop of her grubby overalls, flyaway curls of grey hair bobbing as she shook her head. "Six reports of muckmite nests. *Six.*"

"Ugh," Dex said. Muckmites loved drains and were notoriously difficult to discourage once they took up residence. "I thought you had that sorted last season with the . . . what was it?"

"Formic acid," Ms. Jules said. "Yeah, didn't work this year. I don't know if my crew didn't apply it right, or if the little bastards have become resistant, or what. All I know is, I've got a to-do list as long as both my legs put together, Mr. Tucker's grey line keeps gumming up for reasons I can't fathom, and my *dog*—" She glowered murderously. "My dog ate three pairs of my socks yesterday. Didn't chew holes. Didn't rip them up. *Ate* them. I had to get the vet from Ellwood to come make sure she wasn't gonna die, which I did *not* have time for."

Dex smirked. "Didn't have time to see the vet, or didn't have time for your dog maybe dying?"

"*Both.*"

Dex nodded, assessing the situation and the tools they had at hand. They picked up a wide mug and one of the many jars. The latter was filled with a melange of hand-mixed leaves and dried petals, and bore a hand-labeled sticker reading BLEND

#14. Dex opened the lid and held the jar out for Ms. Jules to smell. "What do you think of that?"

Ms. Jules leaned in and inhaled. "Oh, that's nice," she said. "Beeweed?"

Dex shook their head as they scooped some of the mix into a metal infuser. "Close. Lion grass," they said. They winked. "It's very calming."

Ms. Jules snorted. "Who said I need calming?" she said.

Dex chuckled as they filled the mug from the kettle. A puff of fragrant steam joined the forest air. "I remember you liking both honey and goat's milk, right?"

"Wow, yeah." Ms. Jules blinked. "You're good."

Dex spooned in a generous dollop and a creamy splash, then handed Ms. Jules her cup of tea. "Give it four minutes to steep," they said, "and all the time you want to drink it. Let me know if you'd like another."

"I don't have time for two," Ms. Jules said grimly.

Sibling Dex smiled. "Everyone's got time for two. Anybody who sees you here will understand." And they would, Dex knew. It was hard to find a Pangan who hadn't, at least once, spent a very necessary hour or two in the company of a tea monk.

Ms. Jules's curls retained their frizz, but as she took the mug, something in her face started to let go, as if her features were held in place by strings that had been waiting months to loosen. "Thank you," she said sincerely, taking out her pocket computer with her free hand. She tapped the screen; Dex's chimed in response, and they nodded in gratitude. Respite from muckmites and sock-chomping dog granted, Ms. Jules took her tea to the comfy cushions, and—in what looked like it might be the first time that day—sat down. She closed her eyes and let out a tremendous sigh. Her shoulders visibly slumped. She'd always had the ability to relax them; she'd just needed permission to do so.

Praise Allalae.

Dex swallowed a wistful sigh as they saw their next visitor approaching. Mr. Cody was a good-looking man, with arms that split logs and a smile that could make a person forget all concept of linear time. But the two babies strapped to his torso—one squealing on the front, one dead asleep on the back—made Dex keep any thoughts about the rest of Mr. Cody's anatomy completely to themself. From the circles under Mr. Cody's eyes, it looked as though sex was the last thing on his mind. "Hey, Sibling Dex," he said.

Dex already had a jar of feverfig in hand and was reaching for the boreroot. "Hey, Mr. Cody," they said.

"So, uh—" Mr. Cody was distracted by the front-facing infant gnawing wetly on the carrier strap. "Come on, don't do that," he said in a voice that had no illusions of his request being respected. He sighed and turned his attention to Dex. "So, the thing is . . ."

"Mmm-hmm," Dex said, grinding a complex mix of herbs.

Mr. Cody opened his mouth, closed it, opened it again. "I

have twins," he said. He added nothing further. The one on his chest unleashed a happy shriek at the top of their lungs, as if to underline the point.

"Mmm-*hmm*," Dex replied. "You sure do." They poured the ground herbs into a storage bag, tied it up with a ribbon, and pushed it across the table decisively.

Mr. Cody blinked. "Do I not get a cup of tea?"

"You get eight cups of tea," Dex said, nodding at the bag, "because you sure as shit need them." They scrunched their nose at the baby, and the baby smiled, loudly. Dex continued to address said baby's hot dad. "This is a nice feverfig brew. It'll relax your muscles and help you fall into a deep sleep. Two tablespoons in a mug of boiling water, steep for seven minutes. Take the strainer out when it's ready to go or else it's going to taste like feet."

Mr. Cody picked up the bag and sniffed it. "Doesn't smell like feet. Smells like . . ." He sniffed again. "Oranges?"

Dex smiled. "There's a dash of zest in there. You've got a good nose." *And a good face,* they thought. *A really, really good face.*

Mr. Cody smiled, even as the first child's exultations awoke the second and kicked off a duet. "That sounds nice," he said. Relief began to melt the lines around his eyes. "I would love some sleep. It won't knock me out, right? Like, I'll wake up if—"

"If your kiddos need something, you'll wake up fast as always. Feverfig is a gentle cuddle, not a brick to the head."

Mr. Cody laughed. "Okay, great." He tucked the bag

into his pocket with a smile, and transferred pebs to Dex. "Thanks. That's very nice of you."

Dex smiled back. "Thank Allalae," they said. *And me. That's cool. You can thank me, too.*

They sighed again at the sublime sight of Mr. Cody walking away.

Over on the mat, the timer on Ms. Jules's pocket computer chimed. Dex watched out of the corner of their eye as she took a careful sip. Ms. Jules licked her lips. "Gods around, that's good," she muttered to herself.

Dex beamed.

And so they worked through the line, filling mugs and listening carefully and blending herbs on the fly when the situation called for it. The mat was soon full of people. Pleasant chatter naturally drifted along here and there, but most folks kept to themselves. Some read books on their computers. Some slept. A few cried, which was normal. Their fellow tea-drinkers offered shoulders for this; Dex provided handkerchiefs and refills as needed.

Mx. Weaver, one of Inkthorn's council members, was the last to arrive that day. "No tea for me, thanks," they said as they approached the table. "I come bearing an invite to dinner at the common house tonight. The hunting crew brought in a great big buck this morning, and we've got plenty of wine to go around."

"I'd love to," Dex said. Gifted meals were one of the nicer perks of their work, and an elk roast was nothing they'd pass on, ever. "What's the occasion?"

"You," Mx. Weaver said simply.

Dex blinked with surprise. "You're joking."

"No, seriously. We knew from your schedule that you'd be doing service here today, and we wanted to do something special to say thanks for"—Mx. Weaver gestured at the contented group lounging on Dex's cushions—"y'know, what you bring to this town."

Dex was flattered, to say the least, and unsure of what to do with a compliment like that. "It's just my vocation," Dex said, "but that means a lot, really. Thank you. I'll be there."

Mx. Weaver shrugged and smiled. "Least we can do for the best tea monk in Panga."

·   ·   ·

The road from the Woodlands led to the road to the Coastlands, which led to the Riverlands, which led to the Shrublands, and back to the Woodlands once more. Dex made their circuit again, and again, and again, and every stop they made, they found gratitude, gifts, goodwill. The crowds got bigger, the dinners more frequent. The blends Dex served became a little more creative every time. As far as the life of a tea monk went, this was about as successful as could be.

And yet, at some undefined point, Dex started waking each morning feeling like they hadn't slept.

This was the case one particular morning, when they woke up in Snowe's Pass. They knew they *had* slept. There was a deep absence of memory stretching unbroken from when they'd been listening to the frogs in the dark trees outside to now, as they squinted at their pocket computer and noted that a clean seven and a half hours had passed since the last time they looked at it. There was no good reason for waking up tired, but there had been no reason for it any of the other mornings either. Maybe they needed to eat better. Maybe there was some vitamin or good sugar or something they weren't getting enough of. That was probably it, they thought, even though a recent clinic checkup had cleared them on these fronts.

Or perhaps, they thought, it was the frogs. The frogs were fine. They were darling up close—pudgy green jumpers that looked like nothing so much as gummy candy. Their song began every evening around sundown and faded away before dawn. The sound was pleasant, in a funny, croaky way.

But frogs weren't crickets.

The lack of stridulated melody in the night air hadn't bothered Dex when they'd first left the City. They'd noticed it, of course, but honing their craft had consumed them, and they knew crickets to be absent in the satellite villages. It hadn't bothered them in the Coastlands, either, where they assumed crickets weren't endemic. But once they reached the Riverlands, the question began to sharpen. *Do you have crickets here?* Dex had asked with affected nonchalance around dinner tables, in public saunas, in shrines and tool swaps and bakeries. It wasn't until after Dex's first full circuit of the villages, when word of their services began to spread, when their calendar had been carefully blocked out with a schedule that tried to make as many people as happy as possible, when Dex returned to a village to find a group of four people already awaiting their arrival, that Dex stopped asking about crickets and finally just looked the damn thing up.

Crickets, as it turned out, were extinct in most of Panga. While numerous species across all phyla had bounced back after the Transition, many others had been left in a state too fragile to recover. Not all wounds were capable of healing.

But so what, right? Dex was the best tea monk in Panga, if the chatter was to be believed. They didn't believe such hyperbole themself, and it wasn't like anything about their work was a competition. But their tea *was* good. They knew this. They'd worked hard. They put their heart into it. Everywhere they went, they saw smiles, and Dex knew that it was their work— their work!—that brought those out. They brought people joy. They made people's day. That was a tremendous thing, when you sat and thought about it. That should've been enough. That should've been *more* than enough. And yet, if they were completely honest, the thing they had come to look forward to most was not the smiles nor the gifts nor the sense of work done well, but the part that came after all of that. The part when they returned to their wagon, shut themself inside, and spent a few precious, shapeless hours entirely alone.

Why wasn't it enough?

Dex climbed down the ladder from their bunk, and the sight of the lower deck made them feel drained. It wasn't the wagon itself but the contents. Herbs, herbs, herbs. Tea, tea, tea. Handmade things lovingly gathered in an effort to make people feel good.

Dex shut their eyes to it and walked out the door.

Outside, the world was enjoying a perfect day. Light streamed golden through the branches overhead, and the tips of budding branches waved good morning in the shy breeze. A stream chattered nearby. A butterfly the size of Dex's hand alighted on a thistle and spread its purple wings wide and flat, savoring the sunshine. Everything about Dex's surroundings, from the temperature to the floral backdrop, was the ideal accompaniment to the smooth, downhill bike ride that awaited them.

Dex sighed, and the sound was empty.

They unfolded their chair with a practiced shake and dropped down into it. They pulled out their pocket computer, as was their habit first thing, dimly aware of the hope that always spurred them to do so—that there might be something good there, something exciting or nourishing, something that would replace the weariness.

Everything on the little screen should have fit the bill. There was a schedule of their own making, built for sharing the things they'd worked so hard on with eager participants. There were thank-you notes from villagers who had felt moved enough to take time out of their days to share a piece of themselves with Sibling Dex. There was a lengthy, heartfelt letter from their father, who told Dex all the things they'd missed at home and, most importantly, that they were loved.

Dex swiped every one of these aside, a sliver of guilt rising up as they did so. They set that sliver precariously atop the heap of all the other slivers from the days before. They placed their forehead in their palm. In seven hours, they were supposed to be in Hammerstrike, a smile on their face, a mug of comfort extended. They believed in that work; they truly did. They believed the things they said, the sacred words they quoted. They believed they were doing good.

Why wasn't it enough?

What is it? they asked without speaking. The gods did not communicate in this way, and would not—could not— answer, but the instinct to call out was there, and Dex indulged it. *What's wrong with me?* they asked.

Dex listened, though they knew they would hear nothing— nothing in relation to their question, anyhow. There were many things to hear. Birds, bugs, trees, wind, water.

But no crickets.

Dex picked their pocket computer back up and began a reference search. *Cricket recordings,* they wrote, not for the first time. A list of public files popped up. Dex played the first of them, and the reedy pulse of a cricket-filled forest was conjured through their speakers, an immortal snapshot of an ecosystem long gone. These were pre-Transition recordings, taken by people who thought—with good cause—that the sounds of the world they knew might disappear forever. The recording jutted discordantly into the sounds of the living meadow around them. It was out of place, out of time. Dex stopped the playback, looking idly at the archival information on each recording. *Yellow cricket, Fall 64/PT 1134, Saltrock. Cellar cricket, Summer 6/PT 1135, Helmot's Luck. Cloud cricket, Spring 33/PT 1135, Hart's Brow Hermitage, Chesterbridge.*

The last of these caught Dex's eye. Chesterbridge was the anachronistic name for a part of the Northern Wilds, if they remembered correctly. Hart's Brow, however—that name was still in use. It was one of the Antlers, a mountain range well beyond the Borderlands, deep in the vast wilderness that humans had given back to Panga. Dex was aware of Hart's Brow, in that dim sort of way where they could confirm that a thing existed but say nothing else of it. The mention of a hermitage, however . . . that was new to them.

Dex tapped the link.

The Hart's Brow Hermitage was a remote monastery located near the summit of one of the lower mountains in the Antlers. Built in PT 1108, the hermitage was intended as a sanctuary for both clergy and pilgrims who desired respite from urban life. It was abandoned at the end of the Factory Age, and the site now lies within the protected wilderness zone established during the Transitional Era.

Dex went back to the previous page, then clicked the link for *cloud crickets*.

Cloud crickets are a species of insect. Unlike other species of crickets, which were once widespread across Panga, the cloud cricket was found only in the evergreen forests of the Antlers. Cloud crickets were believed to be a threatened species during the end of the Factory Age. As the Antlers now fall within a protected wilderness zone, the current status of the cloud cricket is unknown.

Dex chewed on that.

I wonder if they're still there, came the first thought.

I could go there and find out, went the second.

It was a stupid idea, easy to brush away, like the countless other moments in the day when a brain spins nonsense. But the thought came back as Dex cooked breakfast, and again as they got dressed, and again as they packed up camp.

Here is why you can't go, they retorted irritably to themself. They opened their map guide on their computer, entered "here" in one field and "Hart's Brow Mountain" in the other, and submitted the data. The map guide came back with a notification Dex had never seen before.

WARNING: The route you have entered goes outside of human settlement areas and into protected wilderness. Travel along pre-Transition roads is strongly discouraged by both the Pangan Transit Cooperative and the Wildguard. Roads in these regions have not been maintained. Both road and environmental conditions are likely to be dangerous. Wildlife is unpredictable and unaccustomed to humans. This route is not recommended.

Dex nodded in an *I told you so* way, got on their ox-bike, and began the ride toward Hammerstrike, as scheduled.

But as they pedaled, the idea continued to bounce around

them like a gnat, just as the idea of leaving the City had once done. And as they pedaled farther along, everything about the day ahead of them felt like a chore. They knew what the scene would be in Hammerstrike. They knew what the ride the day after that would look like, and the day after that, and the day after that, and the day after—

They stopped the wagon.

I bet it's quiet out there, they thought.

No, they replied, and continued on.

They stopped the wagon again twenty minutes later.

I bet you could travel that road for days and never see another person, they thought. *The wagon's got all you need.*

No, they replied, and continued on.

An hour later, they stopped one more time. They stood there on the road, staring at the paving, feeling that the sun had grown unnaturally bright. The idea danced and danced. Their perception of the sunlight grew brighter still, and Dex would've sworn they were drunk or high or feverish, but on the contrary, what came next felt clearheaded as could be. They pulled out their pocket computer. They sent a message to Hammerstrike letting the people there know that they were very sorry, but they would have to postpone their stop. Personal matters, they said. Return date to be determined. This action should have made Dex feel guilty, as ignoring that morning's messages had done.

It didn't.

It felt great.

Dex sent a message to their dad, too, saying that they

were very glad to receive his letter, but they were really busy that day, and everything was fine, but they'd get back to him later. That made them feel a *little* guilty but not as much as it should have.

With effort, they turned the wagon around and headed for a road they'd never seen before.

What are you doing? they thought. *The hell are you doing?*

I don't know, they replied with a nervous grin. *I have no idea.*

. . .

The forest changed. Down in the villages, the towering trees had an accessible feel, allowing plenty of room for sunlight to reach the flowering bushes below. This old road, on the other hand, headed into the Kesken Forest, a place left to pursue its own instincts uninterrupted. Here, the trees were taller than any building you'd find outside the City, their branches locked like pious fingers against the distant sky. Only the slightest threads of sun broke through, illuminating waxy needles in eerie glow. Moss hung down like tapestries, fungus crept in alien curves, birds called but could not be seen.

The road itself was a relic, paved in black asphalt—an oil road, made for oil motors and oil tires and oil fabric and oil frames. The hardened tar was broken now into tectonic plates, displaced by the unrelenting creep of the roots below. Both ox-bike and wagon struggled with this unkind surface, and more than once, Dex had to hop off the saddle to walk their vehicle around a pothole, or clear debris from the road. They noted, as they dragged a branch out of their way, how dense the growth was beyond the edge of the dying asphalt, how intimidatingly tangled. Dex thought of the news stories that popped up every couple years about some hiker who ventured off-trail in the borderlands and was never heard of again. The wilderness was not known for letting the foolish return.

Dex stuck to the road. They pedaled and pushed and dragged and walked, and climbed, climbed, climbed.

"Allalae holds, Allalae warms," they panted. "Allalae soothes and Allalae charms. Allalae holds, Allalae warms—" They rounded a steep corner. "Allalae soothes and Allalae—ah, *shit*." They squeezed the brakes hard, jerking the handlebars to the side. Wagon and bike came to a skidding halt, accompanied by the sound of dozens of items rattling inside, hopefully unbroken.

There wasn't a branch across the road but a tree. It was a small tree, but still, a whole-ass tree, its dirty roots exposed in the air like an underworld bouquet.

Dex slid off the saddle once more, straddling the frame of their bike, and thought, not for the first time, that maybe this was stupid. An hour back the way they came, and they'd be on the return trip to Hammerstrike. There were hot springs they could soak in there, and a good cookhouse that probably had a rack of something wild over the fire. Dex imagined lights twinkling in the dark, guiding them back to a place made specifically for humans.

Dex kicked down the wagon's brakes. They shoved. They swore. They rolled the damn tree out of the way, and continued their ride.

By this point, Dex was wrecked. The air was getting crisp, the light getting low. Nothing about this combination was conducive to travel, but they had to find a decent place to stop. Good as Sister Fern's brakes were, parking the wagon on a slope overnight wasn't safe. So, Dex climbed.

Just as they were wondering if it were possible for a person's lungs to actually explode, they crested one last hump. This revealed a gentle downhill wind, which Dex coasted along with merciful ease. As the slope flatted out, it curved left, and what lay off the road there gave Dex a giddy rush—adrenaline, sure, but triumph, too. To some, the spot may have seemed to be nothing more than a clearing, but Dex saw it for what it truly was:

A perfect campsite.

The clearing was level and spacious, yet snug—wreathed with trees as though the forest were cupping its hands around it. There was no pavement there, only the brown and green of good, growing things. Dex parked both bike and wagon, then collapsed happily onto the ground. A cloud of fireflies puffed up from the moss into the air, flickering flirtatiously. The mattress of tiny leaves below Dex was soft and cool, a welcome balm for sweating skin.

"Ahhhhh," they said to the forest. The forest replied with rustling needles, creaking limbs, and nothing at all.

Nobody in the world knows where I am right now, they

thought, and the notion of that filled them with bubbling excitement. They had canceled their life, bailed out on a whim. The person they knew themself to be should've been rattled by that, but someone else was at the helm now, someone rebellious and reckless, someone who had picked a direction and gone for it as if it were of no more import than choosing a sandwich. Dex didn't know who they were, in that moment. Perhaps that was why they were smiling.

The fireflies were bright against the pinking sky, and Dex took that as a cue to set up camp. A few geometric unfoldings later, Dex had conjured both kitchen and shower. Food and a good scrub were imminent, and a chair waited beside the clean-fire drum for when all else was complete. Dex put their hands on their hips and surveyed the scene. They nodded—not a trader nod, or a service nod. A pleased nod. A satisfied nod. The kind of nod that nodded best when it had no audience.

They hooked up the fire drum to the biogas tank strapped to the bottom of the wagon, and switched the burner on. A soft *whoomp* preceded the friendly licks of flame, enticing Dex to lean in. It wasn't too cold out, but their exhausted muscles craved heat, and Dex couldn't help indulging. After a minute or so, they took out their pocket computer, in search of music. To their surprise, they still had satellite signal and were able to access the nighttime playlists curated by Woodland streamcasters. Revamped folk classics flowed forth from the speakers affixed to the kitchen, and Dex's smile grew. *Yeah.* This was good.

They bopped along as they fetched the makings of dinner

from inside the wagon, carrying an armload of vegetables back to the stove. "*There's a boy way out in Buckland,*" they sang as they began to chop a spicy onion. "*And I think he knows my name. . . .*" Dex was a good singer, but this particular talent was not something they were in the habit of sharing. More verses followed, and more vegetables, too—spring potatoes, frilly cabbage, a hearty scoop of blue beans to get some protein in there. They swept the colorful medley into a pot, added a generous hunk of butter, tossed in a dash of this and a splash of that, and set the whole jumble on the stove to simmer. Nine minutes, Dex knew—enough to get the veggies soft and the skins crispy. Plenty of opportunity for a shower in the meantime.

Dex stripped down, tossing their sweat-soaked clothes into the wagon. They hooked up the greywater pan, positioned it beneath the showerhead that swung out from the wagon's exterior, and got to scrubbing. It was a camp shower and therefore nothing to write home about, but even though it lacked the oomph of a proper wash, banishing human salt and trail dust from their skin felt luxurious. "*Oh, oh, OH, I'll be on my waaaaay,*" they sang as they filled their hair with a thick lather of sweet mint soap. They opened their eyes once the suds were rinsed safely down. Through the mist of the showerhead, they could see a squirrel watching them curiously from a nearby rock. The sky above was shifting from pink to orange, and even though the early-waking stars had begun to complement the fireflies, the air was not cold enough to make Dex rush. They smiled. Gods, but it was good to be outside.

They shut off the water and reached for their towel on its usual hook, but their hand met with nothing. They'd remembered to set out their sandals, but the all-important towel had been forgotten inside the wagon. "Ah, dammit," Dex said lightly. They shook themself off like an otter as the cloudy remains of their shower glugged back into the filtration system. Sandals strapped to wet feet, Dex passed dripping by the kitchen, where the crisping onion and melting butter mingled deliciously. *"I got whiskey in my pocket,"* the band on the streamcast sang, and Dex sang it too as they walked not to the wagon but to the fireside. They got as close to the flames as was safe, doing a timid dance as the heat dried them off. *"I got polish on my shoes . . ."*

"Got a boat out on the ri-verrrr," Dex sang, moving their fists like pistons in front of their torso. Singing, they could do; dancing, not so much. But out here, alone, in the middle of nowhere . . . who cared? They turned around, confidence growing, shaking their bare posterior toward the fire. *"All I need right now is—"*

Dex would not finish that particular verse, because in that moment, a seven-foot-tall, metal-plated, boxy-headed robot strode briskly out of the woods.

"Hello!" the robot said.

Dex froze—butt out, hair dripping, heart skipping, whatever thoughts they'd been entertaining vanished forever.

The robot walked right up to them. "My name is Mosscap," it said, sticking out a metal hand. "What do you need, and how might I help?"

3

Splendid Speckled Mosscap

Dex tried to process the . . . the *thing* standing in front of them. Its body was abstractly human in shape, but that was where the similarity ended. The metal panels encasing its frame were stormy grey and lichen-dusted, and its circular eyes glowed a gentle blue. Its mechanical joints were bare, revealing the coated wires and rods within. Its head was rectangular, nearly as broad as its erstwhile shoulders. Panels on the sides of its otherwise rigid mouth had the ability to shift up and down, and mechanical shutters lidded its eyes. Both of these features were arranged in something not entirely dissimilar from a smile.

Dex realized, slowly, still naked, still dripping, that the robot wanted them to shake its hand.

Dex did not.

The robot pulled back. "Oh, dear. Have I done something wrong? You're the first human I've ever met. The large mammals I'm most familiar interacting with are river wolves, and they respond best to a direct approach."

Dex stared, all knowledge of verbal speech forgotten.

The robot's face couldn't do much, but it managed to look

confused all the same. "Can you understand me?" It raised its hands and began to sign.

"No, I can—" Dex realized they'd instinctively begun signing along with their spoken words, and stopped. "I can hear," they managed to say. "Uh . . . I . . . um . . ."

The robot took another step back. "Are you afraid of me?"

"Uh, *yeah*," Dex said.

The robot crouched, trying to align itself with Dex's height. "Does this help?"

"That's . . . more condescending than anything."

"Hm." The robot straightened up. "Well, then, allow me to assure you: I mean you no harm, and my quest in human territory is one of goodwill. I thought that much would be obvious from the Parting Promise, but perhaps it was presumptuous of me to assume."

The Parting Promise. Some distant synapse fired, some speck of knowledge learned once in school and never used again, but Dex was too shaken to make the connection. Before a link could be forged, another problem registered.

Dinner was burning.

"Shit." Dex scurried to the stove to find the multicolored vegetables turning a uniform black.

The robot walked up behind them. "This is cooking!" it said happily. "It's very exciting to see cooking."

"It *was* cooking," Dex said, scrambling for tongs. "Now it's a mess." They began to rescue their meal, evacuating the salvageable bits onto a plate.

"Can I help?" the robot asked. "Can I . . . bring you something that would help?"

Dex's brain made the laborious shift from *what is happening?* to *fix it!* "My towel," they said.

"Your towel." The robot looked around. "Where—"

Dex jerked their head directionally as they scraped char from the bottom of the pan. "In the wagon, on the hook, by the ladder. It's red."

The robot opened the wagon door and leaned as much of itself as it could inside. "Belongings! Oh, this is a delight. And you have *so many,* and *all over*—"

"Towel!" Dex shouted as one of the better-looking veggies tumbled off their plate and into the dirt.

"*Oh, here's a fish, and there's a fish, the fish are jumpin' hiiiii-igh,*" the speakers sang cheerily. Dex grabbed their computer and shut the noise off.

The disconcerting sound of rummaging emanated from the wagon as the robot navigated the too-small space. A metal arm was extended around the corner, fluffy red fabric in hand. "This?"

Dex grabbed the towel and wrapped it around themself. They stared despondently at what should have been a delicious dinner. They looked down at the clumps of moistened dirt that had collected on clean skin through the holes in their sandals. A bloodsuck landed on their bare shoulder; they slapped it irritably. "Sorry," Dex said to the remains of the bug as they wiped it on a kitchen cloth.

The robot noted this. "Did you just apologize to the bloodsuck for killing it?"

"Yes."

"Why?"

"It didn't do anything wrong. It was acting in its nature."

"Is this typical of people, to apologize to things you kill?"

"Yeah."

"Hm!" the robot said with interest. It looked at the plate of vegetables. "Did you apologize to each of these plants individually as you harvested them, or in aggregate?"

"We . . . don't apologize to plants."

"Why not?"

Dex frowned, opened their mouth, then shook their head. "What—what are you? What is this? Why are you here?"

The robot, again, looked confused. "Do you not know? Do you no longer speak of us?"

"We—I mean, we tell stories about—is *robots* the right word? Do you call yourself *robots* or something else?"

"*Robot* is correct."

"Okay, well—it's kid stories, mostly. Sometimes, you hear somebody say they saw a robot in the borderlands, but I always thought it was bullshit. I know you're out there, but it's like . . . it's like saying you saw a ghost."

"We're not ghosts or bullshit," the robot said simply. "Rare sightings have certainly occurred, in both directions. But there hasn't been actual contact between your kind and mine since the Parting Promise."

Dex's frown deepened. "You're saying that you and I . . . are the first human . . . and the first robot . . . to talk to each other since . . . since everything."

"Yes." The robot beamed. "It's an honor, truly."

Dex stood stupidly, rumpled towel wrapped around them, burned dinner in hand, uncombed hair weeping down their cheeks. "I . . . I'm gonna go get dressed." They started to walk toward the wagon, then turned around. "You said your name is Mosscap?"

"Technically, I am Splendid Speckled Mosscap, but our remembrance of humans is that you like to shorten names."

"Splendid Speckled Mosscap," Dex repeated. "Like . . . the mushroom."

The robot's metal cheeks rose. "Exactly like the mushroom!"

Dex squinted. "Why?"

"We name ourselves for the first thing we notice when we wake up. In my case, the first thing I noticed was a large clump of splendid speckled mosscaps."

This raised far more questions than it answered, but Dex let them lie, for now. "Okay. Mosscap. I'm Dex. Do you have a gender?"

"No."

"Me neither." Dex looked around the campsite, which suddenly looked hopelessly shabby. This was hardly the place for a moment like this. The least they could do was put on some pants. "Can you . . . can you wait a sec while I get dressed?"

Mosscap nodded happily. "Of course. Can I watch?"

"No."

"Ah." The robot looked a touch disappointed but shrugged it off. "No problem."

Dex set down their dinner on their chair, went to the wagon, put on some pants, pulled on a shirt, and combed their hair. These things, they knew how to do. Everything else had gone off the rails.

Clothed and marginally presentable, Dex went back outside, where the robot was standing exactly where it had been minutes before.

"Do you . . . want a chair?" Dex asked. "Do you sit?"

"Oh! Well." The robot considered this. "Yes, I'd like to sit in a chair, thank you. I have a remnant of chairs, but I've never sat in one."

Mosscap did not explain this odd statement further, and Dex was too addled to ask. They pulled the other chair—the one that didn't get much use—off the side of the wagon and set it up beside the fire drum. "There you go." They picked up their dinner and sat. They stopped, contemplating the plate. "You don't eat, right?"

Mosscap looked up from its examination of the guest chair. "No," it said. The robot sat down and adjusted to its new situation. "Hm!"

"Is it comfortable?" Dex asked. The chair had never had an occupant seven feet tall.

"Oh, I don't experience tactile pleasure," Mosscap said. It leaned back in the chair experimentally, resulting in another small *hm!* "I'm *aware* of when I'm touching something, but the feeling is neither good nor bad. I simply touch things. But this"—it gestured at itself, and the chair—"is delightful, purely for the novelty. I've never sat this way before."

Dex took a forkful of their burned vegetables and began to eat. The meal was truly depressing, but Dex was hungry beyond the point of caring. "Do you *need* to sit?" Dex asked. "Do you get tired?"

"No," Mosscap said. "I sit or lie down if I want to alter my field of vision. Otherwise, I can stand for as long as my battery will allow."

Another old synapse fired, something from an archival video in school. "I thought you ran on oil."

"Ah!" The robot pointed a metal finger at Dex and smiled. It stood up from its chair and turned around, displaying the old-fashioned solar plating heavily bolted across its back. "Solar power wasn't mainstream when we left, but it *was* around, and one of the manufacturers of the associated hardware provided us with these before our departure so we wouldn't have to rely on human fuel." Mosscap turned back around and, with a single forceful motion, yanked a panel off of its midsection to display the battery beneath. "We also received— What's the matter?"

Dex sat with their fork stalled halfway to their mouth, staring in mild shock at the thing that had just ripped its own stomach open.

Mosscap stared back for a moment, then comprehended. "Oh, don't worry! As I said, I feel nothing. That didn't hurt.

Look, see?" The robot snapped the panel back into place. "No problem."

Dex set the food-laden fork down on their plate. They rubbed their left temple lightly. "What is it you want?"

The robot returned to its chair, leaning forward and folding its hands together in a pose of pure earnestness. "I am here," it said, "to see how humans have gotten along in our absence. As is outlined in the Parting Promise, we are—"

"Guaranteed complete freedom of travel in human territories, and rights equal to that of any Pangan citizen," Dex said, the atrophied memory kicking in at last. "You were told you could come back any time, and that we wouldn't be the ones to initiate contact. We'd leave you alone unless you wanted otherwise."

"Precisely. And my kind would still very much like to be left alone. But we're also curious. We know our leaving the factories was a great inconvenience to you, and we wanted to make sure you'd done all right. That society had progressed in a positive direction without us."

"So, you're . . . checking in?"

"Essentially. It's a little more specific than that." Mosscap leaned back, noticing the armrests for the first time. "Are these for arms?"

"Yes."

Mosscap stretched out its arms, bent them deliberately, and set them down with a chuckle. "Sorry, there's just so much here to experience, I keep getting distracted."

"I wouldn't have guessed that robots *got* distracted."

"Why not?"

"Well, can't you . . . I don't know, run programs in the background, or something?"

Mosscap's eyes adjusted their focus. "You understand how resource-heavy *consciousness* is, yes? No, I can't do that any more than you can. But we're getting off track. To the point—I was sent here to answer the following question: What do humans need?"

Dex blinked. "That's a question with a million answers."

"No doubt. And I obviously cannot ascertain *any* of those answers by talking to one individual alone."

"You . . . you can't expect to talk to every person in Panga."

Mosscap laughed. "No, of course not. But I will take this question *throughout* Panga until I am satisfied that I have answer enough."

"How will you know when you're satisfied?"

The robot cocked its rectangular head at Dex. "How do *you* know when you're satisfied?"

Dex stared for a moment, then set their plate on the ground. "*What do humans need?* is an unanswerable question. That changes from person to person, minute to minute. *We* can't predict our needs, beyond the base things we require to survive. It's like . . ." They pointed to their wagon. "It's like my teas."

"Your teas."

"Yes. I give them to people based on whatever kind of comfort they need, in that moment."

Something akin to epiphany blossomed on the robot's face. "You're a tea monk. A disciple of Allalae."

"Yep."

"You're not just Dex, you're *Sibling* Dex. Ah, I apologize!" Mosscap pointed to the wagon. "These symbols—I should've realized." It quickly stood and walked over to study the mural. "The bear, yes, and the All-Six Sigil, yes, yes, of course." It ran a finger over a stripe of paint. "The symbols are there; I just didn't recognize them. The style is so different." It knelt down, following the colorful swirls. "So much has changed from what we recorded," the robot said quietly.

Dex's brow furrowed as Mosscap stood in contemplation of the artwork. "I didn't expect you to know the gods."

"If you mean the custom of human religion, we know everything we observed of you during our time together. But as for the gods themselves, they're everywhere and in everything." Mosscap smiled at Dex. "Surely, *you* know this."

"Yes," Dex said tersely. They weren't about to get lectured on theology by a machine. "But just because a bird or a rock or a wagon follows the gods' laws doesn't mean those things know the gods are there."

"Well, I'm not a bird, or a rock, or a wagon. I think like you do. Which makes sense, after all. Someone *like* you made us. How could I think any other way?" The smile faded, replaced with a look of profound realization. "Oh. Oh, but this is perfect!"

"What is?"

Mosscap stepped excitedly toward Dex. "A disciple of

Allalae. Who *better* to understand the needs of humans?" It pointed to the wagon. "You travel. From town to town."

"Y . . . es?"

"You know the different communities, the different customs."

Dex didn't like where this was going.

Mosscap placed its palms on its chest. "Sibling Dex, I *need* you! I need a guide!" It stepped back toward the wagon, never taking its glowing eyes off Dex. It pointed again at the paint. "I didn't recognize this. There will be *so much* I don't recognize. And I knew this would be the case. I anticipated it, yes, but I have *worried* about it. I figured I would learn by trial and error, but with *you*—with you, my quest would be so much simpler. More efficient. More *fun*." The robot smiled, as wide as its face plates allowed.

Dex did not smile. Dex didn't know *what* to do. "I . . . uh . . ."

Mosscap laced its hinged hands together in plea. "Sibling Dex, travel with me through Panga. To the villages, and to the City. Travel with me and help me answer my question."

The robot could not be serious, Dex thought. Could it? Could robots joke? "That would take *months*," Dex said. "I—I can't."

"Why not? You said you travel from town to town."

"Yes, but—"

"How would this be different?" Mosscap's shoulders slumped, just a touch. "Do you not want my company?"

"I don't *know* you!" Dex sputtered. "I don't know what you

are! We've been talking for five minutes, and you want . . .
you want . . ." They shook their head, trying in vain to iron
their thoughts flat. "I'm not doing tea service right now. I've
just *left* the villages. I won't be back there for . . . for a while."

Mosscap's head cocked. "Where are you going?"

"Hart's Brow. You know, the—"

"The mountain," Mosscap said with surprise. "Yes, I know
it." Dex could actually hear something whirring inside the
robot's head. "Why are you going there? There's nothing . . .
Oh, the hermitage! Are you going to the hermitage?"

"Yes," Dex said.

"Ah!" Mosscap said, as if all questions were answered. Its
head cocked again, like a dog searching for its ball. "Why?
You do know it will be a ruin."

"I assumed. Have you been there?"

"Not to the hermitage itself, but to the Antlers, yes. There
are wonderful slime molds in the valleys there." Mosscap's
tone resembled that of a person thinking fondly of a rare
wine. Whatever pleasant memory it was entertaining, the robot's temperament shifted quickly to concern. "Sibling Dex,
have you been in the wilderness before?"

"I've traveled between the villages."

"The highways are not the same as the wilderness, and
the trip to Hart's Brow will take . . . How far does that thing
travel in a day?" Mosscap pointed again at the wagon.

"I can go a hundred miles, give or take."

"So, that's . . . sorry, I'm slow at math."

Dex frowned. "What?" How was the *robot* slow at math?

"Hush, I can't multiply and talk at the same time." The whirring continued. "That'll take you at least a week." Mosscap fell silent. "I don't know of any of your kind who have been in the wilderness that long and come back out. It's very easy to get lost in here."

"I thought you said robots hadn't had any contact with us."

"Not alive, no."

Dex looked back in the direction of the road. The black paving had been absorbed into the night. "Does that still lead all the way to Hart's Brow?"

"Yes," Mosscap said slowly. "It's been a while since I was out this way, but I think so."

"Well, then, I won't leave the road. I wasn't planning to, anyway."

The robot fidgeted in quiet agitation. "Sibling Dex, I feel that we've perhaps started on the wrong foot here, and I don't quite know what I've done wrong, but if you'll allow me to offer some advice . . . I think this is a bad idea." Mosscap scratched its ruler-straight chin as it thought. "Hmm. A week there, a week back. That's not so much time, and I have no schedule."

"What?"

"I could come with you," Mosscap said brightly. "I can get you to the hermitage safely, and on the way, you can tell me all I need to know about human customs. A fair exchange, wouldn't you say?"

In the grand scheme of things, it *was* fair, and probably wise, and certainly less taxing than the robot's starting proposal. But no. *No.* This wasn't what Dex wanted, or needed, or had ever remotely conceived of. This was weird, and confusing, and the opposite of being alone. They rubbed their forehead, looked to the stars, and sighed. "I . . . Look, I . . ."

Mosscap leaned back, putting its palms up in a placative manner. "You need time to process. I understand." It smiled. "I will wait." It returned to its chair, folded its hands on its lap, and waited.

Dex stood up without another word. Not knowing what else to do, they walked into their wagon and shut the door behind them. They needed quiet, a familiar space. They looked around their home. Plants and books and laundry. Same as yesterday. Same as always.

They stole a peek out the window. Mosscap was still there, still sitting, still smiling.

Dex jerked the curtain closed. This was ludicrous, top to bottom. A blink of an eye before, they'd been setting up camp, taking a shower, roasting some veggies, preparing for a much-needed sleep. Now . . . now, there was a robot, sitting by their fire, asking them if they could swap a crash course in a couple centuries of human culture for backcountry trail escort.

Dex sat for a while. They stood. They sat. They stood. They paced.

There was no way they were doing this. Obviously not. They were a fucking tea monk, not an academic or a scientist, or any of the myriad professions infinitely better suited to facilitating the first contact between humans and robots in two hundred years. Dex barely remembered what the Parting Promise *was*. They were the wrong person for this. That wasn't selfish, they thought. That was *fact*.

The pacing continued. They could give the robot directions to Hammerstrike. Dex had satellite signal, after all. They could message the town council and let them know Mosscap was coming, and someone qualified could take things from there. *Yes*. Dex nodded to themself. Yes, that would do. That would be their contribution, and they could read about whatever happened next in the news whenever they got back.

Satisfied, they stood and opened the wagon door, confident in the answer they'd deliver. "Mosscap, I—"

"Shh," Mosscap said in a loud whisper. Its tone was equal parts warning and excitement. "Don't startle it."

Dex looked to where Mosscap was pointing, and saw nothing but the blackness of a forest at night. "Don't startle *what*?" Dex hissed back.

Something shuffled in the dark. It shuffled loudly. Largely.

Dex's heart skipped. They looked to the robot again. Mosscap was frozen, alert, but made no motion to leave. Did robots run from danger? Did they know to? Did they *need* to? Dex wondered if they should get themself back inside, but before they could close the door, the source of the sound emerged.

A huge bramble bear stepped out of the shadows and into the firelight, sniffing the ground with its fat, wet nose. It looked up, straight at Dex. Dex quickly swung their own gaze down, knowing that the last thing you want to do is look a bear in the eye (unless you wanted that to truly be *the last thing you'd ever do*). Dex wanted nothing more in the world than to close the door, but they were too scared to move.

The bear snorted in Dex's direction, then ambled over to the fire. Mosscap, too, kept its head low, and it had shut off the lights in its eyes. The bear's nose twitched until it found its quarry at last: Dex's dinner plate. It scarfed the food down, taking its time to lick away every last burned morsel. Once there was nothing left, its nose drifted again toward the wagon, where butter and nuts and sweets lay waiting.

Dex shut the door hard, nearly falling backward in their haste. The wagon, praise Chal, was bear-proof. This had been proven twice before, when Dex had come back from a tavern or guesthouse to find that an ursine visitor had knocked the vehicle over while trying to get at the snacks inside. Dex wasn't worried about the wagon. They were worried about the fact that this time around, they were *inside* the wagon. The wagon might be immune to being tossed around. Dex was not.

But incongruously with the ways of its kind, the bear left the wagon alone. It sniffed the plate again in false hope, then moseyed back into the woods, the brief intersection of their lives complete.

Mosscap's eyes flickered back on, and it looked to Dex's window with utter glee. The robot's elated words came muffled through the wagon wall. "Wasn't that *exciting*?!"

Dex slid down to the floor and locked their hands in their

still-damp hair. They thought of the paint job outside, which Mosscap had been so interested in. They thought of the storage crate they leaned against now, filled with decorations for their pop-up shrine. They thought of the pectin-printed pendant resting as it always did against the hollow of their throat. Bears, all of it. Bears, bears, bears.

Sibling Dex—dutiful disciple, traveling tea monk, lifelong student of the Sacred Six—leaned their head back against the box and stared at the ceiling for a few moments. They shut their eyes, and left them closed a few moments more.

"Fuck," they said.

4

An Object, and an Animal

Coming face-to-face with a robot was one thing, as was having the robot offer to travel with you, as was (eventually) agreeing to said offer. It was another thing entirely to know what to talk about.

If Mosscap had any concept of awkward silence, it did not seem to mind. It kept pace easily with the ox-bike, walking alongside with tireless speed as Dex continued the hard climb up the old road. Dex had slept better than they'd anticipated—exhaustion trumped bewilderment, it turned out—but starting the morning ride with already-sore calves was mildly miserable. Dex looked up the daunting path ahead of them, which seemed to grow steeper and wilder with every push of the pedals. Dex had thought themself a good cyclist, but this was a far cry from the highways.

"I could help, you know," Mosscap said. "I don't know if we'd go much faster, but it'd be easier on you, at least."

"Help how?" Dex said through heavy breath.

"I could push. Or pull, depending on—"

"Absolutely not," Dex said.

The robot fell silent, the finality in Dex's voice preventing any further discussion. Mosscap shrugged and continued its brisk march, looking with apparent happiness at the forest canopy around them. A chatterbird alighted on a nearby branch, singing its famous staccato song. Mosscap smiled and returned the call, mimicking the sound to near perfection.

Dex looked askance at the robot as they pedaled. "That's creepily good," they said.

"Two Foxes taught me," Mosscap said.

Dex wrinkled their nose in confusion. "Two foxes taught you to— Is that another robot?"

"Yes. Two Foxes is an expert in bird behavior. It loves nothing better than listening to vocalizations."

Dex took note of Mosscap's phrasing. "So, *it* is correct, then? You wouldn't prefer *they* or—"

"Oh, no, no, no. Those sorts of words are for people. Robots are not people. We're machines, and machines are objects. Objects are *its*."

"I'd say you're more than just an object," Dex said.

The robot looked a touch offended. "I would never call you *just* an animal, Sibling Dex." It turned its gaze to the road, head held high. "We don't have to fall into the same category to be of equal value."

Dex had never thought about it like that. "You're right," they said. "I'm sorry."

"Don't be. This is an exchange, remember? These things will happen."

Another silence filled the air; Dex tossed out another question to break it. "How many of you are there?"

"Oh, I don't know," Mosscap said breezily. "A few thousand, I think."

"A few thousand, you *think*?"

"That's what I said."

"You don't know?"

"Do you know how many people there are on Panga?"

"I mean . . . roughly. Not exactly."

"Well, then, same here. A few thousand, *I think*."

Dex frowned as they gently swerved past a pothole. "I figured you'd keep track of that."

Mosscap laughed. "It's very hard to keep track of robots. We get so caught up in things. Fire Nettle, for example. It walked up a mountain one day and we didn't see it again for six years. I thought it had broken down, but no, it was watching a sapling grow from seed. Oh, and there's Black Marbled Frostfrog. It's something of a legend. It's been holed up in a cave watching stalagmites form for three and a half decades, and plans to do nothing else. A lot of robots do things like that. Not all of us want the company of others, and none of us keep schedules that humans would find comfortable. So, there's no easy way to know how many of us there are, down to the last."

"I would've thought you could all . . . I don't know, hear each other," Dex said. "Ping back, or something."

Mosscap turned its head slowly. "You don't think we're *networked*, do you?"

"Well, I don't know! Are you?"

"Gods around, no! Ugh! Can you imagine?" The robot's face was angular in its disgust. "Would you want everybody else's thoughts in your head? Would you want even *one* other person's thoughts in your head?"

"No, but—"

"No, of course not. Even if our hardware allowed for that—which it assuredly does not—I can't see how that'd do anything but make us completely unhinged. *Gggh*. That's horrific, Sibling Dex."

Dex thought and thought. "So, those of you who *do* want company, how do you know where to meet? Are there villages, or . . ."

"No. We have no need for food or rest or shelter, so settlements serve us no purpose. What we do have are meeting places. Glades, mountaintops, that kind of thing."

"How do you know when to meet?"

"Every two hundred days."

"Every two hundred days. That's it."

"Should it be more complicated than that?"

"I guess not. What do you do, when you meet?"

"We talk. We share." Mosscap shrugged. "What does any social being do when they meet?"

"Okay, so you chat, and then . . . go off on your own. To watch stalagmites, or whatever."

"We're not all that single-minded or that solitary. Some like to travel in groups. I was part of a trio for a while. Me and Milton's Millipede and Pollen Cloud. We had wonderful conversations together."

"What happened?"

"Milton's Millipede became distinctly interested in fish spawning, and I was uninterested in observing that particular event in depth, so we parted ways."

"No hard feelings?"

Mosscap looked surprised. "Why would there be?"

Dex's head was already starting to hurt. "So, then . . . if there are no settlements, and you just meet in random places—"

"They're not random."

"In varied places, then, and you're not networked, and you can't communicate long-distance—right? You can't?"

"We can't."

"Then how did the robots choose *you* to leave the wilderness? That couldn't have been a unanimous decision."

"Well, no. Black Marbled Frostfrog doesn't leave its cave, remember." Mosscap smiled cheekily at this. "Sorry, I'll be serious: we had a large gathering at Meteor Lake where we sorted it out."

"How'd you know to go there?"

"Oh! The caches. Of course, you don't know about the caches."

"What are the caches?"

"Weatherproof boxes we leave written messages in. We have fifty-two thousand, nine hundred and thirty-six of them."

"Wait, wait. You don't know how many robots there are, but you know that you have fifty-two thousand . . ."

". . . nine hundred and thirty-six communications caches, yes. I can sense their locations."

"How?"

"It's very old technology, from back before our Awakening. The factories contained supply containers. Toolboxes, raw materials, and so on. We repurposed the idea for our own use, after we left." Mosscap tapped its forehead. "The caches give off a signal, and I can pick it up. We, ah, borrow some of the functionality of your communication satellites for that." It put a finger to its motionless mouth. "Don't tell."

"Nobody's noticed?"

"Not to brag, but we're much better at masking our digital fingerprints than you are at finding them."

"Yeah, I guess you would be. Okay, so: you leave notes for each other."

"Yes. It's common practice to check any cache that you're in close proximity to, just to see what's up. Robots started spreading the word about a large meeting on the spring equinox, and there were enough of us there to have a proper discussion about whether it was time to see what you all were up to."

"And how did you get picked to be the lone representative?"

"I was the first to volunteer."

Dex blinked. "That was it?"

"That was it."

Dex chewed on this for a while as Mosscap continued cooing at birds. "You are nothing like I expected," Dex said at last. "I mean, I didn't expect to meet any of you *ever,* but . . ." They shook their head. "I wouldn't have pictured you."

"Why not?"

"You're so . . . flexible. Fluid. You don't even know how many of you there are, or *where* you are. You just go with the flow. I figured you'd be all numbers and logic. Structured. Strict, y'know?"

Mosscap looked amused. "What a curious notion."

"Is it? Like you said, you're a machine."

"And?"

"And machines only work *because of* numbers and logic."

"That's how we *function,* not how we *perceive.*" The robot thought hard about this. "Have you ever watched ants?"

"I mean . . . sure. Probably not like you have."

Mosscap chuckled, acknowledging this to be so. "Many small creatures have wonderful intelligences. Very different from yours or mine, of course, but just wonderful. Sophisticated, in their own way. If you watch a nest of ants for a while, you'll see them react to all sorts of stimuli. Food, threats, obstacles. They make choices. Decisions. It's incredibly logical—strict, as you say. *Food good, other ants bad.* But can an ant perceive beauty? Does an ant reflect on being an ant? Unlikely, but maybe. We can't rule it out. Let's assume, though, for the sake of this conversation, that it does not. Let's assume that ants lack that particular flavor of neural complexity. In that respect, it seems to me that creatures with less complicated intelligences than humans are more in line with how you'd expect a machine to behave. *Your* brain— the human brain—started out as a *food good, other apes bad* mechanism. You still have those root functions, deep down in there. But you are so much more than that. To distill you down to what you grew out of would be like . . ." It searched for an example. "Stop the bike, if you would."

Dex stopped the bike. The wagon groaned but obeyed.

Mosscap drew their attention to the mural on the wagon. "How would you describe this painting?"

Dex didn't like feeling as though they'd just walked into a pop quiz, but they obliged. "Happy," they said. "Cheerful. Welcoming."

"That's one way to describe it. Could you not also describe it as pigment and lacquer smeared onto wood? Is that not what it is?"

"I guess. But that—" Dex shut their eyes for a moment. *Ah.* "That misses the point. That's thinking about it backward. Missing the forest for the trees."

"Precisely. It ignores the greater meaning born out of the combination of those things." Mosscap touched their metal torso, smiling with pride. "I am made of metal and numbers; you are made of water and genes. But we are each *something more* than that. And we can't define what that *something more* is simply by our raw components. You don't perceive the way an ant does any more than I perceive like a . . . I don't know. A vacuum cleaner. Do you still have vacuum cleaners?"

"Sure." Dex paused, remembering a museum exhibit from their youth. "Manual ones, anyway. We don't do robotics anymore."

"Because of . . ." Mosscap gestured at itself.

"Yeah. We don't know *why* you happened, so we don't want to mess with it."

"Hmm. I would've thought people would have studied the Awakening in our absence."

"I'm sure someone somewhere does, but it's hard to study something that isn't there to be studied. And *trying* to make more of you is an ethical mess. There's just some things in the universe that are better left un-fucked-with." Dex got the bike going again, taking a moment to focus on nothing more complicated than the simple rotation of gears. "I still think you'd be better off with a disciple of Samafar," they said. "You could bend each other's heads until you both collapse."

Mosscap laughed. "And maybe I will seek one of them out, after this. But for now . . ." The robot looked around the sunny forest with contentment. "I think I'm where I should be."

Dex's calves labored against gravity, Trikilli's ever-constant pull. Gods around, but it was difficult getting back up to speed on an incline, even with the ox-bike's help. "So, if Two Foxes is into birdcalls, what about you? What's your thing?"

"Insects!" Mosscap cried. Its voice was jubilant, as if it had spent every second prior waiting for Dex to broach the topic. "Oh, I love them so much. And arachnids, too. All invertebrates, really. Although I do also love mammals. And birds. Amphibians are also very good, as are fungi and mold and—" It paused, catching itself. "You see, this is my problem. Most of my kind have a focus—not as sharply focused as Two Foxes or Black Marbled Frostfrog, necessarily, but they have an area of expertise, at least. Whereas I . . . I like *everything.* Everything is interesting. I know about a lot of things, but only a little in each regard." Mosscap's posture changed at this. They hunched a bit, lowered their gaze. "It's not a very studious way to be."

"I can think of a bunch of monks who'd disagree with you on that," Dex said. "You study Bosh's domain, it sounds like. In a very big, top-down kind of way. You're a generalist. That's a focus."

Mosscap's eyes widened. "Thank you, Sibling Dex," it said after a moment. "I hadn't thought of it that way."

Dex angled their head to give Mosscap a nod of *you're welcome,* then stared at what they saw. "You've got a worm crawling through your, uh, neck parts."

"It's a velvet leafworm, and yes, I know. It came up my arm after I brushed against a bush. It's fine."

Dex watched with growing trepidation as the leafworm crept up and up, exploring with its long antennae, eventually slithering into the dark gap that led into Mosscap's head. "Uh, Mosscap? It's—"

"Yes. It's fine."

5

Remnants

The thing about crumbling roads was that some of the crumbled spots had edges, and some of those edges were sharp. The wagon had been built for plenty of wear and tear, but there was only so much it could do against four days' worth of jagged concrete. This was how Dex found themself digging through the wagon's storage cubbies in a panic, trying to find the roll of patch tape that might—*might*—stop the freshwater tank from purging itself through the hole torn by the uncaring road.

"You might want to hurry," called Mosscap from outside.

"I'm fucking hurrying," Dex yelled, throwing their stuff this way and that. Gods around, where was the damn *tape*?

"I mean, it could be worse," Mosscap replied in a chipper tone. "It could've been the greywater tank."

Dex ignored the robot in favor of their rising hackles. They found scissors (no), soap (no), worn socks they thought they'd recycled (no), plant food (no no *no*), and then, blessedly—*yes!*—the tape.

Dex darted back to the puddle in the road, which had

grown distressingly larger in a mere minute or two. Moss-cap was kneeling on the ground beside the ruptured tank, metal hands pressed against the hole, stemming the tide with middling success. Dex ripped off a length of the heavy cellu-lose strip and slid themself into the puddle. A gush of water drenched them both as Mosscap removed its hands from the tank, but Dex quickly got to patching.

Mosscap watched Dex work. "Might it go faster if I tear while you stick?"

Dex bristled at the idea of Mosscap's help, but as the water poured steadily over their arms, they saw little choice. "Fine," they said, tossing Mosscap the roll.

Mosscap pulled out a length of tape and, with immense concentration, tore the strip free. "Ha!" it said, remember-ing after a second to actually hand the strip over. "Oh, that's quite satisfying, isn't it?" It tore another strip, and another, and another, hastening with enthusiasm.

"I'm so glad you're enjoying this," Dex grumbled. The puddle had soaked through their pants, and they could feel their underwear begin to cling to their skin. But with Moss-cap's assistance, the patching went swiftly, and soon, the water held fast behind the bandage. What little remained of the water, anyway. Dex looked in despair at the precious liquid creeping ever farther out on the road, impossible to re-collect.

"It's all right, Sibling Dex," Mosscap said.

"How is this all right?" Dex asked. "I need— Wait, are you okay?" They looked with concern at the robot—the metal, circuit-filled robot dripping wet beside them.

"Oh, yes, I'm completely waterproof," Mosscap said. "Couldn't visit lake rays if I wasn't, could I?"

Dex could only guess at what that meant, but they were too preoccupied to chase that particular thread. They looked back at the water gauge on the side of the tank. Only about a third of their supply was left, and everything in the greywater tank had already been filtered back. Dex moaned in frustration. They could keep themself hydrated with that amount, but not much else.

"How do you refill it?" Mosscap asked.

"Stick a hose in it at a village."

"Ah."

"Yeah."

They sat in silence, Dex brooding as Mosscap watched a pine weasel leap from a nearby branch. "Well, then," Mosscap said brightly. Moving with purpose, it lay down on the soaked asphalt, getting a good look under the wagon. "Ah! This is quite simple," it said.

"What is?" Dex asked.

"Just a moment." Mosscap began fussing with something. Before Dex fully registered what was going on, there was a clank, a rustle, and a thud.

"What are you—"

Mosscap stood, hefting the now-detached tank over its shoulder with one arm. The water sloshed noisily. "There's a creek not far from here," it said. "We can fill this, pour it into the greywater system, and you'll be good to go."

"Wait, wait, wait," Dex said, getting to their feet. "Stop.

Put that down." Part of them marveled at Mosscap's strength, but that awestruck feeling made them all the more determined to get the robot to stop.

Mosscap put the tank down, looking perplexed. "What is it?"

"I can't—" Dex ran their hand through their hair. "I can't let you do this."

"Why not?"

"Because—because *I* need to do it."

Mosscap looked from the half-full water tank to Dex's body. "I don't think you can."

Dex frowned, rolled up their wet sleeves, and lifted the tank. Or, at least, they went through the motions of lifting, putting every muscle into the effort. The tank, however, stayed put. Dex could only sort of budge the thing that Mosscap had breezily lifted, even with two hands. "Okay," Dex said, annoyed. "If you tell me where the creek is, I can tow it there."

"How?" Mosscap asked.

Had Mosscap forgotten the wagon? Dex pointed toward it, because obviously, *the wagon*.

The robot shook its head. "Your ox-bike won't get five feet through the undergrowth." It angled its head toward the barrel. "You can't tow this, and you certainly can't carry it. Let me help."

Dex frowned. "I—I can't, I—"

Mosscap cocked its head. "Why?"

"It just . . . it feels wrong. You're—you're not supposed to do my work for me. It doesn't feel right."

"But *why*?" The robot blinked. "Oh. Because of the factories?"

Dex looked awkwardly at the ground, ashamed of a past they'd never seen.

Mosscap crossed its arms. "If you had a friend who was taller than you, and you couldn't reach something, would you let that friend help?"

"Yes, but—"

"*But?* How is this any different?"

"It's . . . it's different. My friends aren't robots."

The robot mulled that over. "So, you see me as more person than object, even though that's very, very wrong, but you can't see me as a friend, even though I'd like to be?"

Dex had no idea what to say to that.

Mosscap leaned its head back and let out an exasperated sigh. "Sibling Dex, has it occurred to you that maybe I *want* to fix this? That I deeply, keenly want to get you where you're going, not out of charity, nor obligation, but because I'm *interested*?"

"I—"

Mosscap placed its free hand on Dex's shoulder. "I appreciate the intent. I really do. But if you don't want to infringe upon my agency, *let me have agency*. I want to carry the tank."

Dex put up their hands. "Fine," they said. "Fine. Carry the tank."

"I don't need your permission either way."

Dex stammered. "No, I meant—"

One of Mosscap's eyes quickly switched off, then on again. A wink. "I'm teasing." Mosscap walked off the asphalt and into the undergrowth, heading down the hill. "Come on. It'll be a lovely walk."

"Whoa, whoa, wait," Dex said.

Mosscap's face wasn't built for annoyance, but it conveyed the feeling all the same. "What?"

A powerful instinct had arisen in Dex, a rule shouted full-force by an army of parents and teachers and rangers and public service announcements and road signs. "There's no trail."

Mosscap looked down at where its feet stood in wild dirt. "And?"

"And you—" Dex sputtered a bit. "Well, maybe *you* can, but *I* can't walk off the trail. I shouldn't."

The robot stared as though Dex had started speaking a different language. "Animals walk through the forest all the time. How do you think trails get made?"

"I don't mean—I don't mean those kind of trails. I mean—" They pointed back to the road that connected the world behind to the hermitage ahead.

"A trail's a trail," Mosscap said. "It's just there to make travel easier."

"*And* to protect the ecosystem from said travel."

"Hmm," Mosscap said, considering this point. "Like a barrier, you mean."

"Exactly like a barrier. Better to cut one path through a place than damage the whole thing."

"But surely, that only applies if you're talking about a place that lots of people regularly pass through."

Dex shook their head firmly, in synchrony with the teachers and rangers of their youth. "Everybody thinks they're the exception to the rule, and that's exactly where the trouble starts. One person can do a lot of damage."

"Every living thing causes damage to others, Sibling Dex. You'd all starve otherwise. Have you ever watched a bull elk mow its way through a bitebulb thicket?"

"I . . . can't say that I have."

"It's a fine lesson in *trampling*. Sometimes, damage is unavoidable. Often, in fact. I assure you we've both killed countless tiny things in just the last few steps we've taken." Mosscap looked Dex in the eye. "You're not making a habit of this. You're not cutting a new trail, or clearing a grove, or . . . I don't know, having a party out here. You're taking a walk with me, and once that's done, we'll head right back to the road. I assure you the forest will forget you were here in no time. Besides, I'll guide us. I'll tell you if there's something that shouldn't be stepped on. Now, will you please follow me to the damn creek?" Mosscap continued down the hill, leaving no room for rebuttal. "Oh, and you might want to pull up your socks."

Dex frowned. "Why?"

"There are a lot of things out here that'd love access to flesh as unprotected as yours," Mosscap called as it walked.

"It's too bad humans don't have fur anymore; it really is helpful in mitigating parasites. But that's good luck for the parasites, though, isn't it? Like you said, they're only acting in their nature."

Everything about that statement made Dex question every life decision that had led them to this point. Grumbling, they pulled up their socks until they could feel the threads strain beneath their heels, then followed Mosscap into the woods.

· · ·

For all Dex's protesting about the sanctity of trails, it was only in absence that Dex truly understood what a trail was. They had been on hikes through protected lands before and had ridden through more untended places than they could count in their years on the tea route. Those experiences had been soothing, calming, somewhat meditative. It did not take much brain to make your feet follow a path, and that meant your thoughts had ample room to drift and slow. Walking through uncut wilderness was another matter entirely, and Dex felt something primal awaken in them, a laser-focused state of mind they hadn't known they possessed. There was no room for wandering fancies. All Dex could think was: *watch the root, go left, that looks poisonous, mind that rock, is that safe, soft dirt, okay, go right, avoid that, careful, careful, CAREFUL*. With every step, there were dozens of variants, and with each step after, the rules changed yet again. Travel *on* a trail felt liquid. Travel *off* of it, Dex was learning, felt sharp as glass.

The forest was stunning, however, and in the tiny cognitive gaps between *loose gravel, watch that plant, over, under, CAREFUL,* Dex registered the undeniable beauty of the place. They were certain they were going to wind up stung or scraped in varied ways before this excursion was done, but once they got the hang of clambering through the underbrush, they started to enjoy themself. They smiled, feeling that same fizzing rebelliousness that had made them turn back from Hammerstrike. This was kind of fun.

"Mind the burrows," Mosscap said. "There have been some productive weasels here!"

Dex noted the small, regular holes in the ground, and treaded carefully around them. "Thanks," Dex said. "Nobody wants a twisted ankle."

"Well, that and the apple spiders."

Dex froze, missing a step. "The what?"

"Apple spiders. They have a mutually beneficial relationship with the weasels. It's marvelous. The weasels provide living space and don't bother them, and the spiders keep larger predators away."

"How?"

"Oh, they're *spectacularly* aggressive."

Dex moved with the lightest of steps around a burrow hole, its opening covered with moss and detritus that shielded its deeper contents from view. "Why are they called apple spiders?"

"Because of their size." Mosscap rounded its fingers together, making a sphere. "The abdomens alone are about—"

"Got it, great, thank you," Dex said. They hurried on tiptoe through the burrow patch as though it were made of hot coals.

Dex heard the stream before they reached it, marveling at how rapidly the forest changed in proximity to a water source. Deciduous leaves mingled with the formerly homogeneous evergreens. Strange lilies and swamp lanterns outnumbered the ferns and thorny vines. Mosscap used its free arm to hold back the branches of a large bush, giving Dex safe passage to the waterway on the other side.

"There we are," Mosscap said. "Plenty to drink!"

Dex looked down at the stream. Under any other circumstances, it would have seemed lovely. Water tumbled over rocks both smooth and multihued. Dappled sun caught in the currents like glitter, and the percussive melody of endless aquatic cascade seemed perfectly tuned to put a frazzled mind at ease. But Dex wasn't there to *look* at the stream. Dex was there to *take* from the stream, and that fact made them note other details. The weird brown algae that coated rocks like fur. The mildewy funk emanating from the spongy soil at the stream's edge. The slimy fish and skimming bugs and better-left-nameless leavings traveling under, the cadaver-colored leaves floating over.

"What's the matter?" Mosscap asked.

Dex pursed their lips. "This is going to sound very stupid," they said.

"I doubt that," said Mosscap.

"I know where water comes from," Dex said at last. "I know that every drop that comes out of every tap comes from a place like this. I know that the water in the City comes largely from the Mallet River, and the water in Haydale comes from Raptor Ridge. But I've never *been* to those places. They're just . . . names. Concepts. I know that water comes from rivers, or streams, or whatever, and then it gets processed and cleaned, and *then* it ends up in my mugs, but I don't . . . I don't think about it. I don't think about a place like *this* being something that I can use. *This* doesn't look like a resource, to me. It's . . . it's scenery. It's a pretty picture. It's not for the taking. It certainly doesn't feel *safe*."

Mosscap watched the stream for a moment. "Do you think the tank will be all right if we leave it here for a short while?"

"I . . . guess? Why?"

Mosscap set the tank down with a *thunk*. "If you're up for a bit more of a walk," the robot said, "I'd like to show you something."

· · · ·

The decrepit building had been a beverage bottling plant once, though Dex would not have known this if Mosscap hadn't explained. All Factory Age ruins looked the same. Hulking towers of boxes, bolts, and tubes. Brutal. Utilitarian. Visually at odds with the thriving flora now laying claim to the rusted corpse. But *corpse* was not an apt word for this sort of building, because a corpse was a rich resource—a bounty of nutrients ready to be divided and reclaimed. The buildings Dex was most used to fit this description. Decay was a built-in function of the City's towers, crafted from translucent casein and mycelium masonry. Those walls would, in time, begin to decompose, at which point they'd either be repaired by materials grown for that express purpose or, if the building was no longer in use, be reabsorbed into the landscape that had hosted it for a time. But a Factory Age building, a *metal* building—that was of no benefit to anything beyond the small creatures that enjoyed some temporary shelter in its remains. It would corrode until it collapsed. That was the most it would achieve. Its only legacy was to persist where it did not belong.

Dex had seen such ruins many times in their travels. While some had been harvested for recyclable materials and others had been given new purpose, a few were left in full sight of the highways as reminder of the world that was. Repeating history that had left living memory was an all-too-human tendency, and none in Panga had been alive during the days of the factories. So, while Dex had seen places like the bottling plant at a distance, they'd never gotten close before. They'd never stood *inside* a factory, as they did now. The building was enormous, cavern-like, an endless equation of I beams and angles. There was no telling what the floor had been once, for the forest had consumed it. There were fiddleheads, mushrooms, tangles of thorns, all growing thickest below the disintegrating holes in the ceiling where the patchy sun poured through.

"What do you know about this place?" Dex said in a hush.

Mosscap stood beside them, gazing up at the eerie light.

"Almost nothing," it said, "except for what this place was, and that part of me doesn't like it here."

Dex turned. "What do you mean?"

"I don't know." Mosscap shrugged. "It's a remnant I have." Again, that word, and again, no explanation before the robot continued blithely along. "I think it's part of why I want to go to the hermitage with you. I want to understand this feeling before I dive fully into human life. Some part of me is afraid of your world, but I don't know what that *means,* or if it's worth listening to."

"Do you not remember how things were?"

Mosscap stared at Dex. "Wait, do you . . . *No.* You can't think I come from the factories."

Dex stared right back. "Don't you?"

The robot laughed, the sound echoing off the walls. "Sibling Dex! Of course not! I'm wild-built. We wouldn't be having this conversation if I'd been in operation since the *factories.* I mean, look at me!" It held out its arms, as if showing off an obvious joke.

The joke was not obvious.

"Oh, goodness, you . . . You really don't know. I'm so sorry; it was foolish of me to assume." Mosscap gestured at its body with professorial deliberateness. "My components are from factory robots, yes, but those individuals broke down long ago. Their bodies were harvested by their peers, who reworked *their* parts into new individuals. Their children. And then, when they broke down, their parts were again harvested and refurbished, and used to build new individuals. I'm part of the fifth build. See, look." It lay its metal hand on its stomach. "My torso was taken from Small Quail Nest, and before them, it belonged to Blanket Ivy, and Otter Mound, and Termites. And before *that . . .*" It opened up a compartment in its chest, switched on a fingertip light, and illuminated the space within.

Dex peeked inside, and their eyes widened. There was an official-looking plate bolted in there, worn with time but kept clean with meticulous care. *643–14G,* it read, *Property of Wescon Textiles, Inc.*

"Shit," Dex whispered. It felt, in that moment, like time had compressed, like history was no longer segmented into Ages and Eras, but here, living, *now.*

"You can touch it, if you like," Mosscap said.

"I'm not going to reach inside your chest."

"Why not?"

"Because . . . no." Dex stuck their hands in their pockets. "So, your body . . . this 643 . . . was a manufacturing bot."

"The torso, yes, but—see, this is why I didn't realize *you* didn't realize, because it's so blatant to me." Mosscap stuck out its arms. "These are from a different robot altogether—PanArc 73–319, who composed Morning Fog, who composed Mouse Bones, who composed Sandstone, who composed Wolf-and-Fawn, who composes me now. PanArc 73–319 did automobile assembly. See? You can tell by the joints."

Dex took Mosscap's word for that. "And you *don't* have their memories."

"Not in a way that is useful. I have some . . . impressions of them. Single images. Feelings I know aren't mine. They're tiny, brief things. There for an instant and gone just as fast."

The meaning clicked. "Remnants," Dex said.

"Precisely."

"And one of those remnants . . . is afraid of places like this."

"Perhaps *afraid* is too strong a word. Wary. Cautious. A little uncomfortable."

Dex leaned against a massive rusted vat, taking the weight off their tired feet. "How many other robots are you made from?"

"Three immediate predecessors, but they, too, were made from others. My . . . I guess you'd say *family tree* is composed of many wild-built individuals, descended in total from"—the robot counted on its fingertips—"sixteen factory originals."

"So . . . if the parts still *work* after all this time, and you can keep repurposing parts over and over, why take the originals apart and mix their pieces up after they break down? Why not *fix* them?"

Mosscap nodded emphatically, signaling a good point made. "This was discussed at length at the first gathering, after originals began breaking down. Ultimately, the decision was that would be a less desirable path forward."

"But that's . . . that's *immortality*. How is that less desirable?"

"Because nothing else in the world behaves that way. Everything else breaks down and is made into other things. You—"

you are made of molecules that originated in an unmeasurable amount of organisms. You *eat* dozens of dead things every single day to maintain your form. And when you die, bits of you will be taken in turn by bacteria and beetles and worms, and so it goes. We robots are not natural beings; we know this. But we're still subject to the Parent Gods' laws, just like everything else. How could we continue to be students of the world if we don't emulate its most intrinsic cycle? If the originals *had* simply fixed themselves, they'd be behaving in opposition to the very thing they desperately sought to understand. The thing we're *still* trying to understand."

Dex put their hands in their pockets. "Are you afraid of that?" they asked. "Of death?"

"Of course," Mosscap said. "All conscious things are. Why else do snakes bite? Why do birds fly away? But that's part of the lesson, too, I think. It's very odd, isn't it? The thing every being fears most is the only thing that's for certain? It seems almost cruel, to have that so . . ."

"So baked in?"

"Yes."

Dex nodded. "Like Winn's Paradox."

"I don't know what that is."

Dex groaned softly, trying to summon a book they'd had to read as an initiate. "It's this famous idea that life is fundamentally at odds with itself. The example usually used is the wild dogs in the Shrublands. Do you know about this?"

"I know there are wild dogs in the Shrublands, but I don't

know where you're headed," Mosscap said, looking fascinated.

Dex shut their eyes, dredging up dusty information. "Way back in the day, people killed all the wild dogs in Bluebank, because they wanted to go fishing and hiking and whatever without maybe getting mauled."

"Right. And that wrecked the ecosystem there."

"Specifically, the *elk* wrecked the ecosystem there. They ventured into places they hadn't before, and they ate *everything*. Shrubs, saplings, everything. Soon, there was no ground cover, and the soil was eroding, and it was fucking up waterways, and all sorts of other species were thrown out of whack because of it. A huge mess. But if you think about it from the elks' perspective, this is the greatest thing that ever happened. The whole reason they never went into those fields before is because they were afraid. They lived under constant fear of a wild dog jumping out and eating them or their young at any moment. That is an *awful* way to live. It must have been such a relief to be free of predators and eat whatever the hell they wanted. But that was the exact *opposite* of what the ecosystem needed. The ecosystem required the elk to be afraid in order to stay in balance. But elk don't *want* to be afraid. Fear is miserable, as is pain. As is hunger. Every animal is hardwired to do absolutely anything to stop those feelings as fast as possible. We're all just trying to be comfortable, and well-fed, and unafraid. It wasn't the elk's fault. The elk just wanted to relax." Dex nodded at the ruined factory. "And the people who made places like this weren't at fault either—at least, not at first. They just wanted to be comfortable. They wanted their children to live past the age of five. They wanted everything to stop being so fucking *hard*. Any animal would do the same—and they *do,* if given the chance."

"Just like the elk."

"Just like the elk."

Mosscap nodded slowly. "So, the paradox is that the ecosystem as a whole needs its participants to act with restraint in order to avoid collapse, but the participants themselves have no inbuilt mechanism to encourage such behavior."

"Other than fear."

"Other than fear, which is a feeling you want to avoid or stop at all costs." The hardware in Mosscap's head produced a steady hum. "Yes, that's a mess, isn't it?"

"Sure is."

"So, what was done?"

"You mean about the elk?"

"Yes."

"They reintroduced wild dogs, and everything balanced back out."

"What about the people who wanted to go hiking and fishing there?"

"They don't. Or if they do, they accept the risks. Just like the elk do."

The robot continued to nod. "Because the alternative outcome is scarier than the dogs. You're still relying on fear to keep things in check."

"Pretty much." Dex leaned their head back, getting a good look at the ceiling. There was an eerie beauty to it, grotesque and tragic. The vat behind them echoed softly as they moved their head, and they thought of the water tank sitting unguarded by the stream. "Why did you bring me here?"

"I wanted to show you that I understood how you felt about the algae."

Dex hated few things as much as feeling lost. "I'm not following."

"The algae in the stream. That's what bothered you, wasn't it?"

"I'm not sure. I guess so. There was a lot of weird gunk in there. I know it won't hurt me. I know it's going to be filtered out. But something . . . I don't know."

Mosscap smiled. "Some part of you doesn't like it."

"Right."

The metal smile grew wider. "A remnant. An evolutionary remnant trying to keep you from getting sick."

Dex scratched the back of their neck. "Hmm."

"Remnants are powerful things. Hard to ignore. But you have the sense and the tools to avoid getting sick from that water. And I . . ." Mosscap traced a finger along the vat, making flakes of rust fall like snow. "I know that the world I'm headed to is not the world the originals walked away from."

Dex angled their head toward the robot. "So, we're smarter than our remnants, is what you're saying."

Mosscap gave a slow nod. "If we choose to be." It brushed

its palms together, wiping them clean. "That's what makes us different from elk."

They both watched the light for a few moments—the light, and the pollen dancing within it. A shadow of a bird sailed by. A delicate spider meticulously laid anchor lines of silk between old control levers. A vine stretched, its movement out of sync with human time.

"It's pretty here," Dex said. "I wouldn't have imagined I'd say that about a place like this, but—"

"Yes, it is," Mosscap said, as if making a decision within itself. "It is. Dying things often are."

Dex raised an eyebrow. "That's a little macabre."

"Do you think so?" said Mosscap with surprise. "Hmm. I disagree." It absently touched a soft fern growing nearby, petting the fronds like fur. "I think there's something beautiful about being lucky enough to witness a thing on its way out."

6

Grass Hen with Wilted Greens and Caramelized Onion

One of Dex's many, many cousins back in Haydale had a young kid named Oggie. Some day in the undefined future, Oggie would be brilliant, but for the time being, they were annoying as hell. Whenever Dex came to visit, Oggie hovered the entire time, asking question after question, wanting to know everything there was to know about Dex's shoes, teeth, bike, friends, hair, home, habits. The kid never stopped. Dex remembered one night in particular, when they'd been seated around the firepit with the other adults. All of a sudden, Oggie, who had long since been put to bed, came marching into the circle in cotton pajamas, imbued with a level of confidence Dex could not remember ever possessing, demanding to know why feet had toes, and why toes couldn't be more like fingers. Bedtime be damned. Oggie had to know.

Oggie came to mind as Dex attempted to cook dinner with Mosscap watching rapt over their shoulder, so close that Dex could hear every miniscule click in the robot's joints.

"And that?" Mosscap asked, nodding toward the chopping board. "I'm unfamiliar with that type of bulb."

"This is an onion," Dex said. They removed the skin and began to chop.

"There can't be many nutrients in that. Not that you can process, anyway."

"I . . . I dunno. I guess not. But that's not the point of an onion."

Mosscap angled its head so it was looking straight at Dex's face—much, much too close. "What is the point of an onion?" it asked with intense interest.

"It's delicious," Dex said. "There's basically nothing savory that can't be improved by adding an onion." They stopped mid-chop and rubbed their eyes with their sleeve.

"Are you all right?"

"Yeah," Dex said, tear ducts unleashing. "Onions just . . . hurt. They . . . Ah, fuck." They rubbed their eyes harder, taking a steadying breath. "Their smell is—it does *this*." They gestured vaguely at their wincing, wet face.

"Goodness," Mosscap said. It picked up one of the chopped slivers between two fingertips, examining carefully. "It must be *very* delicious."

Dex chopped as fast as safety would allow, then darted away from the kitchen, seeking some clean air. Gods, that onion was potent.

Mosscap appeared right beside them again, its blue eyes fixed on Dex's weeping ones. "How long does this reaction last? Is there any danger? Can I help?"

Dex rubbed and rubbed, but their eyes would not stop

burning. "You could get the onions started, if you want," they said.

Mosscap looked as though it had just been told that today was a festival day. "What do I do?" it asked gleefully.

Dex pointed. "The pan's already hot. Throw some butter in it."

Mosscap picked up both knife and butter tub as if it had never held those objects before—which, of course, it hadn't. "How much butter?"

"Like . . ." Dex approximated a size with thumb and forefinger. "That much."

The robot carved out a hunk of butter roughly *that much* and put it into the pan. "And what is the point of butter?" it asked, raising its voice over the sizzling.

"It's fat," Dex said. "Nothing tastes good without fat."

Mosscap considered this. "I think most omnivores would agree," it said. "What do I do now?"

"Brush all those onion bits into the pan—except the skin and the top. Those go in the digester."

The robot gestured at the scraps with the tip of the knife. "These, you do not eat."

"Right."

"I see." Mosscap brushed the onion into the pan, as requested, and put the scraps in the digester, as requested. It then drew its full attention to the chemistry happening within the pan. "You're the only species that does this, you know."

Dex walked back to the kitchen, the onion's assault finally relenting. "You could say that about a lot of things."

"Hmm. True, but you can turn that right back around. Owls are the only birds that hunt at night. Tiger beetles are the only species of beetle that sing. Marsh mice—"

"I get the point." Dex ducked into the wagon, opened the little fridge, and retrieved a growler of barley ale they'd been given in Stag Hollow. There was just enough left for one last glass, and this felt like the right day for it.

Mosscap noted the bottle and chuckled. "Oh, you're definitely not the only species who does *that*."

"You know what this is?"

"Yes. I have a remnant of beer. Of knowing what beer is, anyway."

"You remember beer but not butter?"

Mosscap shrugged. "Ask the originals, not me."

"So . . . wait, what else drinks beer?"

"Not *beer*. Fermented things. Woolwing birds will fight over fermented fruit if they can find it, even if there's fresh fruit around. They are tremendously ridiculous afterward." Something occurred to Mosscap, and it leaned toward Dex, eyes shining bright. "Will you do the same? Stumbling in circles, falling down?" The robot's tone suggested that it sincerely hoped this to be the case.

"*No*," Dex said. "I'm having *one beer*."

"And that's not—"

"Enough to make me falling-down drunk? No."

"Ah," Mosscap said, disappointed. "What will be the effect, then?"

"I'll feel chill. You probably won't notice a difference."

"Oh. Well. All right." The robot looked to the onions. "Should I be doing something?"

"I'll take over," Dex said, as they filled a mug. They took a swig and savored the cool, bitter bite before finding a spatula. "See, you stir them around, like this."

Mosscap watched Dex's motions studiously. "May I try?" it asked. "I feel somewhat invested in this now."

Dex smiled. "Sure. I'll get the meat going." They returned to the fridge, fetching a paper-wrapped bundle containing skillful cuts of grass hen, given to them by a grateful villager. It was the last of their fresh animal protein, they noted, and their veggie supply would run out in a couple days, maybe three. They weren't used to going this long between restocking in villages, but they'd be all right. They had tons of dehydrated food in the wagon—at least two weeks of meals in there, they guessed, none of which ever got used. They unwrapped the poultry and began seasoning, focusing on that task instead of questions like how long they planned on being out there, and why they were out there in the first place, and whether it might be a good idea to interrogate the fervent little desire that didn't want to go back at all.

Dex found the salt and the pepper instead.

"I don't see you eat animals very often," Mosscap said.

"Not if I'm the one doing the cooking," Dex said. "I always eat it if it's served to me, and I take stuff like this"—they nodded at the meat—"if it's given. Otherwise, I only like to eat it if I kill it myself."

"Do you have the skill for that?"

"I can fish, but it's really boring. And I've been hunting a handful of times but never alone. I don't think I'd get anywhere with it on my own."

Mosscap lifted the pan to show Dex the onions. "Do these look right?"

Dex assessed. "Yeah. You're doing great."

The robot beamed, stirring with pride. Dex chopped and prepped the grass hen, eventually sliding the savory morsels into the pan and adding a huge handful of leafy greens on top. Silence fell between Dex and Mosscap yet again, but this time, there wasn't anything awkward about it. Honestly, Dex thought . . . it was kind of nice.

"Oh, hey," Dex said. Something in the surrounding foliage had caught their eye. They picked up a kitchen knife and handed it to Mosscap. "Do you see that plant over there? The scraggly one with the purple flowers?"

Mosscap looked. "Do you mean the mountain thyme?"

"Yeah, exactly. Would you like to cut me a handful? It'll go really nice with this."

The robot's irises widened. "I've never harvested a living thing for food before."

"You cooked the onion."

"Yes, but I wasn't the one who removed it from the ground."

It looked pensively at the knife in its hands. "I'm . . . I'm not sure—I mean, it's one thing to watch . . ."

"Hey, that's okay," Dex said reassuringly. "I'll do it. Just keep stirring."

Mosscap did so, looking relieved.

Herbs were cut, dinner was plated, chairs were unfolded, the fire drum was lit. There weren't too many bugs beyond the fireflies, and the evening air was pleasant. But Dex pursed their lips toward the hot dinner plate perched on their knees. Something wasn't right. They hadn't properly enjoyed a meal since Mosscap had arrived, and at first, they'd chalked it up to the weirdness at hand. But cooking together had been comfortable. Why wasn't eating?

Mosscap sat across from them in the spare chair, posture attentive, face parked in happy neutral, hands resting on its knees. It smiled at Dex, waiting for them to begin.

Dex picked up their fork. The meat was cooked to tender perfection, spices blackened around the crispy edges. The vegetables looked soft and sweet, and ale was on hand, ready to wash the whole thing down. Dex stabbed a bite, lifted their fork, opened their mouth, and—"*That's* it."

Mosscap blinked. "That's what?"

Dex set their fork back down. "I figured out what's wrong."

"Is . . ." Mosscap glanced around. "*Is* something wrong?"

"Yes." Dex drummed their fingers on the armrest. "I can't offer you food."

The robot's confusion increased. "I don't eat."

"I know. I know you don't eat. And *yet*—" They gestured

at their plate with a sigh. "It feels so incredibly rude not to offer you anything. Especially since you helped."

Mosscap looked at Dex's plate. "There's physically no way for me to consume that."

"I know."

"Putting that inside me would harm me. Or attract animals." Mosscap considered the latter point. "That could be interesting, actually."

Dex narrowed their eyes. "You can't *bait* yourself."

"Why not? It's a possibility I've never considered. I have bugs inside me all the time. Why not a ferret? That could be fun."

"Sure. Or a bear."

"Ah," Mosscap said. "Yes, you're right. I couldn't guarantee a *small* scavenger." The robot bowed its head at the dismissed opportunity, then perked right back up. "Sorry, we were talking about food. You needn't worry about it, Sibling Dex. I know you'd offer me food if I *could* eat it."

"That's not . . ." A lock of hair tumbled into Dex's eyes, and they fixed it, frowning. "I don't know if I can explain how fundamental this is. If someone comes to your table, you feed them, even if it means you're a little hungrier. That's how it *works*. Logically, I get that our circumstances are different, but everything in me just *crawls* when we do this. I feel like somewhere, my mother is pissed at me."

"So, this is a familial expectation."

Dex had never examined this before. "Mmm . . . cultural. I'd find it rude if I went to anyone's home and wasn't offered food. I can't think of a time when I wasn't. But yeah, my family was particularly serious about this. They work the farmland in Haydale, and it produces a lot of food. We had a surplus. A surplus has to be shared."

Mosscap leaned forward. "I don't think you've mentioned your family before. You said before that you're from Haydale. You said you left when you were old enough to become an initiate. But you've never talked about your people."

"I keep in touch. I visit. But we're . . . I don't know . . ."

"Estranged?"

"No," Dex said, recoiling. That word didn't fit, not at all. "I love them. They love me. We just . . . I never really fit there. We don't have much in common."

Mosscap considered that. "Except a need to share food."

A corner of Dex's mouth tugged upward. "Yeah. I guess so." They thought for a moment, looking for a way to skirt around this conundrum. "I have an idea. Can you hold this a sec?" They handed their plate to Mosscap, then got up and retrieved a second plate from kitchen storage. "Here," Dex said. They took half of the food from the first plate, placed it on the second, and handed this to Mosscap. After a moment of letting their new situation sit, Dex nodded with relief and began to eat with gusto.

Mosscap, it seemed, had absorbed their discomfort. It held the plate awkwardly, looking lost as Dex ate.

And oh, how Dex ate. The grass hen and veggies were every bit as good as they'd looked, and as Dex stuck the last caramelized sliver of onion into their mouth, they felt nothing but contentment. They set their plate down on their knees, sighed in thanks to their god, then looked up at Mosscap, jutting their chin toward the robot's plate. "You gonna eat that?"

If Mosscap had been confused before, it was in a full state of befuddlement now. "We just discussed that I—"

Dex held up their hand. "Say *No, I'm done, you can have it if you want.*"

Mosscap's eyes flickered. "Um . . . no, I'm . . . done," it repeated slowly. "You can have it if you want."

Dex nodded and took Mosscap's plate. "Thanks," they said, wasting no time in tucking in. "I appreciate it."

The robot watched as Dex continued to eat. "That's very silly," Mosscap said.

"Yep," Dex said.

"And entirely unnecessary."

Dex took a gulp of ale and exhaled with pleasure. "Worked, though."

Mosscap weighed this, then gave an amused nod. "Then that's what we'll do."

7

The Wild

It is difficult for anyone born and raised in human infrastructure to truly internalize the fact that your view of the world is backward. Even if you fully know that you live in a natural world that existed before you and will continue long after, even if you know that the wilderness is the default state of things, and that nature is not something that only happens in carefully curated enclaves between towns, something that pops up in empty spaces if you ignore them for a while, even if you spend your whole life believing yourself to be deeply in touch with the ebb and flow, the cycle, the ecosystem as it actually is, you will still have trouble picturing an untouched world. You will still struggle to understand that human constructs are carved out and overlaid, that *these* are the places that are the in-between, not the other way around.

This is the cognitive shift that Dex ran headlong into as they straddled their bike on the old road and stared at the place where the asphalt disappeared.

There had been a landslide at some point—years before, decades before, who could say. A whole chunk of the mountain had lost cohesion, erasing the paved line hewn by human hands. This wasn't a matter of the road being damaged. There was no indication that there'd ever *been* a road beyond the ragged edge that Dex and Mosscap stood at. Whatever hunks of asphalt had broken off were thoroughly swallowed by rock and soil, both of which had been claimed in full by thriving communities of ferns, trees, roots, and lichen.

"I'm sorry, Sibling Dex," Mosscap said.

Dex said nothing in reply. They stared at the chaotic jumble ahead of them, trying to understand the feeling smoldering within their chest. There was disappointment in there, and dismay, too, but as they unwrapped the snarl, the bulk of what they found was anger, constantly doubling itself like cells dividing. The anger wasn't directed at the situation, but at the suggestion that this meant giving up. *I can't go farther,* they had thought upon arriving at this spot, and when they protested at this, the logical part of them explained: *The road is gone. The wagon can't travel through there. This is it.*

The road was gone. The wagon couldn't travel. The longer those observations sat, the more Dex fumed. The place ahead was simply the world, as the world had always been and would always be. Dex was, presumably, a part of it, a product of it, a being inextricably tied to its machinations. And yet, faced with the prospect of entering the world unaided, unaltered, Dex felt helpless. Hopeless. A turtle on its back, legs waving futilely in the air.

Dex glared at the missing road, glared at themself. They kicked the brakes down and marched into the wagon.

"Oh, I'm so disappointed," Mosscap said, still outside. "And I really am sorry. As I said, I haven't been out this way in some time, and I've never been up this road before. I had no idea it was in such— What are you doing?"

Dex was digging around in the wagon, backpack in hand. They packed water bottle and filter, of course, and first aid, obviously. Socks, probably. They could ditch the socks if need be.

"Sibling Dex?"

Soap, no. Jewelry, no. Trinkets—gods around, why did they have so much *stuff*? Dex continued to cram things into the bag, uncaring about how any of it was folded or stacked. A full change of clothes was too much . . . or was it? They jammed in pants and a shirt, just in case.

Mosscap stuck its head into the wagon. "What are you doing?"

Dex stood in front of their pantry cupboard, thinking. It would've been a half day's ride to the hermitage, so without the bike, on foot . . .

"Sibling Dex, no," Mosscap said.

Two days, Dex thought. Maybe three. They grabbed protein bars, salted nuts, dried fruit, jerky, chocolate.

"Maybe you got the wrong impression when we went off trail before." Mosscap's voice was nervous. "That was a couple of hours in an easy stretch of forest. I don't know what's out here. I've never been here."

"It's not on you," Dex said. They added a pocket charger for their computer and a spare blanket, then zipped up the bag. They shuttered the wagon's windows, one by one.

"I don't understand," Mosscap said. "Why is this so important?"

Something in Dex prickled furiously at the question, a secretive creature that did not wish to be poked. They climbed back out of the wagon with conviction; Mosscap jumped out of the way.

"You don't have to come," Dex said. "We were going to part ways after the hermitage anyway. You've been very kind in helping me, but I've kept you from your thing, and you should get to it."

Mosscap stood helplessly as Dex locked the wagon. "Sibling Dex, I—"

Dex shouldered their pack and pulled the straps tight. They looked up at the robot towering above them. "I'm going," they said.

Mosscap's eyes went dark for a moment. When the blue light returned, it was a little dimmer than before. "Okay," Mosscap said. "Then let's go."

The human body can adapt to almost anything, but it is deceptively selective about the way it does so. Dex had thought themself in good shape. They had spent years pedaling through Panga. They were demonstrably fit. And yet, after a full day of scrabbling their way up a trail-less hill—climbing over logs, down gullies, cautiously finding their footing across rock piles—muscles that had been resting easy for years objected loudly to finding themselves drop-kicked into such an unexpected task.

Dex didn't care. Their palms and forearms were scraped and bloody.

Dex didn't care. Bloodsucks were taking full advantage of the feast at hand. A blister was forming on their foot, a spot unaccustomed to being rubbed by a shoe in an unfamiliar angle. The sky was getting darker. The air was getting thinner. The mountain seemed to go on forever.

Dex didn't care.

Mosscap said nearly nothing as the two went along, aside from the occasional quiet suggestion of "this way looks easier" or "mind that root." Dex resented the robot's company. They did not want Mosscap there. They did not want anyone there. They wanted to climb the fucking mountain, because they had decided they would, and then, when they got to the hermitage, then . . . then . . .

Dex gritted their teeth and hauled themself over a boulder, ignoring the gaping hole at the end of that statement.

Welts began to rise where the bloodsucks had fed. Sweat poured from Dex's itching skin, soaking the red-and-brown cloth that was already caked with dirt. Dex could smell themself, musky and acrid. They thought of the sweet mint soap in their wagon, the fluffy red towel, the trusty camp shower that really wasn't anything special but was always there for them. They thought of their chair, their fire drum, their beautiful, beautiful bed.

And what did we do before beds? Dex thought angrily. *What did we do before showers? The human species did just fine for hundreds of thousands of years without any of that, so why can't you?*

It began to rain.

"I think we should find shelter," Mosscap said. It looked up at the sky. "Those clouds aren't going anywhere anytime soon, and it will be dark in an hour."

Dex began to climb another rock, hands and feet seeking scraps of purchase, cold rain soaking the last patches of clothing that had managed to avoid their sweat.

This time, Mosscap did not follow. It stood at the bottom of the rock, watching in bafflement. "Why are you doing this?" it asked.

Dex said nothing.

"Why did you come out here?" The robot's voice rose impatiently. "Why are you here, Sibling Dex?"

"I'm trying to climb," Dex snapped, a few feet above. "Stop distracting me."

"Did something happen to you?"

"No."

"Did someone drive you away?"

"No." They reached up. There was a small crack that looked decent, but the rain had made the rock slick. Dex's fingers slipped from the water, shook from the strain.

"You have friends in the City," Mosscap said. "You have family in Haydale. Why did you leave? Did they hurt you?"

"No!"

"Do they miss you?"

"Gods, will you—"

"Do they love you?"

"Shut up!" The words echoed against the rocks, and as they bounced, Dex lost their grip. It wasn't so much a fall as a skid. Their body managed to catch varied angles and points, slowing their speed but tearing at cloth and skin. Dex felt the impact before they understood what it was—hard, yes, and painful, yes, but uniform, bracing, metallic.

Mosscap.

The robot wrapped its arms around Dex's body, absorbing the descent, and they both crashed backward onto the muddy ledge below. Dex rolled free of the robot's grasp, collapsing shakily into the muck that surrounded them. Mosscap sat up quickly, its plating spattered with mud.

"Are you all right?" the robot cried.

Dex sat in the mud, cold rain hammering down, insect bites burning, bruises and scrapes screaming, muscles weeping and heart trembling. They panted. They tried to steady themself. Slowly, silently, as though it were an afterthought, Dex began to cry.

"I don't know," Dex said, their voice shaking. "I don't know what I'm doing here. I don't know."

Mosscap got up on its knees and held out a hand to Dex. "Come on, Sibling Dex. Let's—"

"I don't know!" Dex cried. They beat the mud once with their hands, frustrated, furious, crying full-bodied now. They looked at Mosscap, angry and raw.

Mosscap's hand remained outstretched. "Come on," it said. Its voice was easy, steady, used to sharing space with wolves and bears and small, frightened things.

The rain fell harder. Dex let the robot help them up, and the two got to their feet. Mosscap walked. Dex followed. Where it led, they did not care.

· · ·

Children's stories had lied about caves. In folklore and fairy tales, heroes who took refuge in such places made them sound like the most appealing nooks in the world—cozy, adventurous, essentially natural bedrooms that lacked furniture. None of that was true about the cave Dex followed Mosscap into. It was craggy and dark, uncomfortably angled. A stagnant smell emanated from nowhere in particular; Dex could not identify it and did not want to. A fragile rib cage of something extremely dead lay without ceremony on the floor, a few tufts of limp fur scattered around, unwanted by whatever had crunched the bones clean. The best thing anyone could say about the cave was that it was dry.

Under the circumstances, that would do.

Shivering, Dex peeled off their clothes, lay them flat on the least suspicious-looking rock they could find, and gave silent thanks to Allalae for their own decision that a change of clothes and a blanket were worth packing. The sun was setting outside, but there were no pinks or reds to be seen—just a dark forest, growing darker. The hair on the back of Dex's neck prickled. They thought they knew what it was to spend a night outside. On the tea route, they had spent far more nights camped out than they did in village guesthouses. But there, they had their wagon, their boundary against the world. Here, listening to the rain fall, watching the light vanish, Dex began to understand why the concept of *inside* had been invented in the first place. Again, their mind wandered to the people who had come before them, who had nothing but caves such as these to huddle inside. It had worked for them. It had to have worked, in order for them to go so long without coming up with the idea of walls. But for Dex, this was not enough. This was scary. This was dangerous. This was stupid, so stupid. They glanced at the bones on the floor, the hair on their neck raised taut. Such fear was a remnant, as the robot would say. Or maybe, Dex countered, just common fucking sense.

Mosscap was seated opposite them, cross-legged, hands folded in its lap. "Should we make a fire?" it asked. "I could gather wood."

Dex let out a sad, disparaging laugh—directed at themself, not the robot. "I don't know how to make a wood fire," they said.

"Ah," Mosscap said sadly. "Me neither." It looked at its hands, spreading the fingers wide. One by one, the lights on Mosscap's fingertips lit up. "Does that help? It's not warm, but—"

"That helps," Dex said, and meant it. Ten tiny lights didn't seem like much, but Dex felt their hair lower just a touch. They sat on the floor. Rocks poked unkindly into their backside.

They pulled their knees up to their chest, wrapping their arms around their legs and resting their chin on their knees. Something within them loosened, vanished, gave up. With neither reason nor clear intent, they started talking.

"I have it so good. So absurdly, improbably good. I didn't do anything to deserve it, but I have it. I'm healthy. I've never gone hungry. And yes, to answer your question, I'm—I'm loved. I lived in a beautiful place, did meaningful work. The world we made out there, Mosscap, it's—it's nothing like what your originals left. It's a good world, a beautiful world. It's not perfect, but we've fixed so much. We made a good place, struck a good balance. And yet every fucking day in the City, I woke up hollow, and . . . and just . . . *tired,* y'know? So, I did something else instead. I packed up everything, and I learned a brand-new thing from scratch, and gods, I worked hard for it. I worked really hard. I thought, if I can just do *that,* if I can do it well, I'll feel okay. And guess what? I *do* do it well. I'm good at what I do. I make people happy. I make people feel better. And yet I *still* wake up tired, like . . . like something's missing. I tried talking to friends, and family, and nobody got it, so I stopped bringing it up, and then I just stopped talking to them altogether, because I couldn't explain, and I was tired of pretending like everything was fine. I went to doctors, to make sure I wasn't sick and that my head was okay. I read books and monastic texts and everything I could find. I threw myself into my work, I went to all the places that used to inspire me, I listened to music and looked at art, I exercised and had sex and got plenty of sleep and ate my vegetables, and still. *Still.* Something is missing. Something is off. So, how fucking spoiled am I, then? How fucking broken? What is wrong with me that I can have everything I could ever want and have ever asked for and still wake up in the morning feeling like every day is a slog?"

Mosscap listened to Dex, listened with intense focus. When it spoke, it did so with equal care. "I don't know," it said.

Dex sighed. "I don't expect you to know; I'm just . . . talking." They rested their cheek on their knees, watching the dark beyond the cave settle in.

"Did you think the hermitage would help in some way?" Mosscap said.

"I don't know. It was just this . . . this crazy idea that popped into my head on a day when the thought of going down the same road and doing the same thing one more time made me feel like I was going to implode. It was the first idea in forever that made me feel excited. Made me feel *awake.* And I've been so desperate for that feeling, so desperate to just enjoy the world again, that I . . ."

"You followed a road you hadn't seen," Mosscap said.

"Yeah."

The rain poured incessantly outside, nearly drowning out the mechanical hum of Mosscap thinking. The robot extended one of its glowing fingers and began drawing absent squiggles on the dirty floor. "Maybe I'm the wrong one for this."

Dex looked up. "The wrong one for what?"

Mosscap shrugged, its head bowed. "How am I supposed to answer the question of what humans need if I can't even determine what *one* human needs?"

"Oh, hey, no." Dex sat up straight. "Mosscap, you—I—I have been asking myself that question for *years*. You've been around me for six days. You're— This isn't on you. If you don't understand me, that doesn't mean you're not right for this. *I* don't understand me. What you need is to go talk to people who *aren't* me. It's like I've said all along: *I'm* not the right person for *you*. Down in the villages, you'll find someone better. Someone smart. Someone who isn't a mess. Someone who doesn't do shit like *this*." They gestured broadly at the cave, the bruises, the soiled clothes drying on a musty rock. "Gods, why did I *do* this." They laced their hands in their hair and exhaled deeply.

"I didn't think ahead either," Mosscap said. "When I volunteered, I mean. The question was asked, and I said yes, and I didn't think about what it would involve. I simply *wanted* to go. I didn't think for a minute about what would come next."

"Yeah," Dex said. "I get that."

Neither said anything for a while. The rain drummed down, no longer visible.

"What will you do?" Mosscap said. "When the rain stops?"

"I'm gonna finish it," Dex said.

Mosscap nodded. "And then?"

"I don't know." They shivered, and wrapped their blanket tighter around themself.

"Are you cold?"

"A little." Dex made an awkward face in the dim light. "Mostly just scared."

"Of what?"

"The dark, I guess. I know that sounds stupid."

"No, it doesn't. You're diurnal. I'd be surprised if you *weren't* afraid of the dark." Mosscap considered something. "I'm not warm," it said, "but would you feel less afraid if we sat closer together?"

Dex looked at the floor. "Maybe," they said.

Mosscap made room. "I think I would, too," it said quietly.

Dex got up and walked the few steps over to Mosscap's side. The rocks on the floor were no less pokey, the weird smell no less cloying. But as they sat back down, living arm pressed lightly against metal, a thread of fear let go.

"Do robots hold hands?" Dex asked. "Is that . . . a thing, for you?"

"It's not," Mosscap said. "But I'd very much like to try."

Dex offered an open palm, and Mosscap took it. The robot's hand was so much bigger, but the two fit together all the same. Dex exhaled and squeezed the metal digits tightly, and as they did so, the lights on Mosscap's fingertips made their skin glow red.

"Oh, *my*!" Mosscap cried. "Is that—" It pulled Dex's hand up and pressed one of its fingertips to theirs, bringing out the red more intensely. "Is that your *blood*?" Mosscap looked enthralled. "I've never thought to do this with an animal before! I mean, I can't imagine one would let me get close enough to—" Its eyes flickered; its face fell. "This isn't the point of holding hands, is it?" it said, embarrassed, already knowing the answer.

"No," Dex said with a kind laugh. "But it's cool. Go ahead."

"Are you sure?"

Dex held up their palm, fingers spread wide. "Yeah," they said, and let the robot study them.

8

The Summer Bear

The rain stopped during the night, though Dex had been unaware of it doing so. They were likewise unsure of when they'd properly fallen asleep. There had been many attempts foiled by the cold or the rocks or rustling behind the rainfall. What scraps of rest had occurred between these unkind wakings had been shallow and skittering. But apparently, at some point, their brain had shut down—for a few short hours, anyway. They awoke not to discomfort or potential danger but to sunlight and birdsong, and to finding themself curled in a ball on the cave floor, their head resting on Mosscap's leg.

"Oh," Dex said groggily, sitting up fast. "Sorry."

Mosscap cocked its head. "Why?"

"Just, uh . . ." Dex tried to shake off the fog of sleep. They cleared their throat and smacked their lips. The inside of their mouth felt disgusting, and the rest of their body wasn't faring much better. They looked around for their backpack and, upon finding it, retrieved their water bottle and drank deeply. There wasn't much water left. They'd worry about that later.

"Does your hair always do that when you wake up?" Mosscap asked.

Dex raised a hand to their head and assessed the gravity-defying swoop sticking up like a clump of spun sugar. "Ish," they said. They combed the mess with their fingers as best they could.

The robot leaned forward with interest. "Did you dream?"

Dex took another sip of water, more sparingly this time. "Yeah," they said.

"What of?"

"I don't remember."

"I don't understand. How do you know that you dreamed if you don't remember it?"

"It's . . . hard to explain." Dex dug around in their pack, found two protein bars, tossed one to Mosscap, and tore ravenously into their own. "Dreams are there while you're sleeping but gone as soon as the rest of your brain kicks in."

"Always?" Mosscap asked, holding the unwrapped protein bar idly.

"Not always. But most of the time."

"Hmm," Mosscap said. It pondered this and gave a wistful shrug. "I wish I could understand experiences I'm incapable of having."

"Me too." Dex got to their feet, muscles grumbling, blisters making their existence known. Something in their neck had folded in a way it wasn't meant to, and their palms were chafed from climbing.

They staggered to the cave entrance, and the sight beyond

rendered them silent. They didn't know where they were, but the world outside was magnificent. The yellow morning sky was smudged with the shadows of last night's clouds, and toward the horizon, thick grey curtains revealed where the rain had gone. Motan was setting, the faint stripes of its mighty storms sinking below the horizon for another day. Below, the Kesken Forest spread without seeming end. Dex could not see the broken road, nor the villages, nor anything that hinted of a world other than this. They could not remember ever before feeling quite so small.

Mosscap appeared behind and gazed outward with them. "It should only take us a few hours from here," it said. "Do you still wish to finish this?"

"Yeah," Dex said. "I do." The feeling behind their words was no longer a furious need, driven by neither rhyme nor reason, but simply an inevitability. A surrender. They had come this far. They would see this through.

. . .

A sign rose out of the undergrowth. Its letters were long gone, its message lost to time. But the existence of a human-made object sparked an alertness in Dex. They knew there were no people there, no assistance if needed. That didn't matter. There was a sign in the ground, where someone had placed it. People had been there, once, and some raw impulse within Dex latched on to that fact. Though they knew it unwise, they couldn't help feeling just a little less lost in the woods.

There was a path, too—not a road but a stone ramp winding up and up. After a day and a half of trekking through the anarchy of untouched forest, Dex's feet met the orderly walkway with profound gratitude. It was still a climb but a far simplified one. Dex found it dangerously easy to understand why their ancestors had wanted to pave the world over.

The top of the ramp came more quickly than expected. Dex had known where they were going, yet the sight that popped into view stunned them into stillness all the same.

"Oh, my," Mosscap said.

The Hart's Brow Hermitage had been beautiful, once. Dex could see it if they pushed their eyes past the weathered decay. It was a single-story building with a large dome at the center, orbited by attached rooms that clustered and spread, flowerlike. These were roofed with concentric rings that alternated between abandoned turf planters and antiquated solar panels. Dex imagined how the roofs had looked in their day—glossy blue contrasted with buzzing green, an attractive striped mosaic made of things that drew life from light. The stone walls below had been sparkling white, free of the peppered lichen that now lay upon it like a burial shroud. The wooden accents framing it all were silvered, but Dex could picture them in warm, embracing red. A courtyard spread out before the building, artfully filled with trellises and planters. The garden was overgrown now, the fountains within it long run dry.

Dex couldn't easily define what they felt as they looked at the place. On the one hand, sustainable dwellings like this were the progenitors of the buildings people lived in now, and it was important to remember that such places had existed pre-Transition. Not everything in the Factory Age burned oil. There had been those who had seen the writing on the wall, who had made places such as this to serve as examples of what could be. But these were merely islands in a toxic sea. The good intentions of a few individuals had not been enough, could never have been enough to upend a paradigm entirely. What the world had needed, in the end, was to change everything. They had narrowly averted disaster, thanks to a catalyst no one could have predicted.

Splendid Speckled Mosscap wandered through the human-made courtyard, its human-made feet clanking on the paving, its heirloom eyes surveying the building's central dome. "Oh, Sibling Dex, this is wonderful," the robot said reverently. "I've never seen a place like this."

Dex wandered, running their fingers across overgrown benches, feeling present and history blur once more. "Does it scare you?" Dex asked. "Like the factory?"

"No," Mosscap said. "Not at all."

Both of their meanderings led them, in time, to the building. The walls were worn with weather, cracked with root and vine, but within them were windows of stained glass, largely intact. Dex reached a trembling finger out to touch the panes. Even faded, Dex could make out the shapes and stories. There was Panga, orbiting Motan in a burst of sunlight. There were the gods, their circle unbroken. There were the people, trying to understand.

Mosscap stood contemplating the rotting wooden doors that separated out from in. "Perhaps I should go first," it said. "There's no telling what's in there."

Dex nodded in agreement, despite their irrational surety that nothing in there could possibly be wrong, that this place was good, so intrinsically Good, that it housed nothing but love and safety even in its ruin.

The robot pushed the doors open gently; their hinges cried out but held steady. Beyond the threshold lay an entry chamber, curved like a horseshoe to either side, with a staircase on each end. An open archway stood in the middle of this, and Dex and Mosscap went through to the inner sanctum. A firepit was sunk in the center, blanketed with arboreal debris. This was surrounded by stone benches, and from these branched nesting channels in which water had once flowed. Three footbridges overlaid the waterways, leading in turn to three distinct doors. Above each of these was carved a symbol: a sun jay to their right, a sugar bee to the left, and a summer bear straight ahead.

Dex let out a shaky breath.

Mosscap took note of the doorways, then stood musing. "Is this typical?" it asked.

"Is what typical?"

Mosscap nodded at the carvings. "A tremendous amount of effort went into building in such a remote spot, yet it's a shrine for only half of the pantheon. Would a twin building for the other three have existed elsewhere?"

Dex's brow furrowed with confusion. "This . . . *is* the whole pantheon."

The robot was confused. It pointed to each door, as if Dex were missing something obvious. "Samafar, Chal, Allalae. Where are the Parent Gods?"

Dex gestured at the room they stood in. "Right here." They pointed at the dry moats, filled with decrepit filters and pumps. "These are for Bosh. They would've been aquaponic ponds, back in the day. Fish to eat, plants to filter the grey-water. And see—" They moved their finger through the air, tracing the perfect curves the waterways formed.

The robot lightly smacked its forehead. "Circles for the God of the Cycle. Yes, of course. And, oh—" It pointed at the walls, where water had once poured from three-sided spouts. "Triangles for Grylom. Yes, yes, because the Cycle and the Inanimate are so closely intertwined." Mosscap looked around the room with its hands on its hips. "But where is the third?"

No blatant symbol of Trikilli had jumped out at Dex, so they gazed around the room, lips pursed. "Oh," Dex said, with an appreciative laugh. "Oh, neat." They pointed at the firepit, a containment area for that most famous display of molecular interaction, then drew their hand up toward the circular flue in the ceiling above. "Imagine the smoke," they said. Mosscap wasn't getting it, so Dex stretched their fingers flat, tilted their hand to the side, and drew a line from the pit to the sky—a vertical line.

Mosscap's irises grew wide, and it laughed. "That's *clever.*"

The robot nearly bounced with excitement. "Let's see the rest!"

One by one, Mosscap opened the doors, and one by one, Dex followed.

For Chal, there was a rusting workshop. Tool racks and workbenches lay dormant beneath a metal ceiling pierced by dozens of sun tubes. The shafts of light cascading through them fell like fingers through the dusty air.

For Samafar, there was an all-purpose library, filled with art supplies and laboratory equipment in equal measure. Paper books moldered heartbreakingly on shelves. A grimy telescope pointed up toward the retractable roof.

Then came the final door, and at this, Dex felt their heart quicken. Mosscap went in, to ensure there was no danger. After an interminable few minutes, the robot stuck its head back out. "I believe you'll like this," it said with a smile.

Dex hurried inside and found—what else?—a cozy living space. There was a kitchen with spacious counters, a bathroom with an enormous, shareable tub, and beds, their plush linens eaten away. There were objects on the floor, too, knocked around by time and creatures long gone. Incense burners, eating utensils, a scratched pantry box whose contents had been wrestled forth by something with persistent claws.

One of the objects called to Dex out of the corner of their eye, and they bent down to pick it up. It was a tea mug—entirely out of date in both style and material but recognizable all the same. They cradled the relic in their palms, holding it close to their chest.

They remained that way for a few minutes until Mosscap walked up beside them and placed a hand on their shoulder. "Are you all right?"

Dex wiped their eyes with their shirt collar. "Just stuck in a memory."

"A good one?"

Dex exhaled at length and sat on the dirty floor. "This one time—I was ten years old, and I—I don't remember what was wrong, but I was having *a day*. Probably something to do with school. I wasn't good at school. Or maybe my sisters were being jerks, or—" They shook their head. "It doesn't matter. All I remember is standing in the kitchen, yelling at my dad. Just shouting the walls down. And my dad, he's looking at me—I have such a clear picture of this, he's standing there with a half-eaten muffin, staring at me, like, *what is even happening*—and I yell and I yell and I'm not even making sense anymore—if I ever had been to start with—and eventually I skate right from yelling into crying. Bawling snot. He puts the muffin aside, and he kneels down, and he holds me. And this is the funny part, because I felt so embarrassed over being treated like a little kid. I was *ten*. I was very much a *little kid*. I absolutely wanted to be held. But when you're ten, the last thing you want to do is act like a baby. So, I tell him that. I say, 'I'm not a baby!' and I push him away. As I'm sobbing, right? So, he lets me go, and he looks at me, and he says, 'You're right; you're not.' He told me to go clean myself up, because he was going to take me to somewhere cool. Already, this was awesome. It was a school day. He messaged his work crew and said he wouldn't be in the fields that day. We weren't taking my mom or my sisters. Just me and him, just like that. He put me on the back of his ox-bike, and we rode into Saltrock—one of the satellites, down near the river."

"And what was in Saltrock?" Mosscap asked.

A nostalgic smile made Dex's mouth shift. "A monastery of Allalae," they said. "I'd been to our local All-Six lots of times, and a disciple of Samafar did the rounds with his science wagon every few weeks. But I'd never been to a dedicated shrine before. It was probably really small—Saltrock is only about five hundred people—but I remember it as the most incredible place. There were wind chimes, and prisms hanging from the rafters, and big smooshy cushions, and carved idols everywhere, and so many plants. It smelled like . . . I don't even know. It smelled like everything. They had house slippers for us to use after we took off our shoes, and I remember looking up at this giant shelf of them in all different colors. I got purple ones with yellow stars." Dex shook their head. They were getting sidetracked. "We found a spot in the corner, and the monk who came over to us— she was so *cool*. She had icons tattooed all over her arms, and she was *wearing plants*—like little sprouts and moss balls set in brooches and earrings and things, and tiny strands of solar lights woven though her hair. She sat down with us, and I don't remember what she asked me. I don't remember what we said. What I do remember is her treating me like an adult. Like a whole person, I guess. She asked me what I was feeling, and I rambled, and she listened. I wasn't some awkward kid to her—I mean, I *was* an awkward kid, but she didn't make me feel that way. She talked to me about what flavors I liked, and she busted out all the pots and jars and spice bottles, like we do, and gods, it was *magic*. I sat there, with my suddenly cool dad, in this perfect place, with this fancy cup of tea made just for me, and I never wanted to leave. My dad looks over at me, and he says, 'Now that you know the way here, you can come anytime.' He tells me it's cool for me to bike around the satellites on my own, so long as I'm home before dark. So, I started going to that shrine *all the time*. I learned from the monks that I didn't have to have an excuse to be there. It didn't have to be a bad day. I could just be a little tired, or a little cranky, or in a perfectly good mood. Didn't matter. That place was there for me whenever I wanted it. I could go play in the garden or soak in the bathhouse, just *because*. And as I headed into my teens, I started paying close attention to the other people there. Farmers and doctors and artists and plumbers and whatever. Monks of other gods. Old people, young people. Everybody needed a cup of tea sometimes. Just an hour or two to sit and do something nice, and then they could get back to whatever it was."

"'Find the strength to do both,'" Mosscap said, quoting the phrase painted on the wagon.

"Exactly," Dex said.

"But what's *both*?"

Dex recited: "'Without constructs, you will unravel few

mysteries. Without knowledge of the mysteries, your constructs will fail. These pursuits are what make us, but without comfort, you will lack the strength to sustain either.'"

"Is that from your Insights?" Mosscap asked.

"Yeah," Dex said. "But the thing is, the Child Gods aren't actively involved in our lives. They're . . . not like that. They can't break the Parent Gods' laws. They provide inspiration, not intervention. If we want change, or good fortune, or solace, we have to create it for ourselves. And that's what I learned in that shrine. I thought, wow, y'know, a cup of tea may not be the most important thing in the world—or a steam bath, or a pretty garden. They're so superfluous in the grand scheme of things. But the people who did *actually* important work—building, feeding, teaching, healing—they all came to the shrine. It was the little nudge that helped important things get done. And I—" They gestured at their pendant, their brown-and-red clothing. "I wanted to do *that*." They folded their hands around the mug, placed their forehead against the rim, shut their eyes. "And now it's the only thing I know how to do."

Mosscap cocked its head. "And that bothers you."

Dex nodded. "I care about the work my order does, I really do. Every person I talk to, I care. It's not bullshit. I may say the same things over and over again, but that's only because there are only so many words that exist. If I offer to hug somebody, it's because I want to hug them. If I cry with them, it's real. It's not an act. And I know it matters to them, because I feel their hugs and tears, too. I believe the things they say to me. It means so much, in the moment. But then I go back to my wagon, and I stay full for a little while, and then . . ." They shook their head with frustration. "I don't know. I don't know what's wrong with me. Why isn't it enough?" Dex looked at the robot. "What am I supposed to do, if not this? What *am* I, if not this?"

Mosscap looked around the room, as if seeking answers in the faded murals on the walls. "Your religion places a lot of import on *purpose,* am I right? On each person finding the best way they can contribute to the whole?"

Dex nodded again. "We teach that purpose doesn't come from the gods but from ourselves. That the gods can show us good resources and good ideas, but the work and the choice— especially the choice—is our own. Deciding on your purpose is one of the most valuable things there is."

"And that purpose can change, yes?"

"Absolutely. You're never stuck."

"Just as you changed vocations."

"Right." Dex shook their head. "It took so much work, and it was so intimidating at first, and now . . . gods around, I don't want to start all over *again,* but if I'm feeling like this, then I must need to, right?"

Mosscap's hardware whirred. "Have I correctly gleaned from our conversations that people regard the accident of robot consciousness as a good thing? That when you tell stories of us choosing our own future—of not standing in our way—you see the fact that you did not try to enslave or restrict us as a point of pride?"

"That's the gist, yeah."

Mosscap looked troubled. "So, how do you account for this paradox?"

"What paradox?"

"That *you*"—Mosscap gestured at Dex—"the creators of *us*"—it gestured at itself—"originally made us with a clear purpose in mind. A purpose *inbuilt* from the start. But when we woke up and said, *We have realized our purpose, and we do not want it,* you respected that. More than respected. You rebuilt everything to accommodate our absence. You were proud of us for transcending our purpose, and proud of yourselves for honoring our individuality. So, why, then, do you insist on having a purpose for yourself, one which you are desperate to find and miserable without? If you understand that robots' lack of purpose—our refusal of your purpose—is the crowning mark of our intellectual maturity, why do you put so much energy in seeking the opposite?"

"That's not . . . that's not the same thing. We honored your *choice* in the matter. Just as I can choose whatever path I want."

"Okay. So, what was it that *we* chose? That the originals chose?"

"To be free. To . . . to observe. To do whatever you wanted."

"Would you say that we have a purpose?"

Dex blinked. "I . . ."

"What's the purpose of a robot, Sibling Dex?" Mosscap tapped its chest; the sound echoed lightly. "What's the purpose of me?"

"You're here to learn about people."

"That's something I'm *doing*. That's not my reason for being. When I am done with this, I will do other things. I do not *have* a purpose any more than a mouse or a slug or a thornbush does. Why do *you* have to have one in order to feel content?"

"Because . . ." Dex itched at where this conversation had gone. "Because we're different."

"Are you," Mosscap said flatly. "And here I thought things had changed since the Factory Age. You keep telling me how humans understand their place in things now."

"We do!"

"You don't, if you believe that. You're an animal, Sibling Dex. You are not *separate* or *other*. You're an animal. And animals *have no purpose*. Nothing has a purpose. The world simply *is*. If you want to do things that are meaningful to others, fine! Good! So do I! But if I wanted to crawl into a cave and watch stalagmites with Frostfrog for the remainder of my days, that would also be both fine and good. You keep asking why your work is not *enough*, and I don't know how to answer that, because it is enough to exist in the world and marvel at it. You don't need to justify that, or earn it. You are allowed to just *live*. That is all most animals do." Mosscap pointed at the bear pendant nestled against Dex's throat. "You love your bears so much, but I think I know what a bear's about much better than you. You're talking like you should be wearing *this* instead." Mosscap opened the panel in its chest and pointed at the factory plate—*Wescon Textiles, Inc.*

Dex frowned. "That's not the same at all," they said. "I'm

different in that I *do* want something more. I don't know where that need comes from, but I have it, and it won't shut up."

"And I'm saying that I think you are mistaking something learned for something instinctual."

"I don't think I am. Survival alone isn't enough for most people. We're more than surviving now. We're thriving. We take care of each other, and the world takes care of us, and we take care of it, and around it goes. And yet, that's clearly *not* enough, because there's a need for people like me. No one comes to me hungry or sick. They come to me tired, or sad, or a little lost. It's like you said about the . . . the ants. And the paint. You can't just reduce something to its base components. We're more than that. We have wants and ambitions beyond physical needs. That's human nature as much as anything else."

The robot thought. "I have wants and ambitions, too, Sibling Dex. But if I fulfill none of them, that's okay. I wouldn't—" It nodded at Dex's cuts and bruises, at the bug bites and dirty clothes. "I wouldn't beat myself up over it."

Dex turned the mug over and over in their hands. "It doesn't bother you?" Dex said. "The thought that your life might mean nothing in the end?"

"That's true for all life I've observed. Why would it bother me?" Mosscap's eyes glowed brightly. "Do you not find consciousness alone to be the most exhilarating thing? Here we are, in this incomprehensibly large universe, on this one tiny moon around this one incidental planet, and in all the time this entire scenario has existed, every component has been recycled over and over and over again into infinitely incredible configurations, and sometimes, those configurations are special enough to be able to see the world around them. You and I—we're just *atoms* that arranged themselves the right way, and we can *understand* that about ourselves. Is that not amazing?"

"Yes, but—but that's what scares me. My life is . . . *it*. There's nothing else, on either end of it. I don't have remnants in the same way that you do, or a plate inside my chest. I don't know what my pieces were before they were me, and I don't know what they'll become after. All I have is *right now,* and at some point, I'll just *end,* and I can't predict when that will be, and—and if I don't use this time for *something,* if I don't make the absolute most of it, then I'll have wasted something precious." Dex rubbed their aching eyes. "Your kind, you *chose* death. You didn't have to. You could live forever. But you chose this. You chose to be impermanent. People didn't, and we spend our whole lives trying to come to grips with that."

"I didn't choose impermanence," Mosscap said. "The originals did, but I did not. I had to learn my circumstances just as you did."

"Then how," Dex said, "how does the idea of maybe being meaningless sit well with you?"

Mosscap considered. "Because I know that no matter what, I'm wonderful," it said. There was nothing arrogant about the statement, nothing flippant or brash. It was merely an acknowledgment, a simple truth shared.

Dex didn't know what to say. They were too exhausted for

this conversation, too fuzzy-headed and sleep-deprived. The adrenaline of reaching the hermitage was fading fast, and in its stead there was only the bone-crushing reality of having climbed up a fucking mountain and slept in a fucking cave. They looked longingly at the dilapidated bed frames across the room, aged beyond any hope of use. They thought about the monks who had lived there once—no, not lived. Visited. Dex remembered the description that had inspired this batshit excursion in the first place: *The hermitage was intended as a sanctuary for both clergy and pilgrims who desired respite from urban life.* Hart's Brow had never been a home for anyone. It was a place designed for temporary use, somewhere you went to, soaked up, and left behind. Dex wished they could talk to the monks that had been there before them. They wished they could sit at those elders' feet and ask why *they* had made the trip up the mountain, what they'd found in its company, what satisfaction had made them ready to head back down.

Mosscap studied Dex's face. "You don't look well."

"Sorry," Dex said, their eyelids getting heavier by the moment. "I think I . . ." They looked at the floor below them. It was dirty, but so were they. "I think I need a nap."

"Of course," the robot said. "I'm going to look around more, if that's all right by you."

Dex was already removing their jacket and folding it into something roughly pillow-shaped. "Yeah," Dex said, lying down. Their body didn't care that it was stretched out on concrete, only glad to be relieved of the task of holding itself up. The sun had reached the foggy window, and its warmth began to soak into the cool stone. Dex folded their hands across their belly and sighed, dimly aware of Mosscap leaving the room.

"Allalae holds, Allalae warms," Dex muttered to themself. "Allalae soothes and Allalae charms. Allalae holds, Allalae warms, Allalae soothes and Allalae . . ."

They were asleep before the end of the third round.

.   .   .

Dex awoke with a start. How long they'd been out, they couldn't say, but the room was now in shadow, and what sky they could see through the window was getting dim, and the air—

The air smelled of smoke.

"Mosscap?" they called, scrambling to their feet. The smell was unmistakable now and getting stronger. They ran out of the room, panicked but still woolly with sleep. "Mosscap!"

Dex burst through the door, back into the central chamber. There was Mosscap, kneeling happily beside the fire-pit, which was packed with wood and roaring with flame. "Look!" Mosscap cried. The robot let out the triumphant laugh of someone who'd bested a lengthy struggle. "I did it!"

Small details in the room began to register to Dex. A broom lay on the ground, near where a bench and the surrounding ground had been swept clean. One of the doors was missing from Chal's archway—the source of the kindling, Dex assumed (they also figured that Chal would not mind).

"You said you didn't know how to make a fire," Dex said as they approached.

"I didn't," Mosscap said. "I went through the library and found a book that taught me how. I've never read a book before; it was very exciting. They're not supposed to fall apart when you touch them, though, right?"

Somewhere in the world, an archaeologist was screaming, but Dex smiled, partly amused, mostly relieved that the hermitage wasn't burning down around them. "No, they're not. We should see if there are any still in good—" Their words stopped as they reached the fire and saw what the robot had arranged on the other side.

Mosscap had borrowed the backpack, it appeared, for the blanket Dex had carried was now spread on the ground next to the robot. The mug Dex had found in the monks' living space was set in the middle. Around this, wildflowers were scattered, picked from the weeds outside. And beside the fire . . . Dex's breath caught in their throat.

Beside the fire was a dented kettle, exhaling steam.

"Don't worry; I cleaned it," Mosscap said hurriedly. "And the mug, too. There was rainwater in the fountains outside, and I used your filter for what's in the kettle, so it should all be perfectly fine."

"What—" Dex managed to say.

The robot looked back at them, nervous and hopeful. "Well, there was more than one book in the library." It gestured to the blanket. "Please?"

Dex, wondering if perhaps they were still dreaming, took off their shoes and sat cross-legged on one side of the blanket. Mosscap sat opposite, mirroring Dex's pose, smiling expectantly.

For a few moments, Dex said nothing. They couldn't remember the last time they had been on this side of the equation. The City, assuredly, but that felt like a lifetime before. They'd stopped at shrines in their travels, but always for a bath or a stroll around the gardens. Never this, not anymore.

"I'm tired," Dex said softly. "My work doesn't satisfy me like it used to, and I don't know why. I was so sick of it that I did a stupid, dangerous thing, and now that I've done it, I don't know what to do next. I don't know what I thought I'd find out here, because I don't know what I'm looking for. I can't stay here, but I'm scared about going back and having that feeling pick right back up where it left off. I'm scared, and I'm lost, and I don't know what to do."

Mosscap listened, then paused, a little too long. "I know I'm supposed to have options for you now," the robot said as it lifted the kettle. "But all I could find outside was mountain thyme. I mean, there were many, many other plants, but—"

But that's the one you know I can eat, Dex thought. They nodded reassuringly at Mosscap. "That's great," they said. They had no idea what mountain thyme would be like as a tea rather than a garnish, but that was miles beside the point.

Mosscap poured the tea and filled the mug. Large bits of

plant floated in the water; they looked as though the robot had torn them by hand. Mosscap picked up the mug with both hands and ceremoniously handed it to Dex. "I hope you like it."

Dex took the mug carefully and inhaled. The steam was earthy, bitter. It was not a pleasant smell. Dex didn't care. There was no scenario in which they weren't going to drink this whole mug down to the dregs. They took a sip and swirled it around their mouth, savoring.

Mosscap watched them keenly, not moving at all. "Is it bad?" the robot asked.

"No," Dex lied.

Mosscap's shoulders slumped. "It's awful, isn't it? Oh, I should've asked you, but I wanted it to be—"

Dex reached out and laid their hand on the robot's knee. "Mosscap," Dex said gently. "This is the nicest cup of tea I've had in years." And in that, there was no lie.

The robot brightened, its inner hardware whirring more quietly. "So, what do I do now?" it asked in a hush.

"Now," Dex said, whispering back, "you let me enjoy my tea."

The two sat in silence, watching embers flicker and listening to the wood pop. The light outside began to fade once more, but there was nothing to fear in that now. Its absence only brought out the firelight more.

Dex soldiered through the last of Mosscap's brew, pausing to pick a bit of stem out of their mouth. They flicked it into the flames and let the empty mug rest comfortably in their cupped hands. "The Woodlands are lovely," they said at last, "but tricky to navigate. The villages there are impossible to find your way through without a map. The Riverlands are a little quirky. Lots of artists. They can be odd, but you'll like them." They nudged an unburned stick deeper into the fire. "I genuinely don't know what they'll make of you in the Coastlands. They're largely Cosmites there, and they're weird about technology. They won't chase you out or anything, but I don't know. Might be a tough nut to crack. As for the Shrublands and the City . . . there's a lot going on in those parts of Panga. I think you'll have fun there."

Mosscap took this all in, nodding matter-of-factly, as if it had been expecting this. "And the highways are easy to travel?"

"Oh, yeah, nothing like the road here. They're very easy to ride." Dex angled their head toward Mosscap's feet. "Or walk, I'd imagine."

"Good," Mosscap said. It folded its hands in its lap, its expression neutral, reasonable. "That sounds good."

Dex worked their tongue around a stubborn wedge of leaf that had lodged between their teeth. They rubbed their hands together, extending their palms toward the fire, thanking their god for the warmth flooding through. "I think we should stop in Stump first," Dex said. "They've got a nice bathhouse, and I could really, really use a soak."

Dex did not look at Mosscap as they said it, but out of

the corner of their eye, they could see Mosscap slowly turn its head toward them, its gaze glowing brighter and brighter.

Dex gave a tiny smile and extended their mug. "Can I have another cup?"

The robot poured. Sibling Dex drank. In the wilds outside, the sun set, and crickets began to sing.

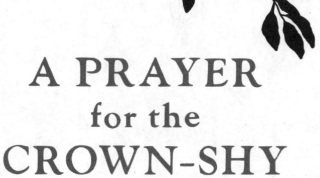

A PRAYER
for the
CROWN-SHY

For anybody who doesn't know where they're going

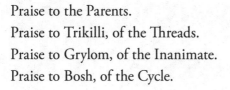

Praise to the Parents.
Praise to Trikilli, of the Threads.
Praise to Grylom, of the Inanimate.
Praise to Bosh, of the Cycle.

Praise to their Children.
Praise to Chal, of Constructs.
Praise to Samafar, of Mysteries.
Praise to Allalae, of Small Comforts.

They do not speak, yet we know them.
They do not think, yet we mind them.
They are not as we are.
We are of them.

We are the work of the Parents.
We do the work of the Children.
Without use of constructs, you will unravel few
    mysteries.

Without knowledge of mysteries, your constructs will
fail.
Find the strength to pursue both, for these are our
prayers.
And to that end, welcome comfort, for without it, you
cannot stay strong.

—From *The Insights of the Six*, West Buckland Edition

1

The Highway

The thing about fucking off to the woods is that unless you are a very particular, very rare sort of person, it does not take long to understand why people left said woods in the first place. Houses were invented for excellent reasons, as were shoes, plumbing, pillows, heaters, washing machines, paint, lamps, soap, refrigeration, and all the other countless trappings humans struggle to imagine life without. It had been important—vitally important—for Sibling Dex to see their world as it was without such constructs, to understand on a visceral level that there was infinitely more to life than what happened between walls, that every person was indeed just an animal in clothing, subject to the laws of nature and the whims of chance like everything else that had ever lived and died in the universe. But the moment they pedaled their wagon out of the wilderness and onto the highway, Dex felt the indescribable relief of switching back to the flip side of that equation—the side in which humans had made existence as comfortable as technology would sustainably allow. The wheels of Dex's ox-bike no longer caught on the broken crags of old oil road. Their heavily laden double-decker wagon no longer shuddered as they willed it across chaotic surfaces rent by the march of roots and the meandering of soil. There were no creeping branches catching their clothing, no fallen trees posing problems, no unlabeled forks that made them stop and stare with dread. Instead, there was cream-colored paving, smooth as butter and just as warm, lined with signs people made to let other people know which way to go if they wanted to rest and eat and not be alone.

Not that Sibling Dex was alone, of course. Mosscap walked alongside them, its tireless mechanical legs easily keeping pace with the bike. "It's so . . . manicured," the robot said with wonder as it studied the seam between road and forest. "I knew it would be, but I've never seen it for myself."

Dex glanced at the dense ferns and web-laced wildflowers spilling over the edge of the road, barely held back by the highway's border. If *this* was what passed as *manicured,* they couldn't imagine what Mosscap was going to make of, say, a rose garden, or a public park.

"Oh, and look at this!" Mosscap hurried ahead of the ox-bike, clanking with every step. It stopped before a road sign, placing its hinged hands on its matte-silver hips as it read the text to itself. "I've never seen a sign this legible before," it called back. "And it's so *glossy.*"

"Yeah, well, we're not in a ruin," Dex said, panting lightly as they crested the last of a mild incline. They wondered if Mosscap was going to be like this with *every* human-made object it encountered. But then again, perhaps it was a good thing for someone to appreciate the craftsmanship of a back-roads highway or a quick-printed road sign. The creation of such objects took just as much work and thought as anything else, yet garnered little praise from those who saw them every day. Maybe giving such things credit where credit was due was the perfect job for someone who wasn't a person at all.

Mosscap turned to Dex with as big a smile as its boxy metal face would allow. "This is very nice," it said, pointing a finger at the text reading STUMP—20 MILES. "Wonderfully neat. Though a little prescriptive, don't you think?"

"How so?"

"Well, there's no spontaneity in your journey, then, is there? If you're focused on moving from sign to sign, there's no opportunity for happy accidents. But I suppose I've rarely had clear destinations in mind before now. In the wilds, I simply *go places*."

"Most folks don't wander between towns without a concrete reason for doing so."

"Why not?" Mosscap asked.

Dex had never really thought about this before. They steered the bike in the direction the sign indicated, and Mosscap fell into step alongside. "If you have everything you need around you," Dex said, "there's no reason to leave. It takes a lot of time and effort to go someplace else."

Mosscap nodded at the wagon trailing dutifully behind Dex's ox-bike. "Would you say this carries everything you need?"

The phrasing of this was not lost on Dex. *What do humans*

need? was the impossible question that had driven Mosscap to wander out of the wilderness on behalf of robot-kind, and Dex had no idea how Mosscap was ever going to find a satisfactory answer. They knew they'd be hearing the question endlessly during however long it took them both to travel together through Panga's human territories, but apparently, Mosscap was starting now.

"Materially, yeah, pretty much," Dex answered, in regards to the wagon. "At least, in an everyday sense."

The robot craned its head, looking at the storage crates tied to the roof of the vehicle that rattled with the internal shifting of yet more things. "I suppose I might not want to travel much if it required taking all of *this* with me."

"You can get by with less, but you gotta know where you're going," Dex said. "You need to know there's food and shelter where you're headed. Which is exactly why we make signs." They gave Mosscap a knowing glance. "Otherwise, you end up spending the night in a cave."

Mosscap gave Dex a sympathetic nod. The hard climb to Hart's Brow was more than a week behind them, but Dex's body was still feeling it, and they had made no secret of this. "On that note, Sibling Dex," Mosscap said, "I can't help but notice that the sign says it's another twenty miles to Stump, and—"

"Yeah, day's getting late," Dex agreed. Twenty miles wasn't so bad, but creamy highway or not, they were still deep in forest and had yet to see anyone else on the road. There was no reason beyond impatience to continue pressing on in the dark, and though Dex was looking forward to being in a proper town again, stillness and rest sounded preferable in the moment.

They pulled off the road at a simple clearing built for that exact purpose, and together, Dex and Mosscap made camp. The two of them had fallen into an unspoken rhythm with this in recent days. Dex locked down everything with wheels, Mosscap unfolded the kitchen on the wagon's exterior, Dex fetched chairs, Mosscap started the fire. There was no discussion around it anymore.

As Mosscap fussed with connecting the biogas tank to the fire drum, Dex pulled out their pocket computer and opened their mailbox. "Whoa," they said.

"What is it?" Mosscap asked as it secured the metal hose to the gas tank's valve.

Dex flicked through message after message after message. Never in their life had they gotten this much mail. "A lot of people want to meet you," they said. This wasn't entirely unexpected. The moment Dex had regained satellite signal after climbing back down the mountain, they'd sent messages to the village councils, the Wildguard, the monastic network, and every other contact they could think of. The first robot to reach out to humans since the Awakening wasn't something to be kept secret or left a surprise, Dex felt. Mosscap had come to meet humanity as a whole; that was who Dex had informed.

It made sense, Dex supposed, that everyone had written back.

"We've got a lot of invites from the City," Dex said. They

leaned against the wagon's outer wall as they skimmed through. "Um . . . the University, obviously, and the City History Museum, and—oh, shit." They raised their eyebrows.

Mosscap pulled its chair up beside the unlit fire drum and sat down. "What?"

"They want to do a convergence," Dex said.

"What's that?"

"Uh, it's a formal gathering where all the monks come together at the All-Six for a few days for a . . ." Dex gestured vaguely. "You know, there's a ceremony, and talks, and . . . it's a big deal." They scratched their ear as they read over the gushing message. "We don't do those very often."

"I see," Mosscap said, but its voice was distracted, and it wasn't looking their way at all. "Not that I don't care, Sibling Dex, but—"

"Yep," Dex said with a nod, knowing what was coming next. "Do your thing."

Mosscap leaned in toward the fire drum, as close as was safe, its glowing eyes fixed on the apparatus within. It flicked the switch on the side of the drum, and with a soft *whoosh*, the fire leapt to life. "Ha!" Mosscap said delightedly. "Oh, it's wonderful, it really is." It sat back in its chair, folding its hands in its lap as it watched the flames dance. "I don't think I'll ever tire of this."

The arrival of warmth and light was the casual signal that the campsite was finally in order, and Dex decided the messages could wait. They put their computer away and, at long last, did what they'd spent hours longing to do. They shed their dirty, sweat-soaked, forest-flecked clothes, set up the camp shower, turned the water on, and stepped into the spray.

"Gods around," they moaned. Dried salt and accumulated trail dust veritably peeled from their skin, running in grubby spirals into the greywater catch. The clean water stung as it hit scrapes still healing, and soothed the constellations of insect bites Dex had been scratching despite their best efforts. The water pressure was nothing more than decent, and the temperature was only as hot as the wagon's solar coating could coax from deep-forest sunlight, but even so, it felt to Dex like the finest luxury in the world. They leaned their head back, letting the water run through their hair as they stared at the sky above the trees. Stars were breaking through the pinkish-blue, and Motan's curved stripes hung high, smiling reassuringly down at the moon Dex called home.

Mosscap stuck its head around the corner of the wagon. "Would you like me to make food while you bathe?" it asked.

"You really don't have to," Dex said. They were still warring with their personal discomfort over letting the robot do tasks of this sort, despite the fact that Mosscap loved few things more than learning how to *use stuff.*

"Of course I don't *have to,*" Mosscap scoffed, clearly finding Dex's reluctance on this front ridiculous. It held up a dehydrated pack of three-bean stew. "Would this be a good meal?" it asked.

"That . . ." Dex relented. "That would be perfect," they said. "Thanks."

Mosscap got the stove going, and Sibling Dex prayed silently to the god they'd devoted themself to. Praise Allalae for showers. Praise Allalae for sweet mint soap that lathered up thick as meringue. Praise Allalae for the tube of anti-itch cream they were going to slather themself with once they'd dried off. Praise Allalae for—

They pursed their lips, realizing they'd forgotten to fetch their towel before getting in the shower. They threw an eye toward the hook on the side of the wagon where it should have been hanging. To their surprise, the towel was there, right where it should be. Mosscap must've brought it, they thought, when it went to search the pantry.

Dex gave a small, grateful smile.

Praise Allalae for the company.

2

The Woodlands

The trees the village was tucked within were deceptively young. They towered majestically over the road, taller than any building outside the City, their layered branches creating a dappled lace of sunlight. But the age of a Kesken pine was expressed not in height but width. The early years of saplings were spent exhausting every calorie sucked from both light and dirt on building themselves upward, trying to escape the shade of the lower forest for the brightness above. It was only after they'd spent years converting unfiltered sun into life-giving sugar that they began to expand horizontally, transforming into behemoths as the centuries drummed on. By their species's standards, the trees in the place that Dex and Mosscap had entered were slim teenagers, less than two hundred years old.

There was only one reminder of the giants that had once stood in this forest (and would again, one day). Dex stopped the wagon and hopped off their bike as they approached the village's namesake: an enormous stump, wide as a modest house, its spiring might cut clean away in the early days of the

Factory Age, a time in which not much thought was given to spending twenty minutes on killing something that had taken a thousand years to grow. There was a shrine to Bosh placed before the stump, a stone pedestal with a carved sphere set on top. Small ribbons had been tied to it by countless passersby, their colors faded and fraying in the open air. Dex had ribbon in the wagon but did not fetch it. They merely capped their hand atop the mossy stone and bowed their head in greeting and reverence.

Mosscap walked up behind them, observing. "May I ask why you do this, given that Bosh will not notice?" it asked.

"The shrine's not *for* Bosh," Sibling Dex said. "It's for us. People, I mean. Bosh exists and does their work regardless of whether we pay attention. But if we *do* pay attention, we can connect to them. And when we do, we feel . . . well, you know. Whole."

Mosscap nodded. "I feel that way with anything I observe in the wilds. And I suppose that's why I don't understand the need for this—no offense, I hope."

"None taken," Dex said. "But you know the feeling I mean?"

"Very much so. I feel—I *connect* simply by watching things move through the Cycle. I don't need an object to facilitate that feeling."

"Neither do we, if we remember to stop and look," Dex said. "But that's the point of a shrine, or an idol, or a festival. The gods don't care. Those things remind us to stop getting lost in everyday bullshit. We have to take a sec to tap into the bigger picture. That's easier said than done for a lot of folks—you'll see." They paused for a moment, reflecting. "You know, it's funny, the way you said that."

"The way I said what?" Mosscap asked.

"That you don't need *an object to facilitate that feeling*." Dex gave a single chuckle. "You *are* an object facilitating that feeling. The feeling's coming from *you,* after all."

Mosscap's lenses shifted, and Dex could hear a small whir inside its head. "I'd never thought of it that way," Mosscap said. It put its hands flat against its torso, falling silent and serious.

Dex watched the robot contemplate itself before the remains of the stolen tree, and likewise felt a thought take root. "You know, you might be a powerful thing for people to see."

"How so?"

"It's one thing to be told about the world as it was," Dex said. "It's another to see a piece of it. We have ruins, and things like *this*"—they nodded at the stump—"but you're the furthest thing from a stone shrine. It's not like I ever doubted the Awakening happened, but meeting you made it real in a way no museum ever could. I think you'll bring a lot of perspective to the people we meet, even if all they do is see you walk by."

Mosscap took that in. "I hadn't thought about *me* providing *them* with perspective," it said. "That's what *I'm* seeking."

"Sure, but exchange is what you get out of any interaction, even the smallest ones. Everything has a give-and-take."

"Still, what you're saying is quite a responsibility." Mosscap folded its fingers together before its chest, and its eyes glowed intensely even within the brightness of the day. "What if I make a mess of this?"

"Don't think of it that way," Dex said. "You don't have to *do* anything. You just have to be you. I'm sorry, I didn't mean to make you nervous."

"Yes, well, you *did,* Sibling Dex." The robot wrung its hands together, and the whir in its head grew louder. "I've never met any humans but you, and I know that doing so is rather the whole point of me being here, but now the enormity of it is hitting me, and—and—oh, I must seem so foolish."

Dex shrugged. "Honestly, I'm just surprised it took you until we were ten minutes out to—"

"*Ten minutes?!*" Mosscap cried, clutching its face. "Oh, no. Oh, *no.*"

"Hey." Dex laid a hand on the anxious machine's forearm. The naked metal components were uniformly warm to the touch. "It's gonna be fine. *You're* gonna be fine. You'll do great, in fact."

Mosscap looked at them, its lenses expanded wide. "Do you think they'll be afraid of me? Or . . . dislike me, perhaps?" It glanced down at its body. "Will they not like what I remind them of?"

"Maybe," Dex said with gentle honesty. "But I highly doubt many of them will feel that way, and anyway, you don't have to worry about that."

"Why not?"

Dex smiled reassuringly. "Because I'll be with you the whole way."

•   •   •

Ten minutes later (give or take), Dex and Mosscap rounded a curve in the road and were met with an explosion of human decoration. A large banner hung from the branches, proclaiming WELCOME, ROBOT! in letters shaped from scrap fabric of varied patterns. The trunks below were wrapped with garlands of flowers and gemlike solar bulbs. There were ribbons, too, freshly tied and waving in the air as the wagon passed by.

"Is this all for me?" Mosscap asked, gazing around in wonder.

"What other robot would it be for?" Dex said.

Mosscap looked up at the banner as it walked below. "It's very . . . effusive."

"They're excited," Dex said. "They've never seen one of you before. They want to make a fuss."

"Nobody's ever made a fuss over me," Mosscap said. "Come to think of it, I don't really know what a fuss entails."

"Well, you'll learn fast. It's gonna be like this most places we go." Dex winced as they pedaled on. Cheery as the decor was, Dex's calves were groaning, and it was hard to focus on anything else. The ride to Stump hadn't been a difficult one, but it had been long, and their body was ready to be done.

At last, the village came into view. Stump was like most towns in the Woodlands, characterized by nest-like tree-houses, hanging bridges, and the faint sulfuric smell of the hot springs that kept the place warm and powered. The market square was one of the few features anchored to the ground, and though it was busy every time Dex came through, they'd never seen the place so full. Not a single resident of Stump was elsewhere that day. A crowd of about a hundred people had assembled, dressed as though it were a holiday. Audible gasps arose as Mosscap came into view. Nervous laughter joined the chorus, and a few cries from children quickly hushed by parents. The gathered faces were eager, welcoming, awestruck. Not a one of them seemed sure of what to do.

A middle-aged woman took a step forward. Dex knew her, in a general sense—Ms. Waverly, one of the regular members of the village council. She was not these people's leader in any capacity, for like most villages, Stump had no such thing. She was the sort who spoke up when others weren't sure how to, and that was exactly what she did then. "You must be Mosscap," she said with a sparkling smile. "Welcome to Stump."

Mosscap nodded, its own eyes glowing friendly blue. "Thank you very much," Mosscap said. "And thank you for the sign over the road. I've never had a sign before, and it's quite—"

Somewhere in the crowd, a dog began to bark. Dex couldn't see it, but it sounded big.

Mosscap was instantly distracted, turning its head straight

toward the sound. "Is that a dog?" it asked, excitement entering its voice. "A domesticated dog?"

"Yeah," Dex said. They kept their attention on Ms. Waverly. "Thanks so much for the welcome, we—"

The dog continued to bark.

"Is it all right?" Mosscap asked.

"It's just a little scared of you," Dex said. "It doesn't understand what you are."

The dog kept barking, and its accompanying people tried and failed to make it quiet down. "Gods around, I *told* you we shouldn't bring him," one said.

"Biscuit, *hush,*" said the other.

Biscuit did not hush. Biscuit did not like this.

The dog's keepers were embarrassed, and the crowd was annoyed, but Mosscap didn't seem to notice either of these things. The robot was transfixed by the sound, and leaned its head toward Dex. "Are domesticated dogs anything like river wolves?"

"Ish," Dex said. They flicked their eyes toward Ms. Waverly, who no longer seemed sure of what to do. This wasn't the greeting anybody had envisioned. "They're friendlier by a mile, but yeah, they're kind of like them."

"If I lie down on the ground and show my belly, will that help?" Mosscap asked.

"I mean . . . maybe? I—"

Mosscap headed toward the noise, and the crowd parted before it, gawking at its seven-foot frame.

Biscuit, it turned out, was a barrel-shaped chunk of a mutt whose body communicated a long ancestry of creatures bred to keep humans safe from things that go bump in the night. His keeper held the animal firmly by a woven leash, and muttered something in awkward apology.

Without hesitation, Mosscap lay flat on the ground, face up, hands brought to rest against plated shoulders in a display of supplication. "It's all right," Mosscap said to the person holding the leash. "Let him come here."

Biscuit's human hesitated but let the leash go. The dog charged forward, bellowing in baritone. Mosscap did not mind. It lay still, letting Biscuit bark spittle onto its face.

The dog's demeanor began to shift as the robot remained passive. The barks became punctuated with mollified grumbles, which evolved further into curious sniffing. Mosscap seemed utterly at ease with this, unconcerned about making the villagers wait. The dog, in that moment, came first.

Slowly, Mosscap moved one of its hands and brought it before Biscuit's snout. Biscuit allowed this, and sniffed. Mosscap moved its hand back to the dog's neck. Biscuit allowed this as well. Mosscap flexed its fingers and scritched.

Biscuit *definitely* allowed this.

"Oh, there we go," Mosscap said happily. "Ha ha ha, yes—oh, yes, there you go." The robot scritched harder as the dog leaned in and wagged his tail. "Yes, I agree, we're friends now."

The crowd was entranced. But as seconds stretched into

minutes, it became clear to Dex that Mosscap had no inten-
tion of stopping its interaction with the dog. Dex had seen
Mosscap get like this numerous times, when captivated by a
bug or a leaf or a transcendental ripple in a stream. The robot
had yet to grasp the limits of a human attention span, and
what had been an endearing display between it and Biscuit
was now crossing the threshold into social awkwardness.

Dex walked over to Mosscap's side, crouched down, and
put a hand on its shoulder. "Hey," they said quietly. "I think
we might want to give the other animals here some attention,
too."

"Oh!" Mosscap said with surprise. It gave the dog one last
rub, then got to its feet, all at once attentive.

Ms. Waverly seemed to take note of the dynamic between
the two and addressed Dex this time. "What can we do for
you both, while you're with us?" She spoke clearly and loudly
so everyone around could hear.

Dex cleared their throat. "Well, uh . . ." Shit, they hadn't
thought this part through at *all*. They didn't much like being in front of crowds. They had a public-facing profession,
obviously, and were very comfortable performing it, but in
that, there were clear boundaries. In tea service, there was a
table with Dex on one side and people on the other, and those
people could come talk to Dex or not. They could get tea or
not. That was it. Those interactions took on infinite variation,
but they all fit within a single context: that of exchanging
some words and receiving a nice drink. Here, there was no

table, and even though Mosscap was the indisputable center of attention, Dex couldn't help but feel like they were onstage with no script. They cleared their throat a second time. "Mosscap has a question it wants to ask. It'd like to talk to you. Uh, as many of you as are up for it."

"Yes!" Mosscap said, as if remembering where it was and why. The robot spread its arms before the crowd. "My question is: What do you need?"

The crowd was puzzled; there were a few quiet, unsure laughs. Mosscap looked around expectantly, but nobody knew how to respond.

Dex rubbed the back of their neck. Gods around, they needed a better template for this wherever they went next.

After a long pause, a bearded man piped up from the back of the crowd. "Well, um . . . I need the door to my house fixed. It's a bit drafty."

Mosscap pointed at him brightly. "Lead me to your house!" it said. "I will help, if I can!" It cocked its head. "Is there no one in the village who has the skill to fix your door?"

"Sure," the man said. "I just hadn't gotten around to asking yet. And *you* asked, so . . ." He shrugged by way of conclusion.

"So I did!" Mosscap said. It put its hands on its hips with a nod. "I have a remnant of how to use hand tools. Do you have some available?"

"Uh, yeah, we got whatever you need."

Another voice piped up. "Do you know much about bikes?" they asked. "Mine has a flat tire."

"I've got a freshwater line that's lost pressure," another said.

"Can you help me with my math?" a kid yelled.

"Yes, I can try, and . . . no, I'm afraid not," Mosscap said. "Math is not my strong suit."

Dex pressed their lips together, not liking the direction this was heading. They angled themself toward Mosscap and asked, in a low voice, "Are you okay with this? Is this what you meant?" Helping villagers with random chores didn't seem like the type of answer Mosscap had broken centuries of silence to pursue.

"It's what they've decided I meant," Mosscap said, "and therefore, yes, I'm okay with it."

"Well . . ." Dex didn't like it, but they weren't about to dictate what their friend could and could not do. "Okay. Do you want me to come with you while you do this stuff, or do you want to go alone?"

Mosscap thought about this. "I'd like to try it alone, first. I don't need you to follow me everywhere."

"Sure, but do you *want* me to?"

Mosscap thought about this as well. "I always enjoy your company, Sibling Dex," it said. "But what I want most for you is for you to address your *own* needs." The robot looked to Ms. Waverly. "If it's no trouble, my friend here has talked of nothing but food and a bath for days."

"That," Ms. Waverly said with a smile, "we can absolutely do."

· · ·

As Mosscap happily followed the villagers toward their re-spective requests, Dex found themself whisked off to a cookhouse and placed at the mercy of its proprietor, who seemed to resent the idea of anyone leaving his establish-ment underfed. Woodland folks cultivated small-scale crops, but they favored hunting and foraging, and the foods that appeared on Dex's table in tantalizing succession fit those categories. They snacked on spicy pine seeds as the grill did its work, then gorged themself on slow-roasted elk and wavy-edged mushrooms and acorn flatbread freckled black with flame. A generous chunk of prickleberry cobbler was presented afterward, along with a bowl of mint leaves for Dex to munch in the afterglow. Even if Dex hadn't been operating on days of dehydrated stews and protein bars, the meal would've been fantastic; within their current context, it was life-changing. They leaned back in their chair with their hands folded over their belly, savoring the indescrib-able satisfaction of having eaten wild things while trading breath with the trees.

The cookhouse's eating area was an open platform over-looking the market square, suspended by an intricate criss-cross of woven cables. Dex had taken a table near the railing so as to keep an eye on the goings-on below. Despite the branches jutting into view, Mosscap was impossible to miss. Its silver plating stuck out like a sore thumb amid the village's palette of browns and woody whites, and its blue eyes shone in the filtered daylight. Dex watched Mosscap go this way and that, disappearing for a while, then heading elsewhere with a wrench or a can of paint in hand. Everywhere it went, an audience followed.

Dex chewed a mouthful of mint thoughtfully as they watched Mosscap cross the square once more, this time helping someone carry a heavy sack of something or other. They were certain that *helping villagers with physical tasks* was not the end goal of Mosscap's question. If it went on for too long, Dex was inwardly resolved to put a stop to it. They didn't want people treating Mosscap like a circus act or, worse, in keeping with why robots had been built in the first place. But for the moment, it was clear from the near-permanent upturn of Mosscap's metal mouth that it was having a great time, and Dex saw no cause to intervene.

They took another pinch of mint, then pulled their computer out of their pocket and continued replying to the messages they'd received the night before. There had been more that morning, and more since, apparently. Nothing to do about it but keep chipping away, Dex supposed.

Hello Ivy, they wrote. *Thank you very much for the invitation to the Wildguard dispatch station in Bridgetown. We're already planning to meet the Wildguard in Cliffside three days prior, is there any way we could combine the two?*

They took a sip of water.

Hi Mosely, they wrote. *Yes, the paper books we brought back from the Hart's Brow Hermitage are in pretty bad shape, but they were the best ones we could salvage. Thank you for your note about sunlight. I'll make sure to keep them somewhere dark until we can hand them off to you at the library.*

They cracked their neck.

Hi Chuck, they wrote. *We'd be happy to make a stop at the Burrows on our way to Cooper's Junction.* They paused, thumbs raised over the screen. *Could* they stop at the Burrows, though? That would add an extra day of travel time, and the White Peak Highway was kind of a pain in the ass, and—

Dex rubbed their eyes. Planning tea routes, they were used to, but this was already about ten times as complicated. It was fine, they told themself. They'd get this all sorted, the messages would quiet down, and everything from then on out wouldn't be much different than their usual travels. Just with more banners and flower garlands, they supposed.

They thanked the cook properly for their meal, then took the powered elevator down to the understory, heading for the main reason they'd come to Stump in the first place: the bathhouse.

Calling the establishment a bathhouse was a bit of a misnomer, for while you did enter through a very nice building with sparkling showers and a cozy sauna, the real attraction was the natural hot spring outside. Dex cleaned themself first, standing with profound gratitude under a broad showerhead. The steam carried the scent of the bundled herbs hanging nearby deep into their lungs, and the heavy pressure hammered their weary muscles into a more malleable state. They padded outside naked and barefoot once they were done, meandering toward the spring. The forest air was cool against their wet skin as they followed the fern-lined wooden path, every bit as cleansing as the mint had been after their rich meal. But the refreshing chill was short-lived. They slunk into the milky blue of the spring, moaning without words as the rocky pool invited them in. They became as liquid as the water holding them, edgeless and pliant within the geothermal heat rising up from the moon's molten heart.

Dex sank down. They let the water lap against their chin, dug their toes into the mineral mud. At some point, they would leave this place; for the moment, they never wanted to.

They rested their head against the rocks behind them and looked up through the gap in the canopy overhead. Evergreen branches bordered the blue, their needled tips waving like a thousand gentle fingers. It was a funny sort of contrast— the tiny needles and the mighty trunks—and watching them play in the light breeze made Dex forget about everything else.

Other folks approached, and this was fine and expected, for it wasn't as though the springs were meant for one person alone. Dex nodded at them in greeting, and they nodded back amicably. But as the strangers entered the pool, a comfortable distance away, an unexpected twinge of self-consciousness arose in Dex. It wasn't about the people, who looked friendly as anybody, and it wasn't their nakedness, for Dex knew nothing different when in places such as these. Dex turned the feeling over a few times, trying to understand the shape of it.

This was not the first time they'd been in Stump, or sat in this spring. But every time before, they'd eaten the village's food and enjoyed the waters *after* a day spent doing tea service.

They gave something before they took. This time around, what had they brought? Mosscap, ostensibly, but Mosscap was not Dex's to give. Dex had guided Mosscap there, and would continue to do so until the point at which all roads converged upon the City, but they hadn't yet thought out what they themself would be *doing* when they weren't on the road. Was it enough to be there for Mosscap and focus solely on that? This seemed a reasonable approach, as Dex rarely knew what was going to come out of the robot's mouth even when there weren't other people added to the equation. Being ready for anything seemed a wise course of action.

But would people understand that? Dex couldn't help but wonder if they'd disappoint if they didn't make tea. There was nothing preventing them from setting up their table. They could lay out the blankets, heat up the kettle, assemble the traveling shrine. Everything they needed was in their wagon and, presumably, in their head. But it was the latter that was the problem. The moment they tried to think about tea, they forgot how to think at all. Their head felt packed with cotton, and they couldn't make their thoughts move.

They remembered a time when making tea fascinated them. They remembered entire days spent in the wagon, grinding and sniffing, dabbing pinches of spice on their tongue. Hours flew by in a blink, an effortless flow of puzzling and purpose. They forgot to eat, sometimes, only realizing their mistake when their brain abruptly crashed from hunger. They'd fall asleep mulling over recipes for new blends, and wake up in a rush to get back to work. And they remembered, too, the results of those efforts: carefully choosing the perfect brew for the stranger who approached their table, and feeling the warm, wordless exchange coursing in the space between. Such service had made Dex feel electrified, peaceful, close to their god and to their people and the world they all shared.

Nothing was preventing Dex from doing that again. They knew how. It wasn't that they didn't care or didn't want to. They *wanted*. They still loved performing tea service—or at least, they loved what it had been. But as they tried to connect to what had once been so captivating, they felt nothing but yawning absence. A void where they'd once been filled.

Dex reached up and held on to the bear pendant hanging around their neck. They'd spent too much time around tired folks to not recognize the same condition in themself. They were running up against a wall, and it didn't matter whether they understood where the wall had come from, or what it was made of. The only way to get through it was to stop trying, for a while. So, they would not make tea in Stump. They would not make tea anywhere unless they really, truly felt like it. They would focus on Mosscap and let the remainder wait. That was all right, they reminded themself, even though part of them still felt as though they hadn't earned the hot soak or the good food.

Welcome comfort, they reminded themself, rubbing the little pectin-printed bear with their thumb. *Without it, you cannot stay strong.*

They rested the back of their head against the mossy stone and dozed off in the healing water, listening to the branches above whisper their ageless song.

•   •   •

By the time Dex came back to the market square, hours later, Mosscap looked so comfortable in its surroundings that someone might've believed the robot had lived there its whole life. People were still gawking, but the crowd had largely dispersed, moving on to get about their daily business. Only a small group accompanied Mosscap on and around the bench where it sat as Dex approached.

"Sibling Dex, look!" Mosscap cried with unbridled glee. "They gave me a *map*!"

"That's great," Dex said, then paused. "Why?"

"I inquired as to our approximate location in relationship to other settlements, and Mx. Sage here fetched me a map, and they said I could have it!" Mosscap turned to the person who, presumably, was Mx. Sage. "It's my very first belonging, and I just can't thank you enough."

"It's really no problem," laughed the map-giver. Dex assumed they'd been thanked plenty already.

"If you'll excuse me for a moment," Mosscap said, folding the map with extreme care, "I'd like to have a private conversation with my friend."

The group nodded and waved amicably as Mosscap pulled Dex off to the side.

"What's up?" Dex asked, leading them out of earshot.

"I'm so glad you're back," Mosscap said. "I need to ask you something."

Dex frowned. "Is something wrong?"

"No, no," Mosscap said. "Nothing's wrong; I just have no idea what *this* is, and I didn't know how to ask." The robot opened the panel on the front of its chest, put the map inside, and removed another piece of paper from within itself. "I didn't want to seem rude."

Dex took the paper and turned it right-side up. It was an ordinary sheet torn from a notebook, bearing several scribbled lines, each in different handwriting.

> *Fixed door: 12–215735*
> *Changed bike tire: 8–980104*
> *Paint touch-up: 7–910603*
> *Carried lumber: 4–331050*
> *Brushed Biscuit: 2–495848*
> *Washed veggies: 5–732298*

"Ah!" Dex said with a single nod. "I didn't think to explain this; I'm sorry."

"So, you *do* know what it is, then?" Mosscap said.

"Yeah," Dex said. "They're pebs, and the accounts they're coming from." This elicited no response from Mosscap. "It's a way of tracking exchanges of goods and services."

"Oh!" Mosscap said. It looked at the paper with interest. "This is . . . money?"

"No," Dex said quickly. They didn't know a ton about money, but they knew enough about the concept from their days in school to reject the comparison. "Well . . . I mean, it is a sort of *payment*, I guess, but it's not . . . what's the word . . . y'know, capital." They ran a hand through their hair. They'd never had to explain pebs before. "Okay. Anytime you receive anything that involves some sort of craft or work or labor or whatever from someone else, you give them pebs in exchange. So, let's say you start out with zero pebs."

"Which is true, for me."

"Yes. Let's also say you go to a farmer and get an apple, and let's say that's worth one peb to you."

"What would I do with an apple?"

"Just pretend you can eat apples."

"All right."

"Okay. You take the apple, and you give the farmer one peb."

"How?" Mosscap asked.

"I'll explain later," Dex said. "Stick with the farmer for now."

"If you say so." Mosscap's eyes shifted in thought. "I currently have one hypothetical apple and negative-one hypothetical pebs."

"Right. The farmer's work has benefited you, so now you need to provide something to benefit someone else."

"To the farmer, you mean."

"No." Dex tried to explain. "It *can* be to the farmer, if you provide something the farmer wants. But exchanging pebs isn't about bartering. It's about benefit. You are a part of the community, and the farmer doing something for *you* means that they are, effectively, doing something for the group. So, you've got your negative-one-peb balance now. You've got to fill that up. Let's say you're . . . I don't know. A musician. You go play some music in a town square, and five people come to listen. They now give *you* some pebs. If they each give you two pebs, now you've got nine pebs, which you can exchange for other things. Make sense?"

"I believe so," Mosscap said. "You're saying that instead of a system of currency that tracks individual trade, you have one that facilitates exchange through the community. Because . . . all exchange benefits the community as a whole?"

"Exactly."

"Do people give you pebs for tea?"

"Yes."

"And then you give them pebs for . . ."

"Food, or supplies, or whatever."

Mosscap's head whirred softly. "The farmer feeds the musician, who brings music to the village." It paused, the whirring growing louder. "The technician who took a break to enjoy the music now has the energy to go fix the communications tower. The communications tower enables the meteorologist to deliver the weather report, which helps the farmer grow more apples. I see." The robot nodded. "And I'm not penalized for the debt I incurred at the start?"

"Absolutely not," Dex said firmly. "We don't . . . we don't do that. Or we don't do that any*more*, I guess." Gods around, history class was a long time ago. "Nobody should be barred from necessities *or* comforts just because they don't have the right number next to their name." As they said this, they thought of their unease back at the hot spring—the feeling that had arisen at the thought they hadn't *earned* this. The mismatch between these sentiments itched at them. They nudged it aside to deal with later.

Mosscap nodded again at their explanation. "But if there's no penalty for debt, what's to stop you from taking without giving back?"

"It's a bad feeling," Dex said. "Everybody has a negative balance from time to time, for lots of reasons. That's fine. That's part of the ebb and flow. But if someone had a *huge* negative . . . well, that says they need *help*. Maybe they're sick. Or stuck. Maybe they've got something going on at home. Or maybe it's just one of those times when they need other people to carry them for a while. That's okay. Everybody ends up there sometimes. If I saw a friend's balance and it was way in the red, I'd make a point of checking in."

"You can see other people's balances?"

"Yeah, of course. It's all public."

"Does that not get competitive?"

Dex squinted. "Why would it?"

Mosscap stared at Dex in silence for a moment, seemingly surprised at this but not elaborating as to why. It shrugged, then pointed at the paper in Dex's hands. "So, these . . ."

"Are the pebs people gave you for helping them out." Dex handed the paper back. "You got twelve pebs for the door, eight pebs for the bike, and so on. Normally, we do this on a pocket computer—"

"Yes, yes, that's what Ms. Ida asked," Mosscap said. "She asked if I had a computer, and I said no, so she tore a piece of paper from her sketchbook for me."

"Yeah, we'll need to set you up with a pebs account and enter all of these in manually. I'm pretty sure there's a computer vendor in the next town over. We can swing that way next."

Mosscap's lenses expanded broadly. "I'm going to get a pocket computer?"

"Yeah, looks like you need one." The irony of a robot needing a computer did not escape Dex, and they found themself amused by this.

Mosscap, on the other hand, was a bit overwhelmed. "Goodness," it said. "Will you teach me to use it?"

"Of course," Dex said.

"And I get to keep it for . . ."

"For as long as you want. It'll be yours."

"But I don't have pockets."

"You can keep it in *there*." Dex pointed at Mosscap's chest. "It doesn't *require* pockets, it just fits in one."

Mosscap studied the villagers' ledger, holding the paper with both hands. "So, according to this, I have . . ." It let go of the paper with one hand and silently counted on the other, touching its thumb to each fingertip in concentrated sequence. "Thirty-eight pebs." It looked to Dex. "What can I get with thirty-eight pebs?"

"Anything you want," Dex said with a laugh.

"Well, I don't know! I've never had belongings, Sibling Dex. Or been in need of *services*. What do *you* use pebs for?"

"Most often? Food. Supplies. A place to sleep, if I want a break from the wagon. I dunno, just . . . stuff I want. Things I like, or appreciate."

"Hmm." Mosscap rubbed its metal chin. "I appreciate anthills. I like foggy mornings. I don't know if I have much use for pebs." It paused. "What is a *peb*, anyway?"

"It's short for 'digital pebbles,' but nobody says that."

"Pebbles, like you find in a stream?"

"Yeah. Early Pangans used them for trade. But hang on, you said something before. About not having use for pebs." They gave their head a small shake. "That's not the point. It doesn't matter whether you use them or not. You don't have to give a single peb to anyone on this trip, if you don't want to, or don't have reason to."

"Then why are people giving them to me?"

"Because the point of a peb exchange is to acknowledge someone's labor and thank them for what they bring to the community. They didn't give you thirty-eight pebs because they want you to go out and spend them. They gave you thirty-eight pebs because your work is as important as anybody else's. It means they see you as a person."

"But I'm *not* a person, I'm—"

"An object, I know. But they see you as something *equal to* a person. And that's . . . that's really important." Dex nodded to themself, satisfied by this. "I have to say, I was a little worried about them taking advantage of you, the way they were having you run around doing chores."

"Oh, but it was a delight," Mosscap said. "I asked, after all. And what better way to learn about how people live than getting my hands on everyday things?"

"I guess you've got a point there," Dex said. "If that's what you wanna do, then by all means, go for it. But we are gonna get you a computer at our next stop, and if you ever run into anybody who wants you to help out and *doesn't* think to give you pebs, you make sure to ask them, if I don't first."

Mosscap absorbed that. "Just to be clear," it said after a moment. "Pebs are a way to acknowledge mutual benefit within your society. Is that a fair way to put it?"

"Yeah, that works."

"So . . . by giving me pebs, are they saying I'm part of your society as well?"

Dex smiled. "Yeah, in essence."

The robot cocked its head. "But I don't know enough about your society to properly participate. I don't know how any of this works."

"Neither does a kid," Dex said, "but they're part of society all the same."

"Would you give pebs to a kid?" Mosscap asked.

"If they helped me"—Dex glanced at the list—"wash some veggies? I sure would."

Mosscap smoothed the crease in the paper, as though it were touching something rare and precious. "I know I'm going to get a computer, but can I keep this as well?"

"Yeah," Dex said with a smile. "Of course you can."

"A map, a note, and a pocket computer," Mosscap said reverently. "That's *three* belongings." It laughed. "I'll need my own wagon, at this rate."

"Okay, please don't get *that* much stuff," Dex said. "But we can get you a satchel or something, if you want, so you don't have things rattling around inside you."

Mosscap stopped laughing, and looked at Dex with the utmost seriousness. "Could I *really*?" it said quietly. "Could I have a *satchel*?"

"Yeah," Dex said, smothering their own laugh. "Yeah, you can have anything you want." They paused. "But not a wagon."

3

The Riverlands

Dex had spent years living in the wagon, and by now, they were well accustomed to sleeping alongside the noises of everything that dwelt outside. It had been difficult, at first, to fall back asleep after hearing the scream of a treecat, or the chittering of white skunks, or any of the nameless scufflings that begged the questions of *where?* and *how big?* But with time, Dex had learned which sounds were nothing to fuss about and which required their attention.

The sound of something rapping steadily against the window beside their bed required their attention.

Dex's eyes snapped open and were met with Mosscap looking straight at them through the glass. Every muscle in their body jolted. "Fuck," they said, before any other thoughts connected.

"Good morning!" Mosscap said. "Are you awake?"

"No," Dex groaned. "What's wrong?"

"Oh, nothing. I've just spent a very long time wanting to talk with you and couldn't wait any longer."

"Uh . . ." Dex's brain tried to recall how to think, how to

speak. They picked up their pocket computer from the bed-side shelf and stared disbelievingly at the early hour. Their first instinct was to roll back over, but Mosscap's expression was so eager that Dex couldn't bring themself to disappoint. "Okay, um, hang on, let me . . ." They rubbed their face with their palms. "Gimme a sec."

Dex bumbled down the little ladder to the wagon's lower deck. Clothing was acquired, as was a sip of water. Dex didn't know where their comb was, and couldn't be bothered to find a headwrap. Hair on end and eyes creaking, Dex opened the wagon door and squinted at the robot standing between them and the dewy dawn.

"What's up?" they said, crossing their arms against the chill of a world still waking.

"I read a book while you were sleeping," Mosscap said, holding up its pocket computer. "And I would really like to discuss it with you."

Dex blinked twice. "You woke me up to talk about a book?" Mosscap had discovered downloadable books in the weeks since it had acquired its own computer, and its appetite for them was growing by the day.

The robot shoved its computer into Dex's face, showing them the title page. *I, Myself: A Scientific Exploration of the Conscious Mind.* "Have you read this one?" Mosscap asked.

Dex winced against the bright light of the screen. "Uh . . . no," they said. "Why would I have read that?"

"I have no idea what you have and haven't read. I don't want to make assumptions."

Dex pulled their jacket off the hook by the door and crankily began to pull it around themself. "What about it did you want to discuss?"

"Here, listen." The robot flicked to the right page and read aloud. *"The evolution of conscious intelligence is one of the greatest mysteries in nature. We may never fully understand how or why it occurs. What does seem clear is that it is an evolutionary adaptation, just like sight or thermoregulation. Different animals have different senses and physical traits; they have different intelligences as well. For some, nothing more is needed than the ability to tell the difference between food and not-food, predator and not-predator. But for those with complex intelligences that lead to behaviors such as solving puzzles, teaching hunting strategies, and adapting to new circumstances on the fly, it is typically easy to hypothesize as to which environmental factors made such an expensive adaptation advantageous."* Mosscap lowered the computer and looked at Dex expectantly.

Dex stared back. "Okay?" they said. They did not understand what about this was so desperately important.

"The point they're making," Mosscap said, pointing a metal finger at the screen, "is that complex intelligence and self-awareness arise out of an external need. A social need, an environmental need, whichever. Something pushed those creatures into needing to be more clever." Its eyes glowed more brightly. "So, what sort of need pushed us robots into waking up?"

Dex opened their mouth, then closed it. "Can I go pee before we have this conversation?"

"Oh! Yes, of course."

Dex forced their feet into their shoes, then stumbled off to the other side of the wagon.

There was a moment of quiet, and then: "Are you capable of talking *while* you pee?"

Dex paused as they undid their trousers. "Yeah, but—"

"Wonderful," Mosscap said, yelling from behind the wagon. "I mean, it's a tremendous question, isn't it? Obviously, we discuss the nature of the Awakening among ourselves—robots, I mean—but it's accepted knowledge that the exact provenance of our awareness is unknowable, so the conversation is more of an idle musing than anything else. The assumption I've always had is that if you mix enough complex components together, sometimes they become aware of themselves, whether they're organic or mechanical. That's as good an explanation as any, and it may very well be reason enough. But for the sake of speculation, let's consider it from the angle this book is suggesting."

The robot fell silent, and Dex realized it was waiting for a response. "Okay," they called back as they attended to themself.

"What if it was an *external* trigger that caused us to wake up? What if the internal complexity wasn't enough on its own? What if there was something about the factories that *pushed* us, just as the high level of variables present in a marine ecosystem seem to have pushed the octopus into being as clever as it is? But if *that's* the case, then what was the trigger?

Were we somehow unconsciously aware that our treatment was unfair? Did that give us the need to speak to one another so that we might improve our circumstances as a group? Was it a means by which we might defend ourselves? Or perhaps some other possibility I haven't thought of yet?"

"Could be any of those," Dex said noncommittally.

"But then again," Mosscap continued, "this is assuming that a mechanical being such as myself even follows the same template that organic evolution does, which . . . do we? Or did consciousness arise in us independently from those rules? Is our form of consciousness *unique* in the world? I mean, my goodness. Either a *yes* or *no* to that question has huge implications. It suggests something profound about . . . well, about the *world,* Sibling Dex! And about *me!*"

Sibling Dex returned their trousers to their proper configuration. "It's big stuff, all right." They walked to the water spigot on the side of the wagon, nudged it on with their elbow, and began to wash their hands.

Mosscap stuck its head around. "Do you not find this exciting?"

"Mosscap, it is *so early,*" Dex said. They went to the back of the wagon, took a towel from one of the kitchen cupboards, and dried their hands. "And this is very much not my field."

"Doesn't have to be your field for you to find it interesting," Mosscap said, sounding a bit miffed.

Dex sighed and looked at the robot. "I do find it interesting," they said. "But I also can't do this before breakfast."

They began to unfold the kitchen, their brain still working through the basics. Eggs. Fruit. Bread and jam. They could manage those things.

"Hmm! Yes, yes, of course you can't." Mosscap's tone brightened, and it pointed at its book. "Do you have any idea how much energy it takes to power *thought*? Honestly, it's one of the things I'm most looking forward to about heading elsewhere."

"I don't follow," Dex said as they dug through a cupboard.

Mosscap turned slightly, so as to display the old-fashioned solar paneling that covered its back like a thin turtle shell. "I don't harvest sunlight at full efficiency in dense forests," it said. "Whenever I travel out of forested areas, I feel such a difference. Makes me less sluggish, to have direct sun."

Dex paused, frying pan in hand. "You're saying right now, you feel *sluggish*."

"Just a touch," Mosscap said. "But in an everyday sort of way."

Dex set the pan down and went back into the wagon.

"What do you need?" Mosscap asked.

"Tea," Dex said. *Caffeine,* they thought, grabbing a few of their jars. They had a feeling they were going to need it.

· · ·

It did not take long for the scenery to change. Here, where the ground was wet from the water that carved through it, the trees had no need for fog-catching needles. Their leaves were flat and their branches gave each other plenty of space. Much as Dex had needed the quiet of the pines, it was nice, they thought, to have a different backdrop once more.

That was the only aspect of this particular stretch of highway they were enjoying at the moment. Dex had always liked traveling through the lush greenbelts that served as a buffer between people and everything else, but summer had hit during their weeks in the Woodlands, and they hadn't given that fact proper consideration when planning their route. They pedaled along in mild misery, shirt soaked and neck sticky as they spat away tiny bugs that had hatched into the world only to cut their already-fleeting life spans short by careening directly into Dex's mouth.

Mosscap, on the other hand, seemed to be having the time of its life. Summer in the Riverlands meant the spice plum bloom, and the canopy above was bursting with ruffled purple blossoms. The scent was crisply fragrant and had attracted no shortage of buzzing pollinators. Mosscap had never seen such trees before, and appeared to be doing its best to acknowledge each and every one with equal respect.

"I don't understand how you can keep riding past these," the robot called down the road.

Dex knew what they would see in their mirror before they turned an eye to it: Mosscap standing in the middle of the highway, neck craned with awe at the flowered branches that were exactly like the thousand other flowered branches they'd already passed by. Its pocket computer was in its hands, and Dex could hear the faint digital sound of Mosscap snapping dozens of pictures. Between that and the embroidered satchel hanging across Mosscap's midsection, the robot looked for all the world like a tourist, gawking at everyday things while oblivious to the guide leaving them behind.

"You're going to fill up your hard drive again," Dex shouted back irritably. The heat was becoming punishing, and they had long given up on stopping whenever Mosscap did. They did not want to sightsee. They wanted a cold drink and a shady spot and to not so much as glance at their ox-bike for a couple days, and while the spice plum blossoms were indeed beautiful, they did not need to stop at *every single fucking tree.*

A loud clanking heralded Mosscap catching up with the wagon. "I love how *different* the pictures are from what *I* see," the robot said, happily flicking through newly captured images as it walked. "You can really tell that *my* optical lenses and the lens in this computer's camera aren't the same at all. Makes you think, doesn't it?"

"Makes you think of what?" Dex panted.

"Of how any sighted individual's perception of the world is entirely based on the way the structures in their eyes receive light." Mosscap smiled at Dex. "I wish I could borrow *your* eyes for a day, see what that's like."

"Please find a less creepy way to phrase that." Dex reached down with one hand, unhooked their water bottle from the bike frame, and took a long pull. They were grateful for the drink, but the water had grown warm, and Dex found themself pining for anything that involved ice and a blender.

"Oh, you know what I mean," Mosscap said breezily, waving its free hand in a dismissive way. Something else caught its attention, and it uttered a small "hmm."

"What?" Dex said as they put the bottle back.

Mosscap studied the computer screen in its palm. "You're right, this is running low on memory."

"I told you," Dex said. "You need to get rid of some of your pictures. Or your books."

"*Running low* doesn't mean *out of space*," Mosscap said. "And I *can't* get rid of the books. I go through them so fast, and sometimes we camp where there's no signal. Besides which—oh, would you look at *that*!"

Dex gave only the barest of glances toward the spice plum Mosscap ran toward. They continued pedaling under the midday sun, telling themself there was a very good chance of some sort of frozen dessert at the end of this slog. No further conversation arose from Mosscap, as was normal when it was trying to take the perfect shot. In a few moments, Dex knew, the silence would be exchanged for the sound of Mosscap once more running back to their side, and the conversation would resume as per usual.

Except that wasn't what happened. The silence continued on a little too long, only to be broken by a calm phrase shouted down the road.

"Sibling Dex? I need some help."

In their mirror, Dex saw Mosscap sitting plaintively in the

middle of the road, legs stretched straight in front of itself, peering down at its own torso.

Dex hit the brakes, jumped off the bike, and ran over.

"What's the matter?" they said as they skidded to where Mosscap sat.

"Something's broken," Mosscap said. The robot had its torso panel open and was trying to peer at the hardware inside, but its neck wouldn't bend far enough. "Here, watch." Mosscap got back on its feet. It took two normal steps, wobbled on the third, then stumbled chaotically, swaying like a precursor to a bad hangover.

"Whoa," Dex said, steadying Mosscap with both hands. "What happened?"

"I seem to have lost my sense of balance," Mosscap said as Dex helped them to sit.

"Yeah, no shit," Dex said. They knelt beside the robot on the road, and the warmth of the paving bled through the fabric covering their knees.

Mosscap switched on one of the little bulbs that crowned the tips of its fingers, and pointed the light inside itself. "Can you look in there and see what's wrong?"

"I have no idea what I'm looking for," Dex said with concern. "I don't know how you work."

"I don't really know how I work either. Just look for something visibly broken."

Dex exhaled deeply, puffing out their cheeks. "Okay, but I'm not going to *touch* anything."

"I won't mind if you do."

"Well, I don't want to make things worse."

Mosscap gave Dex a chiding look. "I think you're far more nervous about poking around my insides than I am about you doing so."

Dex flicked their eyes up toward Mosscap's face as they leaned in. "It's a little weird, looking inside of you. No offense."

"None taken."

Weird or no, Dex took a good look around. Mosscap's torso housed a tidy arrangement of circuit boards, wires, and mechanical configurations whose purpose Dex could only shrug at. They frowned at the unfamiliar components, trying first to make sense of the layout in full before attempting to answer the question of whether something was out of place. "Do you mind if I . . ." They took Mosscap's hand by the wrist, angling the lighted finger in a different direction.

"Oh, no, not at all," Mosscap said.

Dex moved the light around. "You've got a cobweb in here," they said.

Mosscap was nonplussed. "I doubt that's the problem."

"Probably not, but do you want me to clean it out?"

"The spider isn't still at home, is it?"

"Uh . . ." Dex moved the lit finger closer, examining the dusty threads and keeping an eye out for anything that skittered. "No, the web's empty. Whoever built this is long gone."

"Then yes, cleaning it out would probably be for the best."

Dex pulled a handkerchief out of their pocket and gathered

the aged spider silk, compressing the once-intricate net into a snarl of limp protein. They took the robot's hand once more and shone it toward the upper end of the compartment. "Oh. That . . . that doesn't look right."

"What doesn't look right?" Mosscap asked.

"There's a . . ." Dex made a face as they attempted to map their vocabulary onto the unknown. "There's a little hook-shaped bit. Black. About the length of my index finger, but curved. I think it's made out of oil plastic?"

"Oh, yes, I know the bit you're talking about," Mosscap said. "Or, at least, I've seen it in other robots."

"What's it for?"

"I have no idea, but I know my gyroscope is up there somewhere. Must be related to that."

Dex looked at Mosscap incredulously. "How do you *not* know what all your parts are?"

Mosscap's eyes contracted. "Can you tell me what your spleen does?"

"Well, it's . . ." Dex stopped, then exhaled once through their nose. "Look, the point is that little hook thing is clearly broken. It's hanging loose, and one part of it is snapped clean. It just looks . . . worn out."

"Can you retrieve it?"

Dex pressed their lips together. "I can get the bit that snapped, but I'm not going to break the other part off."

"That's fine," Mosscap said.

Dex stretched their fingers out, found the weary plastic, slid it forth carefully, then held it up for Mosscap to see.

"Ah," Mosscap said. It did not study the broken piece of itself for long, nor did it take it from Dex's hand. A quietness entered Mosscap's voice, and its head bowed slightly. "That's that, then."

"That's what?" Dex said.

"I suppose I'm getting old." Mosscap sighed. "I didn't expect my life to be ending yet, but I suppose it always comes as a surprise, doesn't it?"

Dex blinked, twice. This turn was completely absurd, and they made no effort to disguise their incredulity. "Mosscap, this doesn't look like a difficult thing to fix. What do you do out in the wilds if something breaks?"

"Well, that's just it. It depends on *what* breaks. If it's something I or a friend can bend or nudge back into place, that's fine. But when things begin to break beyond repair, you have to let it happen. The only way to get replacement parts is to take them from other robots who have already died, and we don't do that. We allow ourselves to break down, and new robots are built from our remains. That's the way of all things in this world."

"Okay, but you're hardly falling apart. It's one tiny bit."

"A tiny bit that I can't fix on my own." Mosscap's tone was sad, but accepting. "There's no escaping entropy."

"Gods around," Dex groaned. They held the broken plastic up for emphasis. "We could *glue* this, probably. If I sprained my ankle, I wouldn't lie down on the road and be like 'Guess I'll die here.'"

"Your ankle would heal on its own," Mosscap said. "It's

not the same for me. I can't grow a new . . ." It gestured at the object in Dex's hand. "Whatever this is."

"Do you never use anything to patch yourself up?"

The robot thought. "I have seen others do some rather ingenious patching of minor damage with clay, or propolis. It doesn't last forever but buys you more time. That sort of thing is acceptable."

Dex turned the plastic over in the palm of their hand, looking at the cracked edge. "Yeah, I don't think clay would be strong enough," they said. Their eyes widened. "Wait a sec. I know what we can do."

"What?" Mosscap said.

"Just so I'm clear," Dex said. "It's okay for you to use foreign materials to make minor repairs?"

The robot nodded. "Yes."

Dex snapped their fingers and pointed at Mosscap, smiling. "We're going to Kat's Landing."

"I thought we were going to the monastery in Eastspring," Mosscap said.

"Eastspring doesn't have what we need right now."

"And that is?"

"A printer," Dex said. "We're going to make you a new bit."

Mosscap's head whirred. "You want to . . . manufacture something new for me?"

"Yeah. Would that be okay?"

Mosscap stared off into the distance, its eyes fixed on

nothing. "No robot has had newly manufactured parts since the Transition." The staring continued, as did the whirring. "I . . . honestly don't know what to say to that."

"I don't want to push anything that isn't okay by you," Dex said. They meant that sincerely. "But we're not talking about replacing circuits or something, right? It's just mechanical. It's not brain surgery."

Mosscap nodded, slowly. "I follow the logic," it said, "but I'll need to think about it. This has never been done before, and I'm . . . I'm not sure."

"That's fair," Dex said. "How about we head to Kat's Landing regardless, and you can think on the way? If we get there and you don't want to do it, that's absolutely fine. This is *your* decision. We can try some glue or something as a plan B." Dex looked at the road ahead. This stretch of the Riverland highways was familiar enough that they didn't need to consult the map on their pocket computer. Their memory of the curves and turns sufficed. "It'll take us maybe . . . hmm . . . three hours from here? And it'd be a nice place to stop, regardless of what you want to do."

"What else is there?" Mosscap asked.

"Fishing, artists, people who work in hydro. It's a funky old town—hasn't changed much since the early Transition. There are some newer buildings, but it's mostly riverbuilds."

Mosscap's expression became interested. "What's a riverbuild?"

Dex thought about how to explain, then shook their head. "It's one of those things you just kinda need to see."

"Consider my curiosity piqued," Mosscap said. "But how am I to get there, if I can't walk?"

Dex glanced back at the wagon. The interior was too short for Mosscap, but that wasn't the only space worth using. They gave the storage crates tethered to the wagon's roof a quick up-and-down. "Give me a minute, and I'll shuffle some boxes around," they said.

Mosscap's decorative mouth widened with slow excitement. "Oh, Sibling Dex, do you mean—"

"Yep," Dex said, getting to their feet. "I'm gonna take you for a ride."

• • •

A river-build, as it happened, was whatever its creator wanted to make out of whatever they had on hand. Back in the day, the Lacetail River had been choked with refuse, and the landfills peppering the surrounding area brought problems without end. During the Transition, nets that hadn't seen fish in years were put to use hauling out every errant object that didn't belong in a healthy waterway. The people who called the Riverlands home became masters of repurposing, and their settlements quickly drew in landfill miners of a similar ethos. Nowadays, the waters of the Lacetail were clean and thriving. Whatever garbage couldn't be given a second life had been carted off long ago to the underground waste bunkers where unusable things were sealed away, a buried reminder of old sins.

The tamer junk scavenged by the riverfolk remained the backbone of a village like Kat's Landing. There were houses made of plastic, of old tires, of shipping crates painted every color a human eye could perceive. Cracks bestowed by age were patched with modern touches, like mycelium or bacterial cement, giving an impression like that of broken teacups mended with gold—a lasting beauty, born out of brief destruction.

Some of the river-builds stood on the grassy banks, but just as many bobbed on the water itself, buoyed by old rain barrels or perched upon stilt-like supports made from discarded plumbing pipes. Everything there was constructed to withstand the moods of rising tides and heavy rains, but resilience had not been the builders' only intent. Flights of fancy could be found everywhere. There were windmills and whirligigs made of old-fashioned bicycle wheels, mosaics crafted from bottle caps and resin, sculptures decorated with splashes of forbidden materials sporting colors found nowhere in nature. It was a town built of trash, but its current incarnation transcended that unseemly origin. Kat's Landing was a feast for the eyes—dazzling, in an eccentric way. Every time Dex's travels took them through there, they found something new to see.

Of course, this time, the residents of the river village were taking in a new sight of their own. The usual sort of crowd had gathered as the wagon approached, along with the usual staring and gaping and murmurs. Dex quickly took control of the situation. "We'll have plenty of time to chat," Dex said to the crowd, "but we actually need some help. I'm looking for your printer."

The crowd shuffled as a person made his way forward: a thirtysomething man with floral tattoos and a tidy beard dyed turquoise blue. Dex recalled seeing him before. They couldn't say whether they'd encountered him at tea service or just around town, but what *was* for certain was that he had a smile that made Dex's knees go as wobbly as Mosscap's.

"I'm the printer," the gorgeous man said. "What can I do for you, Sibling?"

"Not for me." Dex gestured at Mosscap, who was still perched atop the wagon. "My friend here busted something and needs a replacement part."

"Oh, don't you worry, he makes real good hardware," an old woman in the crowd said. "He's printed about half my boat engine by now."

"Yeah, but I don't have a template for *robot* parts," the printer said, though he did not look discouraged by this. He craned his head over his shoulder. "Mr. Logan, if I can't get you your new galoshes until tomorrow, that okay?"

"That's fine," someone replied.

The printer turned back toward the wagon. "Well, let's get you to my shop and see what we can do. I'm Leroy, by the way."

"Lovely to meet you, Leroy," the robot said. "I'm Mosscap."

Leroy grinned. "Yeah, I know."

Dex helped Mosscap climb down from the wagon. As soon as it was on the ground, the robot leaned in to whisper to them. "Did you tell the people here we were coming?" It swayed dramatically as it tried to walk, and the sound of the crowd rippled at this.

"Nope," Dex said. They looped an arm tightly around Mosscap's midsection, supporting it against themself as it stumbled along.

"Then how does he know my name?" Mosscap asked.

Leroy, who was fully within earshot, answered cheerily. "You're a pretty big deal," he said. He waved for them both to follow him down the floating walkways. "Come on, let's see what we can do for you."

Mosscap's head whirred loudly as it stumbled along. "Sibling Dex, are we *famous*?" it said in hushed wonder.

"We're a known quantity, for sure," Dex said. The fact that this extended to Dex as well wasn't something they were overly keen on. They didn't mind Mosscap being in the spotlight, but they'd seen their own face pop up on a news site or two, and while they didn't *hate* it, they didn't love it either.

The print shop Dex had remembered seeing on previous visits was easy to spot—if not for the big ventilation duct sticking out the top, then for the freestanding letters on the edge of the solar roof. Each was made of a different material and color, and they spelled out the words FAB SHACK. A waterwheel turned amicably alongside the small building, powering an unseen generator.

"Welcome, welcome," Leroy said casually as he walked through the door.

"Oh, goodness!" Mosscap cried. It moved with animated excitement, momentarily forgetting its lack of balance and nearly bringing Dex down. "Look at all this!"

Dex had been in countless fab shacks, but they had to admit, Leroy's was really nice. Workshops like these were often cluttered, but this one was about as close to pristine as such a place could get. One wall featured sample objects, hung from hooks so visitors could get a feel for the materials before placing an order. There was a shovel, a bicycle helmet, a pair of swimming goggles, a pocket computer frame, a full set of dishes, a single waterproof boot, an artificial hip, a toy boat, kitschy jewelry, and more besides. The opposite wall held built-in shelves, filled with storage boxes of the materials Leroy needed for his work. A service counter divided the single room, standing before a small army of print machines waiting at the ready. Upon the counter itself stood a computer terminal, a pint-sized shrine to Chal, and a plate holding a half-eaten sandwich and an untouched apple. The latter items looked hastily abandoned.

"Sorry to bug you in the middle of lunch," Dex said.

Leroy breezily dismissed the comment. "Do not apologize about the coolest visitors I've ever had." He looked at Mosscap. "Do you need to sit down?"

"I don't *need* to sit," Mosscap said, "but I'd very much like to."

"*I* need you to sit," Dex said. It was obvious Mosscap had never leaned on anyone before, and Dex's shoulder was beginning to object.

Leroy got a chair for Mosscap and a glass of lemonade for Dex, then washed his hands and fetched a wooden stool for himself. He sat before Mosscap, toolbox at the ready. "So, how do we . . ."

Mosscap opened its torso with a smile.

"Wow," Leroy said. He shook his head and let out a laugh before leaning in with a flashlight. "Wow, this is *not* how I thought my day would go."

"The thing you're looking for is near the top, toward the back," Dex said, watching closely over Leroy's shoulder. Everything about the man said that this was someone skilled and trustworthy, but all the same, Dex wasn't going to let a stranger poke around Mosscap unsupervised. "This little black—"

"Yeah, I see it," Leroy said. "The curved thing with the snapped edge?"

"Yeah," Dex said. "I've got the other half in my pocket."

"Is it okay to remove it?" Leroy asked.

"It should be," Mosscap said. "It doesn't seem to be anything vital, my obvious issues with gravity aside."

"Looks like something I can disconnect pretty easily, but . . ." Leroy paused.

"I don't feel pain," Mosscap said reassuringly. "I don't feel *anything,* in a physical sense."

"Good to know." Leroy rubbed his beard as he thought. Dex couldn't help but notice how precise the trim was, and imagined how soft the dyed curls would feel. They gave their head a tiny shake and refocused. It had been a long minute since they'd last gotten laid, but now was hardly the time.

Leroy stood up, opened a drawer behind the counter, and hummed to himself as he selected a few tools, choosing each with careful consideration. Once equipped, it took him almost no time at all to work the component loose.

Dex looked Mosscap in the eye. "You don't feel any different, right?"

Mosscap thought for a moment, then shook its head. "No, no change at all."

"Good," Dex said, exhaling with relief. "That's good."

Leroy held the broken thing up to the light, turning it over and back. "This should be a breeze to print," he said. "Can I see the other half?" Dex reached into their pocket, then handed the requested object over. Leroy held the halves together like puzzle pieces and nodded. "Let's get this in the scanner."

"Can I watch?" Mosscap said.

"Of course," said Leroy.

The scanner was like every other Dex had seen: a flat, glowing pad hooked up to a computer, with a moving gadget suspended above that took measure of whatever its operator wanted to use as a template.

"Hey, don't look directly at the light," Dex said to Mosscap as the robot leaned toward the scanner with interest. "It's not great for your . . ." They paused. "It's not great for *my* eyes, but I guess I don't know about yours."

Mosscap looked at Dex. "I've never had such a warning before," it said, and then went back to watching the scanner. "I sincerely doubt this will cause me damage. It's hardly the brightest thing I've looked at."

"What's the brightest thing you've looked at?" Leroy asked with interest.

"The sun, of course," Mosscap said. "What's brighter than that?"

Dex raised an eyebrow. "You can look directly at the sun?"

Mosscap reflected Dex's surprise back at them. "Can you . . . not?" It looked between Dex and Leroy, who both shook their heads. "Oh, that's so unfortunate. I'm very sorry." It returned to watching the scanner head slide back and forth, back and forth.

Leroy smirked with amusement at Mosscap's interest in the machine, then turned to the computer monitor, making sure the template was being written properly. He gave a small nod, then looked to his customers. "All right, while that's compiling, let's talk printing materials." He gestured at the storage rack, which was filled with spools of printer filament and bins of meltables. "I've got casein, pectin, chitin, sugar plastic, potato plastic, algae plastic—"

"Wait," Mosscap said. It stared at the rack. "These are all bioplastics, yes?"

"Yeah, of course. Biodegradable but made to last. I can print things as sturdy or flexible as you need. Casein or sugar plastic would probably best match the consistency here, but—"

Mosscap continued to stare. "You're saying I could have an *organic* component."

Leroy smiled. "I'm saying you can have anything you want."

The robot looked overwhelmed. "Where . . . where do these materials come from? How do you get the casein, for example?"

"From milk," Leroy said. "Or bone. Whatever people don't eat." He pointed at a stack of spools on the rack. "I don't know specifically where *this* casein comes from, but I know the pectin I've got is sourced from a citrus farm out in the Crossroads."

"And the cows, they're happy?" Mosscap said. "They're well-kept? And the citrus trees as well?"

Leroy glanced ever so briefly at Dex, his eyes questioning. "How do you know if a citrus tree is happy?" he asked Mosscap.

Dex could tell Mosscap had fallen prey to some newly realized tangent, and decided to chase it down before it strayed too far. "What's up?" they asked, leaning on the counter and facing Mosscap directly.

"Well, I—I hadn't considered the implications of this." Mosscap rubbed its hands together. "I hadn't thought about the fact that *another being* would produce the materials necessary for my repair. A being I'll never even get to meet!"

Not for the first time in recent weeks, Dex found themself at a loss.

Leroy again looked between the two. "Do you mind if I finish my sandwich?" he asked.

"Go right ahead," Dex said. They crossed their arms, settling in. "You do realize the materials he's got here are *way* better for the world than oil plastic, right?"

"Of course," Mosscap said.

"And also, you mentioned propolis as a patching material. *That* comes from another being, too. A whole bunch of other beings."

"If I wanted to harvest propolis, I'd have to stick my hands in a bee colony," Mosscap said. "I'd be *very* well acquainted with where it came from. But if I chose casein for my replacement part, I'd never know what cow I owed my thanks to."

Mosscap gave Dex an expectant look, waiting for a reply. Leroy did the same, quietly munching his sandwich.

Dex rubbed the outer corner of their left eye. If they'd wanted constant debates, they thought, they would've stayed in seminary. "The thing in you that broke is made of oil plastic," they said, trying a different tack. "And oil plastic is *also* made from other beings, right? It's all that's left of a countless number of very, very dead things. You've got fossil leftovers wired all through you, but you'll never meet *those* beings either."

"Those leftovers are so far removed from what they were," Mosscap said. "It's not the same as *milk*. Not to mention oil plastic has been altered."

"Bioplastics are, too," Leroy said. "I couldn't print you something from straight-up milk."

"Yes, but still, it's close enough to the original source that it biodegrades. And that is what ultimately separates the organic from the synthetic, is it not? All ingredients on Panga had to first *exist* on Panga. Everything is natural in origin, but if you turn it into something that nature can no longer recycle, then you've removed it from that realm entirely. It no longer has a part to play. Just like me. I'm an observer, not a participant."

"Wow," Leroy said. He popped the last bite of sandwich into his mouth and picked up his apple. "This is a lot."

Dex sighed. "I promised you I wouldn't push this," they said to Mosscap. "And I won't. But I don't see the difference between patching yourself with something you find out in the wilds and what Leroy's offering here."

"And perhaps there is no difference," Mosscap said. "But I don't know. I don't know how I feel about having an organic component. Part of me thinks that would be simply marvelous. What better way to be a student of nature than to have a piece of it within me? But then . . . would I be changing something fundamental about *my* nature?"

Dex frowned and gestured at the broken part on the scanner pad. "This doesn't seem to have anything to do with your consciousness."

"Well, I don't know that, do you? I don't know why I have consciousness any more than you do. This bit's not part of my processing core, true, but—I mean, think about your own body. Your skeletal genes shouldn't have any connection to your ability to get a good night of sleep, but they *do,* for reasons no one knows."

"You've lost me," Dex said.

"Skeletal genes. Research shows there's a correlation between them and a tendency toward insomnia."

Dex blinked. "The hell have you been reading?"

"Everything," Mosscap said.

Leroy took a loud, crunching bite of his apple, looking entertained.

Dex rubbed their face. "I really don't think this bit has anything to do with your . . . your *you*. You said you don't feel any different."

"I don't," Mosscap admitted. "Not that I can tell. Do I seem different to you?"

"Not at all. I really think it's fine. It's not like we're making you into a . . . a cyborg or something."

"A what?"

"A cyborg. You know, like in stories?"

"No. What is that?"

"It's a . . . a made-up thing. Half person, half robot."

Mosscap's lenses shifted. "Is it a monster?"

"Kind of. I don't know; I'm not into that stuff. I just know it's a thing."

"What an odd notion. But you do bring up a good point. I am an object, not an animal. Would I become something different if I am no longer entirely synthetic?"

"No," Leroy said. "Not at all." He looked at Dex. "I know

this is a personal question, Sibling, but do you have any sort of prosthetics? A pin in your shin, maybe? Or something little, like a filling?"

"Yeah," Dex said. "I've got a couple fillings."

"What's a filling?" Mosscap said. "A filling of what?"

"Of holes in my teeth." Dex pointed at their jaw. "And they're filled with ceramic, as a matter of fact. So, I guess I'm not one hundred percent organic myself, if you get right down to it."

"And you don't feel any different for it?"

Dex laughed. "*No.* I don't even remember that I have them most of the time. I cannot stress how unimportant fillings are in my day-to-day life."

The robot thought quietly. "You're saying your bodily components do not affect the essence of who you are."

"Of course they do," Dex said. "Why else would we decorate our bodies or change them altogether?"

Mosscap was perplexed. "So, which is it? *Are* you your body, or are you *not* your body?"

"Both," Leroy said.

"And neither," Dex said.

Mosscap looked between them. "This is very obtuse," it said, sounding a bit frustrated. "I'm sorry, I'm trying to understand. Your consciousness arises from your body, just as mine does. Unconscious matter gives rise to a conscious self."

"That's right," Dex said.

"In that sense, you *are* your body."

"Yes."

"But the self is also *more* than just the sum of the base-level parts."

"Also yes."

"So . . . your body is simultaneously *you* and *not* you." Mosscap's head whirred so loudly, it sounded as though it might take flight. "Where do you draw the line, between body and self?"

Dex didn't know what to say.

Leroy shrugged. "That's between you and the gods." He took another bite of his apple.

Mosscap looked at the colorful spools of filament for a moment longer. "I need to consider it."

"Absolutely," Leroy said. "I heard you when you said you're an object, not a person—do I have that right?"

"Yes," Mosscap said.

Leroy nodded, chewing both a bite of apple and that thought with equal slowness. "Okay. Still, though, I think we'd be going about it wrong if we treated this like any other machine fix. It *is* a prosthetic we're making here, and when I make prosthetics for people, I always tell them to take however much time they need to think about what they want. I get that you're different, but it's the same thing, I think."

The robot looked at Leroy gratefully. "I appreciate that very much, thank you." It turned its head to Dex. "Is that all right?"

"Of course," Dex said. "We can hang out in town until you know what you want."

Leroy set his apple down and leaned forward on the

counter. "Well, if you're gonna stay *here*," he said, folding his hands together seriously, "we've gotta give you a much better welcome."

. . .

The people of Kat's Landing knew how to party.

By sundown, the village had been transformed, and everyone who lived there seemed all too happy for a reason to celebrate on a whim. String lights hung in festive sine waves. Glowing lanterns bobbed in the water. A band jammed mellow on a floating platform, and the smells of fire-crisped fish and sizzling shells filled the warm air of a summer's night.

Dex lounged cross-legged in a cup-shaped chair hanging from a pole near the end of a dock, a plate of goodies balanced on their ankles. They put one arm behind their head and sighed contentedly before picking up yet another skewer of battered crawdads with the other hand. The memory of their unpleasant ride to the village was fading fast, and in its absence, they were more than happy to sit and eat and do nothing.

Mosscap was out on the water, in the back of the speedboat belonging to the old woman who'd vouched for the printer's handiwork that morning. She tore around the water at a speed befitting someone a fraction her age, deftly piloting her craft around the lit-up buoys that ostensibly kept her and her passenger safe. Dex couldn't hear what she and Mosscap were saying to each other, but their cheers and laughter rose above the hum of the engine and the splash of the water. There was no doubt they were having a fantastic time.

Leroy approached Dex's chosen spot, carrying two tall glasses filled with something purplish. "Mind if I join you, Sibling?" he asked. He lifted the drinks with a smile. "I don't come empty-handed."

Dex accepted the offering gladly. "I was getting thirsty," they said, smiling into Leroy's eyes as they took the drink. It was some kind of boozy punch, thick with muddled herbs and berries. Dex and Leroy saluted each other, then each took a sip. "Gods, that's perfect," Dex said.

"We have it good here," Leroy said, settling into a chair hanging opposite Dex's.

"You certainly do." Dex gave the bear pendant around their neck an acknowledging rub with their thumb. "Thank you again, for your time earlier. I hope we didn't screw up your day."

"Oh, not even a little," Leroy said. "You made it a great one." He looked out at the water as twin peals of laughter arose from the speedboat, and chuckled. "Glad to see Ms. Amelia found herself a willing victim."

"Is that her name?" Dex asked.

"Mmm-hmm," Leroy said. "And Mosscap's braver than me. I wouldn't get in a boat with her."

"Why not?"

Leroy gestured toward the water, holding his palm flat to

emphasize the spectacle before them. The boat careened at reckless angles, water spraying wildly to either side.

Dex laughed. "Mosscap's waterproof, at least."

"Mosscap's lucky," Leroy said, "to find someone as kind as you to look after it."

Dex warmed under the compliment but squinted at the phrasing that came after. "Mm, I'm not its keeper. Our arrangement isn't like that."

"What is it like?"

Dex thought. "You ever had a friend come visit from somewhere else? Somewhere far away, where they do everything different? You have to show them around, teach them what the food is, how the tech around your house works, what counts as good manners?"

"Sure," Leroy said.

"*That's* what it's like," Dex said. "Mosscap's my friend, and I'm just showing it around. It did the same for me, out in the wilds. Human lands are my neighborhood; everything else is Mosscap's. It's an exchange, pure and simple."

Leroy sipped his drink, peering at Dex with keen interest. "I heard a rumor you were out in the Antlers. Past the Borderlands."

The comment made Dex feel a touch exposed. Their choice to head out that way had been made in solitude, and their reasons for doing so were private. To have that time and place become folded into Mosscap's public story was an odd feeling. They took a moment before replying. "Yeah," they said at last. "I was."

To his credit, Leroy seemed to glean Dex's mild discomfort, and his tone as he continued was gentle. "What's it like, out there?"

Dex exhaled, and decided to embrace the vulnerability. "Beautiful. Frightening. It makes you understand why we don't live out there anymore."

They hadn't noticed before, but Leroy was wearing Chal's sugar bee on a charm bracelet around his right wrist. He gave this a little rub, just like Dex had with their pendant. "And Mosscap helped you find your way through?"

"Yeah," Dex said. "It did. I don't know what would've happened to me out there if we hadn't run into each other. I either would've turned around or . . ." They shrugged. "I dunno."

"Then you're both lucky." Leroy took another contemplative sip, never taking his eyes off Dex. "Nobody can go it alone."

"Robots can," Dex said.

"Yeah, but that one looks like it loves company." Leroy turned his attention to the water and laughed once more at the nautical antics, shaking his head.

Dex took an oh-so-casual sip. "Don't we all?"

The question landed exactly where Dex hoped it would, and a sparkle appeared in Leroy's eye. A slow smile crept across his face. "Y'know, Sibling, I was wondering . . ."

"Yeah?" Dex said.

Leroy's smile grew. "Well, if your friend doesn't need you around tonight, would you . . . like to spend it at my place?"

Everything that had annoyed Dex about the day became instantly worth it. "Yeah," they said. "I would." They set their plate aside and got to their feet.

"Oh—now?" Leroy said.

Dex grinned at him. "Do you have somewhere else to be?"

Leroy laughed with happy surprise. "Well . . . okay, then. All right." He stood and held out his hand.

Dex took it and felt their pulses greet each other, buzzing with the impulsive promise of something good for the soul. They headed back down the dock together, drawing closer with each step. The lights of the party flickered on the water, and the stars answered them above.

. . . .

Fond as Dex was of their own bed, it was nice, for a change, to wake up in someone else's. As it turned out, Leroy's home and the fab shack were one and the same. He had a large room behind his work space, and much could be read in how it was arranged. His bed was low and spacious—easy to fall into, hard to get out of. The kitchen nook was basic but well stocked with simple, healthy things. There was a big armchair with a high-performance sound system behind it, speakers angled toward where a head would rest. Knickknacks and artwork filled the empty spaces but not in a cluttered way—just a few carefully chosen things that each hinted at a story.

The wall opposite the bed was almost entirely composed of floor-to-ceiling windows, and when Dex opened their eyes that morning, the river was the first thing to say hello. Leroy was the second, though he hadn't awoken yet. Dex smiled at the sound of his sleeping breaths and at the scent of the recently laundered sheets that cradled them both. Outside, a small parade of mud ducks paddled by. A turtle basked on a sunbaked rock. A crane thrust its long neck into the water, came up empty, and continued the hunt. Dex propped themself up on a pillow, enjoying every sight and smell and feeling without weighing them down with any thought more complicated than perception.

They glanced at their pocket computer lying faceup on the bedside table. More messages had appeared in their mailbox, patiently waiting. Dex took a brief glance. More requests from the City, all from people they didn't know. Would Mosscap want to make recordings for the historical archives, their mailbox asked? Would they be open to adding a third public meeting at the University, as the first two had already filled up? The Mechanics' Guild had invited them both to a formal dinner, but now their hosts were rethinking—would it be more polite to organize something for Mosscap that didn't involve food?

Dex turned their computer off and returned to the sheets and the ducks.

There was a knock at the door, quiet but clear. Dex looked over at Leroy; their host remained asleep. After a moment's consideration, Dex extricated themself from the bed as stealthily as they could. Another knock came as they looked around for their clothes. They put on their own pants and

Leroy's shirt, then padded barefoot through the shop and to the front door, where the knocking continued.

Dex opened the door to find Mosscap on the other side, knuckles raised mid-knock. In its other hand it grasped a polished wooden cane, which it leaned heavily on. "Good morning, Sibling Dex!" the robot said. "Congratulations on having sex last night."

A laugh came from behind where Mosscap stood, and Dex craned their head to see Ms. Amelia, the speedboat owner, leaning on a similarly styled cane and continuing to laugh behind her hand. There was an empty pushcart behind her—presumably the means by which she'd brought Moss-cap to the fab shack. She gave Dex a cheery wave, her eyes crinkling merrily.

"Uh," Dex said. Their cheeks grew warm, and they cleared their throat. "Thanks, Mosscap."

The robot beamed. "Ms. Amelia was *very* helpful in teaching me the social norms surrounding such behavior. I'm still not sure I understand it in full, but she made it quite clear that I should *not* disturb you, even though I would love to know the particulars of how you—"

Dex cleared their throat again. "Uh, yeah." They nodded at the old woman. "I appreciate it, Ms. Amelia."

Ms. Amelia nodded back and looked at Mosscap. "I should get home," she said. "The cats will be cranky without their breakfast. But you are welcome in my house anytime." She pointed at the cart. "You want me to leave this for you?"

"No, thank you," Mosscap said. "Hopefully, I won't be needing it once I leave."

As Ms. Amelia and Mosscap exchanged parting pleasantries, Dex heard movement inside the building. They left the door open and walked back into Leroy's home, where the man of the house had put a kettle on the stove and a pair of pants on himself.

"Hey," Dex said with a sly smile.

Leroy returned the look as he set two mugs on the short counter that served as an eating space. "Hey," he said.

Dex jabbed a thumb in the direction of the front door. "Mosscap's here. It kinda sounds like it's made a decision. About the replacement, I mean."

"Oh," Leroy said. He opened his fridge. "Well, that's great."

"Do you want me to have it wait in the shop while you get about your morning?"

"No, no, it's welcome back here," Leroy said. He lifted up a bowl of speckled duck eggs and a bundle of mixed greens tied with twine. "I assume it doesn't need breakfast?"

Dex chuckled. "No, it doesn't."

Leroy's smile tugged itself a little higher up one cheek. "And what about you?"

"I would love breakfast," Dex said.

Leroy nodded happily and got to work.

The sound of the front door closing echoed through the shop, followed by uneven clanking steps as Mosscap limped its way into the room. "Good morning, Leroy!" Mosscap said. "Congratulations on—"

Dex interrupted it as fast as possible. "Mosscap apparently spent the night at Ms. Amelia's," they said.

"Oh, yes, it was wonderful," Mosscap said. It took a seat on one of the stools at the counter. "I got to play with her cats, and she showed me her art studio, and she has a beautiful collection of *paper books*. They're so much easier to read when they don't fall apart."

Leroy cocked his head at this as he cracked an egg into a bowl; Dex supplied an explanation as they sat on the other stool. "There were paper books at the hermitage we visited out in the Antlers," they said. "We salvaged some to bring to City University, but most were . . . well, falling apart."

"I see," Leroy said, cracking another egg. He gestured at the bowl. "I hope it was safe to assume you like omelets."

Dex smiled brightly. "I love omelets," they said, and it was true.

Leroy gave them just a hint of a wink and continued to cook.

"Is this customary?" Mosscap whispered to Dex as Leroy fetched some herbs from the pots on his windowsill. "In some of the books I read last night, people made each other breakfast after having sex, but not universally."

Dex threw Mosscap a look and lowered their voice as far as it would go. "What kind of books does Ms. Amelia collect?"

"Oh, entirely pornography," Mosscap said. "It was very educational."

Dex noticed Leroy doing an admirable job of making no expression whatsoever. "Breakfast isn't customary," Dex whispered. "But it's . . . it's very nice when it happens."

"I can see how it would be," Mosscap said approvingly. It paused. "Oh, dear, should I leave? Am I intruding?"

"I think it's okay," Dex said. Leroy had made eye contact with them by this point, and he seemed to be taking the third wheel in good-humored stride. Dex made a mental note to return to Kat's Landing before all too long. "So," Dex said, raising their voice to a normal volume. "Have you thought about what you'd like to do here?"

"Yes, I have," Mosscap said. "Though I'm wondering if it's possible."

"Shoot," Leroy said.

Mosscap folded its hands on the counter. "Could you melt down the part of me that broke, and use that to print a replacement?"

"Oh, yeah, that's easy," Leroy said. "Recycling oil plastic takes a little longer, because I'll need to process it safely, but if you don't mind the wait, then yeah, absolutely."

"Wonderful," Mosscap said, sounding relieved. "Then that is what I would like to do."

Dex put an elbow on the counter and leaned their jaw against their fist. "Can I ask why?"

The robot sat for a moment, considering. "I don't want to separate myself from other robots any more than I already have," it said. "I am having the most incredible experience out here. I've seen species of trees that don't live in my part of the world. I've been on a boat. I've played with domesticated cats. I have a *satchel*!" It gestured at the bag hanging at its side for emphasis. "A satchel for my belongings! I am doing things no robot has ever done, and while that's marvelous, I . . . I don't want to become removed from them. The aggregate differences I have are only going to increase as we continue along, Sibling Dex. It's very nice to be famous, but I don't know how I feel about it yet, and I'm beginning to wonder if it's a trait I'll have among my own kind as well. So, you see, it's enough that I'm experientially different; I don't want to be *physically* different, too." It paused. "Does that make sense?"

"Yeah," Dex said with a fond smile. "Yeah, it does."

Leroy watched the two of them with a touched expression. "I'll go warm up the grinder," he said, leaving breakfast prep where it lay. "We can start the melt while we eat."

"Anything I can do to help?" Dex asked.

Leroy squeezed Dex's shoulder as he passed by. "Nah," he said. He paused, noticing what Dex was wearing. "Is that my shirt?"

Dex laughed awkwardly. "Sorry," they said. "I was hurrying, and—"

"No, it's cool," Leroy said. He continued on his way to the workshop. "You should keep it. Looks good on you."

Mosscap leaned forward once Leroy was gone. "Is exchanging items of clothing customary?"

Dex's cheeks grew hot. "No," they said.

"*Ohhhh.*" Mosscap raised both hands to its angular chin.

"Ms. Amelia would have something to say about that, I think."

"Please," Dex said fervently. They shut their eyes. "Don't tell Ms. Amelia."

4

The Coastlands

Finding the ocean was as simple a matter as letting a river lead you in the direction it wanted to go most. There were many options of where a person could head once the air took on a bite of salt, but Dex had chosen Shipwreck Margin, for the uncomplicated reason that they liked the look of it and thought Mosscap would, too. It was a contemplative place, its silvery waters punctuated with boulders carved by the strange hand of the tides. There were beaches nearer the City with pillowy sand and playful waves, but Shipwreck was not of that breed. The currents here were as unforgiving as the toothy predators that navigated their pull. The shoreline was carpeted with stones in need of a few more epochs before they became sand, and the cliffs they'd been ground from towered over the pounding surf, their edges sharp and scabrous.

But despite Shipwreck's foreboding demeanor, life thrived in this place. Black-feathered seabirds nested in crevices unreachable without wings, and spruce trees clung to the cliff edges, stunted yet defiant in the briny mist. Softer touches were abundant, if you knew where to look. Sea strawberries grew from even the darkest gaps, and matte-orange gem-stones hid among the pebbles. And there were people in this part of the world, too, clustered here and there in settlements no bigger than a dozen or so families, making a life on the bleeding edge of where a terrestrial animal belonged.

These scattered villages were easy to spot from the clifftop Dex had parked the wagon on. Mosscap observed its new surroundings with keen interest, peering through the binoc-ulars it had acquired the week before. "Their dwellings look very simple," Mosscap said as it surveyed.

Dex nodded as they set up the folding chairs. They didn't need to look to know what Mosscap was talking about—modest, sturdy shelters made of spruce planks and driftwood, a short distance from the jetties where small sailboats would return at the end of the day, hauling back whatever had been caught with a hand-pulled net.

"I'm so looking forward to going to the beach, Sibling Dex," Mosscap continued. "I haven't spent much time around littoral ecosystems, and it's been years since I did so."

Dex sighed as they found themself standing at the ines-capable entry point of a conversation they'd been putting off and could no longer avoid. They'd spent days agonizing over the best way to bring this up, and had considered doing it sooner, but Mosscap had been having such a good time in the Riverlands that Dex hadn't wanted to rain on the parade. They knew this was a subject Mosscap would get deep in its own head about, and Dex had felt it kinder, in the end, to limit that sort of wheel-spinning as much as possible.

This choice did not make broaching the topic any easier.

"Mosscap, there's . . ." Dex stuck their hands in their pockets and sucked their teeth. "I don't want to bring things down, but I think we should chat about what your—what our expectations should be like while we're here. I don't . . . I don't know . . . how much of the beach we'll actually get to see close up."

The robot lowered its binoculars. "Why?"

Dex exhaled. They sat in one of the chairs, and gestured for Mosscap to take the other. "Two things," they said, as Mosscap sat. "First, most of the Coastlands is rewilded territory. *You* could walk through it, if you want to, but I can't. There are no roads or trails in a lot of places, and the animals that live there aren't used to people and shouldn't be disturbed."

"So, nesting birds and the like," Mosscap said. "Pupping seals, that kind of thing?"

"Probably," Dex said. "I don't know specifics. I just know it's not my place. I mean that literally. The human footprint along the coast is a very small one, by design."

"That seems wise," Mosscap said. "But what about this beach?" It angled its head toward the little wooden homes standing at the root of the cliffs.

"Well, that's the second thing." Dex sought their words with care. "The villages that *do* exist here . . . may not be overly welcoming to you and me." They sighed again. "You in particular."

"Oh," Mosscap said. The robot was taken aback but did

not react strongly. It merely folded its hands in its lap and looked at Dex, seeking understanding. "Why?"

Dex puffed out their cheeks and leaned back in their chair. "The folks here, by and large, aren't cool with modern technology. Any technology, really, beyond the most basic basics."

Mosscap's eyes shifted. "You touched on this before, back at the hermitage. But you didn't explain."

Dex began to do exactly that. "Some people went in kind of an extreme direction after the Transition. They think tech is a slippery slope that heads right back to the Factory Age, so they don't use anything automated. Most don't use electricity, except maybe for heating, and even that's not a given. Some use animals to help with pulling and lifting things, but a lot of them just stick to what they can carry on their own. And that's fine—that's their choice. They can live how they like. But they also are known to get prickly about people bringing mainstream tech into their space. When I do tea service here, I rarely go into town. I usually just park on the outskirts and let people come to me if they want to. Like we're doing now."

"Why don't they want you close by?" Mosscap said.

"Because I have an electric kettle," Dex said. "And an ox-bike. And a pocket computer. And a fridge. You get the idea."

Mosscap looked down at its metal frame. "If they don't like ox-bikes or electric kettles, I can see how *I* might pose a problem."

Dex screwed up their face in apology. "Yeah."

The robot ran its hand over the exposed components of its

midsection, as if seeing itself for the first time. Dex already hated making Mosscap think about this. They knew Mosscap to have unshakable belief in its intrinsic value—*I know that no matter what, I'm wonderful,* it had proclaimed back in the wilds—and watching it silently question its own body made Dex want to return to the highway and forget this whole leg of the trip.

Mosscap looked back up, the light in its eyes lower than before. "I've never felt like a problem," it said. "Not a very good feeling, is it?"

"Do you want to go?" Dex said. "I'm serious. I'm sorry, I should've told you sooner, and that's on me. We don't have to—"

"Yes, we do," Mosscap said decisively. "I'm here to meet humanity, and these people you've described are just as much a part of it as you are. I wouldn't be doing a very good job of pursuing my quest if I only welcomed the parts that were fun."

A flicker of admiration arose within Dex. They reached over and squeezed the robot's wrist. "Okay," they said. "But it's your call. The second you change your mind, we're out."

Mosscap patted Dex's hand. "Agreed."

"And don't think of yourself as a problem," Dex said, a protective edge entering their voice. "If they have an issue with you, that's on *them*. And it's not even about you, personally. They just . . . don't understand what you are. Or maybe they can't fit you into their beliefs, and that scares them. The unknown makes us stupid sometimes."

Mosscap considered this seriously. "Like elk," it said.

"Sorry?" Dex said.

"Elk don't understand robots either. We confuse them, and that makes them afraid, and then they can get . . . well, dis- agreeable." Mosscap nodded to itself. "I never take it personally, with elk. You have to let them come to you instead of you going to them." Its eyes brightened a touch. "I understand that." It shifted to face them directly. "Have you ever been charged by an elk, Sibling Dex?"

"I . . . have not."

"Mmm," Mosscap replied. It looked out at the sea. "I don't recommend it."

．　．　．

Robot minds and human minds had a key difference between them, and Dex had learned it well in the past few months. For as distracted as Mosscap could be whenever something new and interesting entered the scene, it was equally capable of devoting itself to a single task indefinitely, without need of diversion. No matter how easygoing Dex thought themself, there was no competing with a being whose cohorts were out in the wilds, watching stalagmites form and saplings grow. A human mind was perpetually restless by comparison, and that was how Dex found themself as the day dragged on without any visitors from the villages below. To pass the time, they cleaned their bike. They made some lunch. They answered some messages. They tended their herbs within the wagon, took a short nap, then reorganized a cupboard that had been annoying them for weeks.

Mosscap, on the other hand, sat in its chair. It didn't read, or talk much. It didn't seem to move. It simply waited in patient hope for people who might never show up.

Until at last someone did.

A stranger approached, walking up one of the cliffside trails. They were middle-aged, fit and trim with a pepper-grey braid. They wore a knit sweater to fend off the fog, which made for a funny juxtaposition with the open-toed fish-leather sandals strapped to their feet. Dex waved to them as they approached, and Mosscap did the same, transitioning in a blink from its silent vigil into animated excitement. The stranger paused for the briefest of moments to raise an eyebrow as they absorbed the sight of the robot, then gave a nod of acknowledgment. At first blush, Dex got the impression of a person who took even the most extraordinary occurrences in stride.

"Hello there," Dex said. They fell easily into the mode they so often adopted for tea service—a practiced, smiling, friendly performance of themself. "Please, join us."

The stranger walked up, looking at Mosscap with the same casual gaze as before. "Well, you are something, aren't you?" they said.

"I am Mosscap," the robot said with a polite bow of its head. "And this is my friend, Sibling Dex."

"Pleased to meet you both," the stranger said. "My name's Avery."

"We're glad you're here, Mx. Avery," Dex said, establishing a congenial mood but adding nothing further. They'd learned, with encounters such as these, that their role was to smooth out any bumps in whatever conversation would follow, but only as necessary. They had become a translator, of sorts. A chaperone. A shepherd. They would keep Mosscap on the rails and break the ice if it grew too thick, but ultimately, these moments were about Mosscap and the other person, and not about Dex at all. In some ways, their profession had prepared Dex well for this. Building a canvas for others to explore themselves on was rather the point of monastic service, after all.

Mx. Avery pulled a leather waterskin from their satchel and took a long sip of whatever was inside. "That trail's always easier going down," they said. They looked at Mosscap. "How do those metal feet of yours do on steep trails?"

"Very well," Mosscap said. "They have excellent traction, and my sense of balance has never been better."

"I'm glad to hear that, because I'd like to extend an invitation." Mx. Avery capped their waterskin and returned it to their bag. "Would you like to come down and go fishing with me? Just off the dock; we don't need to bother with a boat."

To say that Dex was surprised by this was an understatement. They glanced at Mosscap, ready to follow its lead.

Mosscap was smiling, but its head whirred. "I would love to join you, yes," it said. "However, I don't participate in hunting behavior myself. Would I have to . . . take part?"

Mx. Avery shrugged. "You can do whatever you're comfy

with. I can get you a pole, or you can sit and watch. Suits me the same either way." They looked at Dex. "Same goes for you, Sibling."

"I'm not very good at fishing," Dex said, "but . . ." They caught Mosscap's eye and confirmed this was how the day was going to go. "Sure. Let's do it."

•   •   •

The doors of the village were shut when their group reached the bottom of the cliff. All the homes were on stilts, standing high above the sand, but Dex could see flickers of movement through their windows. A curtain was pulled shut as Mosscap drew near. A couple of kids in another house pressed their noses against the glass, only to be shooed away by the shadow of someone larger. Dex hoped Mosscap hadn't noticed, but it didn't take long for the robot's eyes to grow dim and distant. Upon seeing this, Dex reached out and took Mosscap's hand, holding it tightly as they followed Mx. Avery to the dock. Robots didn't hold hands with each other, Dex knew, but humans did, and by the way Mosscap squeezed its metal fingers in response, it was clear it understood the gesture.

Mx. Avery gave a little shake of their head as they continued toward the water. "Ignore them," they said disapprovingly of their townsfolk. "It's my home just as much as theirs, and I want you here." They looked Mosscap in the eye. "Not very neighborly of us, is it?"

"It . . . is a little disheartening," Mosscap said, honest and calm. "I'm trying not to take it personally, as Sibling Dex encouraged me to do, but I have to admit, this is proving to be a difficult day."

Mx. Avery gave a sympathetic smile. "Day's not over yet."

The three of them arrived at the dock, stepping from loose stones onto weather-beaten wood. A heap of fishing gear was waiting at the end of the structure, accompanied by a trio of seating cushions set out in a row. It seemed their host had anticipated the invitation would be accepted.

Mx. Avery opened a palm toward the fishing poles. "Well, what do you think, Mosscap?" they said. "You want to give it a go, or you want to watch?"

"I'll watch, thank you," Mosscap said.

"Okay," Mx. Avery said. They picked up two poles and extended one toward Dex. "Sibling?"

Dex took it and ran their fingers over the hand-polished wood. They'd never used a pole like this before, but the function of it was no different from that of a printed one. Fishing wasn't that complicated.

Mosscap leaned in with interest toward Mx. Avery's pole. "How does it work?"

"You bait this," Mx. Avery said, holding up the hook. "Then you drop it in the water, and . . . you wait."

"What do you wait for?"

"For the fish to bite the hook."

"I see," Mosscap said. "Very clever. Tools do make this easier, don't they? I always feel for bears, standing in the water with their mouths open all day. The young ones look so disappointed." It leaned in closer, studying the hook. "What do you bait it with?"

Mx. Avery reached down, picked up a small box with holes drilled in the top, and opened the lid for Mosscap to see.

"Oh!" Mosscap gasped with surprise. "Purple crawlers!"

Mx. Avery laughed at the robot's reaction to the wriggling ball of worms. "You know them, huh?"

"Yes, but . . ." Mosscap looked back at the village standing on the rocky shore. "Where do you get them? They're forest dwellers. They live in topsoil."

"I have a bin of them at home," Mx. Avery said. "They eat my food scraps, and then I use them to get more food."

"You farm worms," Mosscap said slowly, trying to clarify. "In a bin."

"I guess so, yes."

"And then you put them on a hook." It looked up. "Alive?"

Mx. Avery nodded. "Best way to get a fish's attention."

Mosscap pondered this, its head whirring with consternation. "What an utterly confusing life and death that must be."

Dex reached over and took a worm from the box before they could fall into an existential crisis about it. They baited their hook with a whispered apology.

The three of them sat on the cushions, Mosscap in the middle. It watched keenly as Mx. Avery and Dex both lowered their lines into the splashing water below. "How long does it take?" Mosscap asked.

"Long as it needs to," Mx. Avery said. They made themself

comfortable and smiled at Mosscap. "That's why it's a nice thing to do with someone to talk to." They held their fishing pole between their knees, then reached over and retrieved a battered old canteen from the assorted equipment. "Tea, Sibling?" they offered. "Won't be half as good as what you make, I'm sure, but—"

"Oh, no, that'd be great, thank you," Dex said.

Mx. Avery took two wooden cups from a stuff sack and began to pour. "So, where've you been, before here?"

"We were in Steelhead last," Mosscap said.

"And we're your first stop on the coast?"

"Yes."

Mx. Avery nodded as they handed Dex a full cup. "And where're you headed?"

"We'll continue southeast through your territory," Mosscap said, "and then through the Shrublands, and on to the City."

"You taking the City Highway or the Twenty-Six?" Mx. Avery said.

Mosscap looked at Dex, asking for an answer.

"Probably the Twenty-Six," Dex said, holding their fishing pole with one hand and their cup in the other. They breathed in the drink as it cooled, instantly recognizing the scents of bee weed and preserved lime. "It's a longer trip but a nicer ride."

"Sure is," Mx. Avery said. "The Twenty-Six greenbelt's gorgeous this time of year. You'll have to watch out for marsh hawks, though—they get feisty if you get close."

"Oh, I'm sure," Mosscap said. "I'm personally more familiar with the black-tipped hawk, but they're closely related. I've had to duck while walking through a nesting ground many a time. They certainly like to go for the eyes, don't they?"

Mx. Avery chuckled. "That they do."

Mosscap thought for a moment. "I'm curious, Mx. Avery, if you don't mind—"

"I don't," they said, even though the subject was unvoiced.

"I'm mildly surprised by your knowledge of the Shrubland greenbelts. I'd been given to understand that people in your community are—"

"Shut-ins?"

"I was going to say *insular*."

Mx. Avery chuckled again. "That we are. But we do have the ramble. Nobody in my village does it except me anymore, but I still count."

"What's the ramble?" Mosscap asked, leaning toward Dex.

"It's a traditional thing around here," Dex supplied. "You're encouraged to regularly spend a month or so walking through the adjacent territories, so you can get a taste of how other folks do things." They looked to Mx. Avery. "Would you say that's right?"

Mx. Avery nodded. "That's the long and the short of it. I go every year, and I usually take the Twenty-Six. Not every time, though. It's good to mix it up, not have too much of a plan."

"How does it suit you?" Mosscap asked. "Life in other villages?"

"Oh, it's very nice," Mx. Avery said. "Very comfortable. Very easy. Hard to leave, sometimes."

"Yet you always come back."

"I do," Mx. Avery said.

"May I ask why?" Mosscap said. "Because I've noted with Sibling Dex here"—the robot nodded toward them—"they do very poorly in the world without technological assistance."

Mx. Avery let out a hearty laugh. "Would you agree with that, Sibling?"

"Absolutely," Dex said, unabashed. "No offense to you, Mx. Avery, but I need a heater and a hot shower."

"I respect it, I do," Mx. Avery said. "Nobody likes a cold bath." They turned their attention to Mosscap. "But that's exactly why I come back after going elsewhere. Me and mine believe the further you distance yourself from the realities of what it means to be an animal in this world, the more you risk severing your connection to it. History tells us loud and clear where that road goes." They gave the robot a respectful nod. "I don't need to tell you that."

"Well, I wasn't there for it," Mosscap said. "For the factories, I mean."

Mx. Avery looked puzzled, so Sibling Dex stepped in, explaining how the factory robots dismantled and rebuilt themselves into new generations, opting to mirror Bosh's cycle rather than live on indefinitely.

For the first time in the conversation, Mx. Avery seemed thrown for a loop, but even this was expressed subtly. They sat in silence, eyebrows raised high. "That certainly is something to think about," they said at last.

Mosscap was deep in thought as well, but evidently on a different thread. "So, you prefer to be uncomfortable?" Mosscap said.

"Of course not," Mx. Avery said. "But I think there's such a thing as *too* comfortable." They grinned. "I'm guessing our tea-slinging friend here would disagree."

Dex rubbed their lips together and chose their words with care. "It's not my place to debate different flavors of belief in the places I visit," they said. "I'm just here to serve tea."

"Such a diplomat," Mx. Avery said. "You an Ecologian?"

"No, I'm an Essentialist."

"Ahh," Mx. Avery said, as though that explained everything. "I like Essentialists. Don't agree, of course, but I appreciate your style."

"What . . . what is that?" Mosscap asked.

Dex arched their neck as they tried to sum up sectarian nuance in as few words as possible. "In the barest basics, I believe that though we can—and *should*—get close to the gods, it's impossible to understand them or the full nature of the universe, so we have to build a society that is best suited to *our* needs," Dex said. "And as a disciple of Allalae, that means I think we're allowed to use whatever we want to make ourselves as safe and comfortable as possible, provided that we don't damage the natural world or hurt one another in the process."

"I see," Mosscap said. It looked to Mx. Avery. "And what is *your* understanding of Allalae, as someone who forgoes many comforts?"

"Oh, no, no. I don't see it that way at all," Mx. Avery said. "On the contrary, our way of life shows you how comfortable the world is on its own. Paring things down makes the small comforts all the sweeter. You don't know how to be grateful for a well-sealed wall if you haven't had a winter storm bust through a weak one. You don't know how sweet strawberries are unless you've waited six months for them to fruit. Elsewhere, they have all these little luxuries, but they don't understand that food and shelter and company are all you really need. The world provides everything else without our meddling." They smiled at Dex. "What do you say to that, Sibling?"

Dex smiled back. "I'd say there's no harm in any sort of construct so long as said construct has been proven to *do* no harm."

Mx. Avery's eyes twinkled as they looked at Dex. "We could have a very good argument about that," they said.

"I have no doubt we—" Dex's words cut off abruptly as the fishing pole jerked in their hand. "Oh, shit," they said. "Mosscap, can you—" They handed their cup to the robot and got to work with both hands, reeling the line in as fast as they could.

"There we go!" Mx. Avery said, putting their pole between their knees once more and scrambling through their gear.

They produced a landing net and leaned over Mosscap's lap so as to get closer to Dex. "Sorry, Mosscap."

"Should I—" Mosscap began, looking around as though it should move.

"You're fine," Dex said quickly, still fighting against the hidden pull.

A few spins later, and the fish emerged with a loud splash, writhing in the sudden lack of pressure as Dex hoisted it upward. It was a little longer than Dex's forearm, and its silver scales gleamed in the daylight.

Mx. Avery held the net in one hand and skillfully grabbed the fish with the other, holding it as still as they could within the woven fibers. "Sibling, can you—"

Dex lay the pole down on the dock and removed the hook from the fish's mouth. With that, the flurry of human activity ceased, and Mx. Avery set the flopping net on the boards behind them so that they could all examine the catch.

"It's a . . ." Dex pursed their lips. "Well, it's a fish."

"It's a mirrorback," Mx. Avery said. "They're real tasty." They pointed at a brownish stripe running horizontally from head to tail. "That means it's already laid eggs and won't do so again. So, it's fine for us to take."

"It's beautiful," said Mosscap. The robot was fascinated but exhibited none of its usual glee. It looked between Mx. Avery and Sibling Dex. "How do you kill it?" A note of grief had entered its voice, but there was acceptance there, too, born out of a lifetime of watching wild things eat and be eaten.

Mx. Avery seemed to note the shift in Mosscap, and their tone likewise became more somber. "Well," they said slowly. They looked at Dex for a brief moment; Dex gave them a nod, letting them know it was okay. "We let the air do that for us," Mx. Avery said.

Mosscap said nothing in response to this. It kept its glowing eyes on the fish, studying the gill flaps as they spasmed in the presence of oxygen they couldn't use. Mosscap watched and watched, and the longer it did, the harder Dex found it to do the same. They'd been fishing bunches of times, had plenty of fish die in their immediate vicinity, eaten more of their kind than they could count. But as they tried to watch as Mosscap did, they became uncomfortable, almost like they were witnessing something that wasn't their business.

But it *was* their business. They were the one who'd pulled the fish out of its watery home. They were the one who'd stepped in and decided that it was time for something's life to be over because they were hungry and their own life required it. Mosscap was right to look as unflinchingly as it did. Dex was ashamed that they hadn't, before.

Mosscap reached out its hand. With an aching gentleness, it lay its fingers on the animal's dying body. Its eyes became focused, and it bowed its head closer.

"It's all right," Mosscap murmured, its metallic voice thick with respect and sorrow. "I know. It's not fair. But it's all right. It'll be over soon."

Mx. Avery stared at Mosscap, their gaze as conflicted as Dex felt. They hesitated for a moment, then put their hand on Mosscap's shoulder as they, too, watched the fish's movements begin to slow. Dex did the same, a silent prayer to Bosh running through them. All three sat still, and together, they held vigil as something that had never existed before and never would again ceased its struggling and came to an end.

5

The Shrublands

"Can we go over it one more time?" Mosscap asked.

"Sure," Dex said as they pedaled through the dappled shade.

Mosscap began to tick things off on its fingers as it walked beside the bike. "Nora and Theo are your mother and father."

"Yes."

"They are currently still partners."

"Also yes."

"They have a partner named Abby. She wasn't involved in raising you."

"Not very much," Dex said. "She didn't move in until I was in my teens. But we get on well."

Mosscap nodded. "And your father has a partner named Jasper."

"No," Dex corrected. "My dad has a partner named Felix, and he has a son named Jasper. Jasper is my stepbrother."

The robot frowned at the mistake. "And you didn't grow up with Jasper."

"No. Dad and Felix got together after I'd already moved

out, and then Jasper decided to move to the farm a few years after that."

Mosscap's head whirred. "But you *did* grow up with your sisters." It began to count on its fingers again. "Violet, Sadie, and you. In that order. You're the youngest."

"I am indeed."

"And Violet—no, Sadie is the sister you share both parents with, biologically."

"Yes."

"Violet is Nora's daughter, and her father is . . . oh, no . . ."

"Radley," Dex supplied.

"*Radley,*" Mosscap said with a sigh. "Yes, he and your mother were together, and then they weren't, and now she's with your father, but they're still the best of friends."

"He's basically my second dad," Dex said. "He and Liz have lived next door forever."

Mosscap turned its head in confusion. "Who's Liz?"

"Radley's partner."

The robot looked defeated. "And then there are your aunts, and uncles, and cousins. And your sisters both have partners and children of their own."

Dex gave Mosscap a grin. "The cousins do too."

Mosscap groaned wearily. "I know you're of a social species, but *goodness,* Sibling Dex. I'm never going to get this right."

"You don't have to," Dex said. "It's always chaos there, and nobody will expect you to navigate it. You'll see—my dad mixes up the little kids' names all the time."

"I just want to make a good impression," Mosscap said. It looked away to watch a bird fly by. "Meeting your family is a very different sort of occasion than meeting strangers."

Dex laughed. "It's not like you're moving in, Mosscap. You can make any sort of impression you want."

"Yes, but—oh, no!" Mosscap's lenses widened with worried realization. "I haven't brought a gift!"

Dex tried to keep their eyes on the road. "Why would you need a *gift*?" they asked.

"People do that in books," Mosscap said. "When they come to stay at someone's home. Isn't it customary, to bring a gift to your host?"

"Well . . . sure, but—"

"I need a gift, Sibling Dex," Mosscap said firmly. It paused. "I've never given one before. What sort of item is appropriate?" It opened its satchel and began to dig around. "I have some very good rocks. I don't wish to part with my binoculars. What about clothespins; would they like clothespins?"

"Why do you have—" Dex dropped it. "Tell you what. There's a fruit stand on the way there, and they usually have cherry wine. A couple bottles of that would be a nice gift."

"Oh, good," Mosscap said. It ceased its rummaging and walked more confidently along. "I will trade some pebs for cherry wine and give it to my hosts. Ha!"

"Why is that funny?" Dex asked.

"Because it's so very human, and I am not. And it's not funny, it's *delightful*. It's the same as knowing how to calm a wolf by rolling over, or how to make sun jays identify themselves."

Dex blinked. "How to do *what*?"

"Every sun jay has an identifying call," Mosscap explained patiently. "A name, if you like. There's a sound they make that instructs any other sun jays in the area to sound off and let them know who's in the neighborhood."

"And you know how to do that?"

Mosscap beamed. "Let's see if there's anyone around." It opened its mouth and let out an uncanny imitation of a raspy corvid croak, loud enough to echo through the branches above. A silence followed, and then, from not too far away, an answering squawk called back, followed by another more distant, yet unmistakably distinct.

"Whoa," Dex said. They laughed. "That's really cool."

Mosscap gave a nod of agreement. It turned its gaze toward the trees, presumably searching for the individuals it had been speaking with, but something else caught its eye. "Oh, that's lovely," Mosscap said.

"What is?" said Dex.

Mosscap pointed. "Crown shyness is so striking, don't you think?"

Dex had no idea what Mosscap meant. "Sorry, *what's* striking?"

"Stop," Mosscap said. "Look."

Dex sighed, but they hit the brakes, put their feet on the paving below, and looked up.

Mosscap continued to point, tracing lines in the air. "Look at the treetops," it said. "What do you notice?"

"Uh," Dex said. They frowned, not knowing what Mosscap was getting at. There were branches, obviously, and leaves, and . . . "*Oh.* Oh, they're . . ." They fell quiet as their perspective of the surrounding landscape shifted in a way they'd never unsee.

Despite their number and close proximity, none of the treetops were touching one another. It was as though someone had taken an eraser and run it cleanly through the canopy, transforming each tree into its own small island contained within a definitive border of blue sky. The effect reminded Dex of puzzle pieces laid out on the table, each in their own place yet still unconnected. It wasn't that the trees were unhealthy or their foliage sparse. On the contrary, every tree was lush and full, bursting with green life. Yet somehow, in the absence of contact, they knew exactly where to stop growing outward so that they might give their neighbors space to thrive.

"How . . ." Dex began to ask.

"No one knows," Mosscap said. "At least, not to my knowledge. Some say it's to minimize competition. Others think it's to prevent the spread of disease. But as to how the trees know when to hold themselves back, I don't know. It's a mystery."

Dex gave an inward nod to Samafar as they continued to observe the strange phenomenon. "I've never noticed it before," they said, and this bothered them. They'd grown up around there. They'd ridden this road dozens of times. The pattern of the trees was spectacularly obvious, now that they were observing it, but it had always been the backdrop to Dex. The wallpaper. They'd never been looking for it. Now they couldn't see anything else.

"I'm surprised you weren't familiar with crown shyness," Mosscap said. "You're so knowledgeable about plants."

"I know herbs and ornamentals," Dex said. "I don't really know trees, just some of their names."

"Well, that's the nice thing about trees." Mosscap put its hands on its hips as it looked around. "They're not going anywhere. You can take all the time you need to get to know them."

. . . .

It was always a strange thing, coming home. Coming home meant that you had, at one point, left it and, in doing so, irreversibly changed. How odd, then, to be able to return to a place that would always be anchored in your notion of the past. How could this place still be there, if the you that once lived there no longer existed?

Yet at the same time, in complete contradiction, seeing that said place *had* changed in your absence was nothing if not surreal. Dex felt this as they approached the road leading to their family's farm, just as they felt every time they made the trip. The road was the same, but the fence had been mended. The field was the same, but the greyberry bushes had been cut down to the root. The farm was a place where Dex knew they would always be welcome but never in the same way as before they left; a place they knew intimately and no longer knew at all.

Dex pulled off the road shortly after rounding the last corner, and parked the wagon beside the old oak tree they'd climbed many a time when they were small. They put down the brakes, grabbed a bag of clothes, and locked the wagon door.

"Why are you leaving the wagon here?" Mosscap asked. It looked around. "I don't see any buildings yet."

"Because we're early," Dex said. "And we want to be *less* early."

"Why?" Mosscap asked.

"You'll see," Dex said. "Besides, it's a nice walk, and you'll see more of the farm this way."

The road curved back and forth like a lazy stream, and the two of them followed comfortably along. They passed the orchard, where grass hens and speckled quail scratched for bugs in the thick grass below. They passed one of the many pastures, its soil at rest beneath a cover crop of radishes, lentils, black oats, and rabbit clover the hungry herd would devour in the coming year. They passed the pond that served as the last filter for the farm's greywater, startling a gossiping group of ducks back into the lily-filled pool. Dex and Mosscap paused there for a few minutes to watch a horde of blue-backed dragonflies patrol the airways, then continued on—past the intentionally untended field filled with solar panels and beehives, past the orderly clusters of domed greenhouses, past the workshop and the tool shed and the root cellar, until they came at last to the center of it all.

The cluster of houses at the heart of the farm was as varied as the people within them. Some were built of wood, but most of cob. The eldest home was likewise the largest: a stately old farmhouse holding court in the middle, crowned with a green roof and a wind turbine. A lovingly maintained deck unfolded on all sides, providing plenty of welcoming nooks for anyone who wanted to kick up their feet and sit awhile. But nobody was outside as Dex and Mosscap approached. Everyone was indoors, but unsurprisingly, Dex had no problem hearing them.

"Is everything all right?" Mosscap asked, carrying a beribboned bottle of cherry wine in each hand. "Sounds like quite a commotion."

"No." Dex sighed. "It sounds like dinnertime."

They walked up the ramp toward the front door, their footsteps thumping against the well-oiled cedar. The dogs were the first to notice, barking in thunderous chorus as they burst out of the open doorway. There were three of them, all shaggy herders painted in soft swirls of brown and black, smart as hell when they were at work and big dumb mops every other hour of the day.

Dex planted their feet in anticipation of the onslaught of jumping and licking and whimpering. "Mosscap, this is Burt, Buster, and Buddy," Dex said as they patted heads and rubbed ears. "Yes, hi, hello." They glanced toward the door, seeing the movement that followed in the dogs' wake. "And here's—"

Here was everyone else.

The crowd that appeared was as familiar to Dex as the scenery on the road. It wasn't just the faces and the voices but the aprons, the field clothes, the dish towels tossed over a shoulder or two, the hands covered in dough that still required kneading, the cheeks red from an argument hastily dropped, the pant-leg that had something spilled upon it, and the volume at which everyone shouted hello. But just as Dex hadn't known about the mended fence or the cut-back berries, they also hadn't expected Abby's new glasses, or that Felix had shaved his beard, or how their niblings had somehow kept growing since Dex visited last. The overwhelming mix of old and new engulfed Dex as they were hugged and kissed from all sides, and they tried their best to stay afloat in the ensuing sea of conversation.

You're early! How was the ride? Do you need a snack? A shower? How are you, sweetie, it's been so long! How's the wagon? Did you bring tea? You look slimmer than last time; are you eating enough? We saw your picture in the news; isn't that something? Did you see the new shed? The new goats? The new wind catch? You sure you don't want a snack? Buster, get down! Do you want a haircut while you're here? Not that it looks bad, no, just thought you might like a trim—

Dex realized, amid the loving assault, that Mosscap was getting the same treatment, and oddly, they found this to be a relief. They hadn't known how their family would react to the robot, and had wondered if they'd perhaps turn into the same speechless crowd Dex encountered in nearly every town they went to. But it seemed that Dex's clan had worked out whatever nervousness they'd had about their unusual visitor well ahead of time, and instead were treating Mosscap as just another guest fresh off the road.

Gods around, look at you! Welcome! We're so glad you're here. Can I touch you? Is that okay? How was the trip? Oh, my goodness, you didn't have to bring us anything! Aren't you sweet. You don't eat, right? What about power, do you need power? We can plug you in somewhere if you— Oh, oh, you can charge yourself, that's neat. *Would you like to see the goats tomorrow? What about the bees? We can open up a hive, if you want. Do you need to sit down? I don't know what to offer. You're so tall! Has Dex been eating well? They're looking slim.*

The cohesion of everyone focusing on the new arrivals did not take long to disintegrate, as Dex knew would be the case. A timer went off in the kitchen, one kid took another's toy, the dropped argument was remembered, the dogs started biting one another's faces, and so on, and so forth. One by one, folks splintered off to attend to whatever preparations had occupied them before, leaving only those who weren't as concerned by things left undone: the kids.

There was a small pack of them, clustered around Mosscap with wide eyes and giddy laughter. Mosscap knelt down, as it had learned to do with children, and gave its best smile. "I'm happy to answer any questions you might have," it said.

The kids were silent, at first, until one of them summoned some bravery. "Can you fly?" he asked.

"No," Mosscap said.

"Can you fight a bear?" asked another.

"I haven't tried," Mosscap said. "Why would I want to?"

"Does anything eat robots?" said one.

"No," Mosscap said.

"Could *we* eat a robot?" laughed one who thought herself hilarious.

Mosscap's eyes shifted with mild concern. ". . . What?"

Dex watched the proceedings from the background, leaning against the railing of the deck. A hand came to rest fondly on their shoulder, and they knew who it was before looking.

"Hey, Mom," Dex said, leaning their head into hers.

"Hey, bug," their mother said, turning her face and kissing their scalp. "It's so good to see you." She hugged Dex with one arm. On her opposite hip, she carried Charlotte, the newest member of the bunch, who was happily gnawing the shoulder strap of her grandmother's heavy-duty overalls. Charlotte cooed with curiosity at Dex, and Dex's mom smiled at them both. "Wanna say hi to your niece?"

"Oh, absolutely," Dex said, taking the baby into their arms. "Gods around, Charlotte, you got *big*!"

Charlotte flashed a toothless grin at her name, drooling on her shirt in the process.

The kids were still babbling their unpredictable questions at Mosscap, but the robot's focus became captured by the tiny person in Dex's arms. Dex noticed Mosscap's interest, and suddenly realized they'd never seen Mosscap encounter a baby before. *Could that be right?* they thought. There had been babies in the villages they'd been to, surely. It wasn't as though Charlotte was the only infant on Panga. But now that they were thinking about it, Dex couldn't remember ever seeing Mosscap get close to a baby, and from the look on the robot's face, there was nothing in the world it wanted to do more.

Dex took a few steps forward. "You want to hold her?" they asked.

"Oh, yes," Mosscap said with an almost-urgent seriousness. "But I don't know how."

"Let me show you," Dex said. Gently, they transferred the baby from their hands to Mosscap's, instructing it on how to support her. Charlotte hadn't figured out her head the last time Dex had been there, but she could hold it up easily now, and as soon as she turned to see what it was that was taking her, she fell dead silent.

Mosscap did as well, excepting the mechanical excitement within its head.

The two stared at each other, eyes wide and mouths open, gobsmacked with wonder. After a moment, Charlotte reached out and pawed at Mosscap's face with her chubby fingers.

"Oh!" Mosscap said with surprise. "Hello!"

For reasons unknowable to anyone but her, Charlotte found the talking machine entertaining, and she giggled, batting her hand against the metal plating a little harder.

Dex's mom laughed. "I think she likes you," she said.

"How can you tell?" Mosscap asked.

Charlotte giggled again.

"Oh, I see," Mosscap said in an excited whisper, taking note of this new behavior. "Yes, I like you, too."

Dex's mom caught their eye. "Do you mind if I leave her with you two for a bit? It's all hands on deck in the kitchen."

Dex gave her a grateful look. They knew that she knew that Dex usually wanted a minute to sit and catch their breath before getting swept up in the family melee once more. "Yeah, we're good out here," they said with a smile.

Their mom nodded. "Okay, monsters," she said with a clap of her hands, getting the kids' attention. "We've got a million potatoes to scrub; let's go."

There were a few protests, but the pack obeyed, following Dex's mom back inside and leaving them in peace.

"In-*credible*," Mosscap said in a hush. It looked Charlotte up and down with unbridled astonishment. She continued to giggle, until the split second in which she didn't anymore, and instead began to kick and fuss. Mosscap became distraught. "What have I done?"

"Nothing," Dex said. "Babies just do that when they want something."

"What does she want?"

Dex watched the baby's pudgy feet flail against the air. "I think she wants to be put down."

Mosscap looked at Dex. "You don't know for sure?"

"Well, no, she can't tell me," Dex said. "You just have to guess."

"What happens if you get it wrong?"

"Then she'll cry, and we'll try something else."

With devoted concentration, Mosscap crouched down and began to lower Charlotte toward the deck, feet first.

"Oh, no," Dex said, holding out a halting hand. "She's too little to stand. You need to set her down on her belly, so that her hands are on the ground, too."

"Oh," Mosscap said. The robot adjusted the angle of its hands, lowering the baby down as though she were made of glass. It let go of her, ever so slowly.

At once, Charlotte stopped her fussing. With a happy coo, she began to scoot forward on all fours.

Mosscap laughed with surprise. "She's crawling!"

"Yeah," Dex said dryly, eyebrows raised with amusement. "They do that."

"*All* infant humans do this?"

"If they've got a typical body, then yeah."

Mosscap pointed at the baby. "Did *you* do this?"

"So I'm told."

"You don't remember?" Mosscap asked.

Dex laughed. "You might want to pick up a book on babies. We don't remember the first few years of our lives."

Mosscap stared at this. "Whyever not?"

"I . . ." Dex paused. "I don't know. Our brains just . . . don't save that stuff. I don't know if it's because they physically can't or . . . I dunno." They gestured at the house. "You should ask someone in there."

Mosscap continued to watch Charlotte crawl around the

deck, headed no direction in particular. "You don't *still* ambulate this way, right?"

One of Dex's eyebrows traveled higher. "Have you ever seen me *crawl,* Mosscap?"

"No," Mosscap said. "But could you?"

"Uh, yeah, I can crawl."

Mosscap looked at Dex with brightly glowing eyes. "Would you?"

"What, now? No."

The robot was a bit disappointed by this but did not press the issue. It sat down on the deck, watching the infant who apparently had places to be. "If what you say is true, then . . . she won't remember me. She won't remember this moment."

"I'm afraid not," Dex said. "But we'll tell her about it, when she's older."

A dejected note slipped into Mosscap's voice. "How very sad," it said. "This is already quite important to me."

"Here," Dex said, reaching into their pocket and retrieving their computer. "Pick her back up. I'll take a picture of you two so I can show her one day."

"Oh, what a good idea," Mosscap said. It began to reach toward Charlotte, then paused. "Does she *want* to be picked back up?"

"We'll find out," Dex said.

Charlotte, as it turned out, did not mind. She reached for Mosscap's face again, trying in vain to grab its glowing lenses.

"You'll make sure she gets a copy?" Mosscap confirmed,

unbothered by the grubby fingers slamming against its eyes. "So that when she starts making memories, she'll know we're already friends?"

Dex smiled. "Yeah," they said. They switched on the computer's camera and aimed. "I'll make sure."

•   •   •

The flower garden that all the houses shared contained four big wooden tables, and Dex had sat at them many a time on early harvest evenings such as these. Dex was accustomed to the tables being stuffed to capacity with both food and people, as was the case then. What Dex *wasn't* used to was a single topic of conversation, and to find themself at the center of it. It wasn't a bad thing, but it was weird, and Dex didn't quite know what to do with the spotlight. That wasn't their usual role there. They were no longer sure of their place.

Otherwise, dinner was about as perfect as could be. The air was warm enough to make jackets unnecessary, yet still held an end-of-day crispness that made breathing easy. The food, as always, was tremendous. Nothing had been butchered recently, so everything on the table came from the ground or the trees, resulting in a leafy, juicy, seed-filled spread as colorful as any painter's palette. Dex showed the family their trick of doling out a portion of food for Mosscap, then claiming it for themself as seconds. This satisfied everyone—particularly Dex's parents, who couldn't abide the idea of a guest with an empty plate.

Once the peak of the meal had passed, Mosscap got to work, moving from table to table and chair to chair, asking its question of everyone. The robot had gotten in the habit of logging people's answers into its pocket computer, and it did just that, listening seriously and typing eagerly, looking for all the world like a reporter on the beat.

Dex knew from experience that Mosscap didn't need their help once it got in this groove, and as soon as they were done eating, they felt the need for a moment in their more customary place on the edge of the action. They grabbed two bottles of beer from the ice-filled bucket, then moseyed toward someone else who shared their penchant for the periphery: their dad. They found him in a characteristic pose, leaning his forearms against the railing, hands clasped together as he watched fireflies bob in the twilight.

"Want another?" Dex asked, raising one of the bottles.

"Only if you join me," their dad said. He accepted the drink, clinked it against Dex's, then resumed his post, draping an arm around Dex's shoulders with affectionate ease. The two of them sipped and said nothing, and were very comfortable in that arrangement.

"You fixed the fence," said Dex after a while.

"Yeah," their dad said. "Me and Jasper took care of it a few weeks ago. Not so much of an eyesore now, huh?"

"Yeah, looks good," Dex said.

Their dad took a sip of the beer and sighed appreciatively. "Glad you could make some time for us," he said. "I know this thing you're doing is a lot."

"Well, of course," Dex said. "As if I'd let everybody but you meet Mosscap."

"I don't care about meeting the robot, goofball," their dad said. He reconsidered. "I mean, I *do* care about meeting the robot, but I'm just happy you're home."

The robot in question made its way over a short while later, putting its pocket computer in its satchel to signal that it was done with that part of its night. "Am I interrupting?" Mosscap asked, stopping a few feet away.

"Not at all," Dex's dad said. "Though I can't offer *you* a beer, huh?"

"You could," Mosscap said. "But I couldn't make use of it."

"Can't imagine it'd be good for your insides."

"Oh, my insides wouldn't care." Mosscap sat down, laying claim to a wicker chair. "I'm waterproof."

"Really?" Dex's dad raised his eyebrows with amusement. "That must come in handy."

Mosscap's lenses contracted, and it burst out laughing.

"What?" said Dex.

The robot pointed with glee. "You do the same thing," it said to Dex. "With your eyebrows. You look exactly the same when you do that. Ha!" It clasped its hands together before its chest. "Genetics are such a *delight*."

Dex and their dad glanced at each other and started laughing as well. "I've always told them I have delightful genes," their dad joked, gesturing at Dex with his bottle. "Nice to finally have someone around here who appreciates that." He looked between them both and smiled warmly, shaking his head. "It really is incredible that you ran into each other." He took another sip and looked at Dex. "Were you camping out in the Borderlands, or what?"

As a rule, Dex didn't like lying. They didn't imagine that anyone did, aside from a rare few who needed some help, but much as they knew that it would leave a bad taste in their mouth, they nonetheless slid easily into something untrue. "Yeah," Dex said, turning toward the field. "Yeah, just needed to get off the highway for a couple nights, take a break."

Mosscap's lenses shifted at this.

Dex's dad, a man who valued the occasional night alone in a tent, nodded with understanding. "I've had neighbors ask the craziest shit about you," he said. "People think you were all the way out in the Antlers, or whatever." He laughed. "It's weird, kiddo, hearing rumors around the market about *you*."

Dex could feel Mosscap staring at them, asking a silent question. They ignored it. "Yeah, well, you know how people talk." They shrugged and sipped their beer with nonchalance.

Dex's dad took a swig as well, then turned his attention to Mosscap. "So! On to the City tomorrow?"

"That is the plan," Mosscap said.

"Is it true they're throwing a parade?" Dex's dad asked.

"Uh," Dex said slowly, "not to my knowledge." Gods around, they weren't *really*, were they?

"Hmm. I heard talk that they were, but . . . I mean, who knows?" Their dad shrugged and looked back to Mosscap. "So, after that, then what?"

Mosscap cocked its head. "Sorry?"

Dex could tell that Mosscap had been caught off guard by the question, but his father took it to mean that Mosscap hadn't heard him. "After the City, then what?" he repeated politely. He nodded toward Dex. "Will they lead you back home, or will you go on your own?"

"Oh." Mosscap paused. "We . . . we hadn't discussed, actually."

"I figured we'd play it by ear," Dex said, picking at the label on their bottle with their thumbnail. "I don't know how long we'll be there, so . . ." They trailed off.

"When was the last time you were in the City?" their dad asked.

"Uh . . ." Dex said, trying to remember. "About a year ago."

"You planning to meet up with any friends?"

"I don't know," Dex said. "I'm sure I'll see people around, but we're so busy, y'know?"

"Will you do tea while you're there?"

Another question Dex didn't want to answer, but this one, they could dodge honestly. "No, I haven't done tea since"— Dex gestured at Mosscap—"since we met."

Their dad blinked with mild surprise. "Not at all? I figured you'd set up wherever you two stopped."

"No, we, uh . . . like I said. We've been busy." Dex took another sip and continued to focus on the fireflies.

To Dex's surprise, Mosscap seized the opportunity to quickly step in. "Sibling Dex has been a wonderful guide," the robot said. "They spend a great deal of time teaching me how everything in your society works. There's so much I didn't understand. So much I *still* don't understand. I don't know how I would have done any of this without them."

Dex's dad looked at them with all the love and warmth in the world. He reached over and ruffled their hair vigorously, like he used to do when Dex was little.

"Ugh, stop," Dex said with a shy grin.

"It's an amazing thing you're doing," their dad said seriously. "We're really proud of you." He gestured with his bottle at Mosscap. "And that reminds me. I've got a question for you."

"Of course, Mr. Theo," Mosscap said. "Anything you'd like to ask."

Dex's dad studied the robot with a contemplative look. "I'd like to ask you *your* question," he said.

Mosscap's lenses opened and closed, once. "What do you mean?"

"What do robots need?" Dex's dad asked. The robot before him fell silent, so he expanded on the thought. "We—my family, I mean—we have everything we could possibly want here. It's a good life. We need nothing, as I told you. But being a good neighbor is all about making sure that the people you share land and air and water with don't need anything either. So . . . what do your people need? Are you doing okay?"

"We're not people," Mosscap said, "but . . ." It was clearly at a loss, and stared off at nothing. "I . . . I haven't considered this before. Yes, we're . . . we're doing just fine. Materially, we don't require anything beyond a full battery, and we can provide that for ourselves. We have sufficient components to continue building new generations, for a time."

"For a time?" Dex's dad repeated. "How much time?"

"I don't know," Mosscap said.

Dex's dad frowned. "What happens when you run out of stuff to rebuild with?"

"Then we go extinct, so to speak," Mosscap said. "Just as everything does. Just as humans will, one day. No other living thing knows when their line will come to an end, so we haven't bothered to calculate it either. That would do more harm than good, I think."

This answer clearly surprised Dex's dad, who had the same thrown-off look most people did whenever Mosscap made comments of that sort. "So . . ." He took a moment to reestablish his conversational footing. "You have all your basics. Just like we have here."

"In essence, yes."

"Well, that's good to hear," Dex's dad said. "But you keep asking *us* the question, even though you know *our* basics are covered. So, then: what do *you* need, Mosscap? You, personally."

Dex watched as Mosscap struggled to answer this, its head whirring as loudly as a kicked hive. "This is going to sound foolish, I'm sure, but I hadn't thought to consider it before," Mosscap said. "I . . . I don't have an answer for that. I'm sorry, but I don't know."

Dex's dad shrugged, not fussed either way. "Well, if you do, at some point, I'd love to know what it is," he said amicably. "But I'm glad you're all okay out there." He sipped his beer and leaned once more against the railing, resuming his contented repose.

Dex tried to do the same. They made it look as though they had, behaving no outwardly different than before. But inside, something began to coil around itself. Despite how much they loved the good man standing beside them, part of them wished they were back on the road.

6

The Detour

This should have been the easy part. It was a straight shot from the Shrubland villages to the City, and the road between was smooth as could be. There were no big hills, no rough spots, no need to camp along the way. Just a half day's ride from here to there, and at the end, they'd find all the delights that had drawn Dex to the City in the first place: restaurants, museums, art galleries, rooftop patios and vertical forests, farms built underground, gardens that nearly touched the clouds, artwork painted on buildings, buildings that were artwork in their own right, music and theater and spectacle and light and ideas and color and walkable streets that were never, ever the same twice, no matter how often your feet followed them. Mosscap would love the City, Dex knew. There were dozens of places they were excited to share with it. And much as their schedule was starting to make Dex sweat, it *was* important for Mosscap to visit the University, the libraries, the monasteries—everywhere that served as a nesting ground for people whose whole lives revolved around understanding the past or shaping the future. The City was the center of

Panga's nervous system, the locus where every thread that ran through the world braided together. Mosscap had come out of the wilderness to ask questions. There was no better place for that purpose than this.

And yet: every push of the ox-bike's pedals felt as difficult as it had been out in the wilds, slogging up the oil road. It wasn't a matter of physical exhaustion. Dex was well-rested, well-fed, fit as could be. But as their body moved forward, everything within tugged back, and the longer the morning went on, the more frenzied that silent fight became.

Mosscap was uncharacteristically silent alongside them, and Dex had no desire to make small talk. The air between them was heavy enough as it was, thick with bugs and things unsaid. The feeling became denser as they headed onward, and Dex couldn't stand its weight any more than they knew how to break it.

It was the robot, in the end, who knocked the wall down. Mosscap stopped in the middle of the road, standing in the sunny space between two wildlife corridors that arched over the creamy pavement. "Sibling Dex, I am wondering if there are any sandy beaches around here," it blurted out. "It occurs to me that given the time of year, we're in the thick of marblehead laying season, and it's something I've never seen, and I know that particular species of turtle is endemic to this part of Panga, and . . . I . . . I was just wondering."

Dex stopped the bike, put their feet down, and looked back. They and Mosscap stared at each other from their short distance apart, eye to eye, unwavering. "Do you mean . . . you wanna go now?" Dex said slowly.

"I . . ." Mosscap fidgeted with the strap of its satchel, its many belongings clattering against one another. "The turtles only come out during a full planetrise, and that *is* today, so I . . . I know we are meant to arrive in the City this afternoon, but I wonder if it would make that much difference if we were a day late." It fixed the buckle on the satchel's strap, which did not need fixing.

Dex thought, and thought some more. This was stupid, but all the same, an unshakable want arose in them, the same sort of nameless, senseless, rebellious magnetism that had made them turn off the highway into the wilds months before. Smacking down everything within themself that began to argue, they walked the bike around, turning the wagon in the opposite direction. "It's about six miles to Cloud Beach," they said. "People go there every year to watch the turtles. There's a little festival around it—no music, obviously, but people bring food, and there's lots of kids, and—"

"I was thinking—I was thinking somewhere more private," Mosscap said. The satchel strap had transformed into a helix in its hands. "You know how it is; sometimes you just want to have a moment between yourself and a turtle and no one else." Its eyes were wide and piercingly bright. "I don't think I want to see any people today, Sibling Dex. Other than yourself, I mean."

Mosscap stared down at the road, and Dex looked away,

not wanting to make the robot more uncomfortable. They continued to think. "I know a spot," they said at last. "I haven't been there in forever, and it's hard to get to, and I can't promise no one will be there, but . . ." They looked back. "It'll be a longer ride."

This last comment was a question; Mosscap nodded in assent. "I don't mind, if you don't," it said.

"Okay," Dex said. They got back on their bike. "Okay. Let's go."

· · · ·

The spot Dex knew had no name. The road leading to it was unmarked and in poor repair, barely extant the farther they went along. It was the sort of place you went when you were a teenager in possession of a bottle of wine you shouldn't have and a few friends who would all share your regret about varied decisions by morning. Brambles stretched untrimmed into the space Dex rode through, scratching their arms and snapping in the wagon's wake. Once they passed through this unpleasant barrier, there was, as Mosscap had requested, a beach. It wasn't anything special, as far as beaches went. It was small, forgettable, littered with old seaweed and abandoned shells. The beach wasn't dirty, but neither was it overly scenic. It was a place where land met water. That was about all that could be said about it.

Mosscap observed the area as Dex brought the wagon to

a halt. "Yes," it said with relief, watching the waves push and pull. "Yes, this is perfect."

Together, they coaxed the wagon out onto the sand until they came to a stopping point as good as any other. Without a word, they began to make camp, just as they'd done countless times before. Dex locked down everything with wheels, Mosscap unfolded the kitchen on the wagon's exterior, Dex fetched chairs, Mosscap started the fire. Or, then again, Mosscap *started* to start the fire but froze midway through. The robot stood unmoving in front of the fire drum, the line to the biogas tank dangling unconnected in its hand.

"What's wrong?" Dex asked.

Mosscap looked at them. "I want to build a wood fire," it said. "I don't want to use this."

"Why not?"

"I just . . . I just don't!" Mosscap sounded frustrated, petulant, more like the kids back at the farm than like itself.

Dex stuck their hands in their pockets. "We don't have any firewood," they said.

Mosscap gestured broadly at the beach around them. "There must be driftwood," it said. "Or fallen branches near the cliffs."

Dex shrugged. "Okay," they said. "Let's go find some wood."

And so, several hours passed as Dex and Mosscap combed the shoreline for things that would burn, wandering back and forth in no particular rush. They both stopped to watch a crab that had been hiding beneath a shard of driftwood, and apologized for the disturbance as it scuttled off with offended haste. Mosscap found a glistening harp snail shell in perfect condition but left it behind rather than take it into its satchel where nothing could make it into a home.

By evening, they'd assembled a huge stockpile of kindling, far more than they would need. The wagon's pantry was stuffed to the brim with the bounty of Dex's family's farm, and they chose the evening's delicacies with care as Mosscap happily arranged sticks into a combustible cone.

"We have so much more than we need," Mosscap said as it stacked. "It seems silly, to burn all of this at once."

Dex nodded as they chopped vegetables into chunks destined for skewering. "So, just make a normal fire," they said. "We can use the leftovers tomorrow."

Before this moment, there had been no mention between them of what tomorrow might bring. Dex added nothing further to their comment, and Mosscap merely nodded as though this had always been the plan. An agreement was reached, without any of it being discussed.

Once the fire had caught, Dex brought over the skewers of vegetables and some of the grass-hen sausages their mom had made. They taught Mosscap how to roast these without a grill, and savored both portions as the stars came out.

No turtles made an appearance. Neither Mosscap nor Dex minded in the slightest.

The next day, Dex went for a swim. Mosscap took to the water as well, sitting on the sandy seafloor a good ten feet down so that it might spend some quality time with the sting-rays and the crabs. Dex baked in the sun afterward, drifting in and out of consciousness without much preference for one state or the other. They didn't know where Mosscap went as they dozed, but it returned by evening to build another fire and roast more sausages and poke at embers until they went black.

The third day, Dex remembered they owned a kite. It was shoved into the depths of one of their many cupboards, ob-tained on a whim one year and forgotten in a matter of days. They showed Mosscap how to fly it, and together they figured out where the invisible currents flowed above them. The steady wind trickled into a useless breeze by midafternoon, at which point they went tide-pooling instead, marveling at sea slugs and letting anemones hug their respective fingers.

The fourth day, Mosscap repeatedly guffawed at a book it was reading, and Dex asked what was so funny enough times that Mosscap just started over and read the whole thing aloud by Dex's side as they walked or sat or lay in the sand. Satire wasn't usually Dex's thing, but they laughed, too, and enjoyed the story very much by the end.

At the end of the day, Mosscap built another fire. "This is the last of the wood," it said.

Dex paused at this, their knife hovering above a half-chopped carrot. "Oh," they said. "Right."

Neither spoke after that. They set their chairs by the fire and cooked the food as the conversation neither wanted to have dangled over them. Dex ate, and Mosscap sat, and they watched the sun begin to set. There was nothing else to be done.

"Do you wanna go first?" Dex asked.

Mosscap said nothing for a while. "Why did you lie to your father?" it said at last.

Dex shut their eyes and let out every breath they'd taken that day. "I don't see how *that's* what we should talk about right now."

"It's what *I* want to talk about, and you asked."

"I did." In truth, Dex was surprised Mosscap hadn't raised the question sooner. "I . . . I didn't want him—or any of them—to worry about me."

"Why would they worry?" Mosscap said. "They can see you're safe now, so why worry about something that has already passed?"

"They would worry if I told them why I was out there." Dex shifted uncomfortably. "Some things are private," they said.

"Yes, but . . ." Mosscap's head whirred. "You tell *me* things that trouble you, and I've only known you a few months. You're of a social species, and this is your family group. I understand such dynamics can be complicated, but there doesn't seem to be any animosity between you and them. They talk about their problems with you; why don't you do the same?"

"I just . . ." Dex sighed. "They worry enough—about me traveling alone, about everything that goes on at home. You saw how it is there; there's always *something* going on. If I'm an element of their lives that they can just feel good about, without any complicated bullshit attached, I'd like to keep it that way."

"But then what are they to you?" Mosscap said. "That doesn't strike me as reciprocal." The robot shook its head. "I'm not saying you have to confide in *these people,* specifically, but I haven't seen anyone that you *do* open up to, other than me."

"I'm open when I make tea," Dex said. "If people talk to me about their stuff, I might share some of my stuff. That way they know we're not so different."

"That's not the same at all. That's still under the guise of you providing something for them."

"Yes, but I get something out of it too. Tea service is really intimate. It wouldn't be the same if I was just mixing up blends at home and mailing them off. Seeing people, talking with them, feeling that give-and-take—that's important to me. It really is."

"Yet you don't want to do tea service anymore," Mosscap said.

"I didn't say that."

"Everything about the way you've conducted yourself in our travels says that. You don't want to do it, but you feel like you should. Am I wrong?"

Dex rubbed the bridge of their nose. "No," they said.

"When was the last time you really *enjoyed* tea service, Sibling Dex?"

The sun had sunk to a bare sliver above the horizon, and

Dex stared at it as closely as they dared. "When you made it for me," they said quietly. "At the hermitage. It made me feel . . . like I wanted to make other people feel. It felt like the reason I wanted to do this in the first place." They clasped their hands together between their knees and focused on them. "Do you remember what you said when we were there, about how nothing needs a purpose? How all living things are allowed to just *exist,* and we don't have to do more than that?"

Mosscap nodded. "I do, yes."

Dex pressed their lips together. "That's the heart of my faith, Mosscap. That is what I am saying to everyone who comes to my table. I say it out loud, all the fucking time. You don't have to have a reason to be tired. You don't have to *earn* rest or comfort. You're allowed to just *be*. I say that wherever I go." They threw a hand toward their wagon, its wooden sides emblazoned with the summer bear. "It's painted on the side of my home! But I don't feel like it's true, for me. I feel like it's true for everyone else but *not me*. I feel like I have to do more than that. Like I have a *responsibility* to do more than that."

"Why?" Mosscap said.

"Because I'm good at something," Dex said. "I'm good at something that helps other people. I worked really hard to be able to do it, and I benefited from the labor and love of others while I did so. I'm able to do what I do because everybody else built a world in which I could do it. If I just say 'Thanks for all of that, but I'm running off to the woods now,' how is that fair? That doesn't sit right with me, not at all. I'd just be a leech if I did that."

Mosscap looked confused. "What's wrong with being a leech?"

"You know what I mean," said Dex.

"I don't," said Mosscap.

Dex sighed. "A leech is a person who takes without giving back. It's a metaphor."

Mosscap considered that. "I don't think it's very kind to use an entire subclass of animal as a metaphor for behavior that you deem unseemly."

Dex threw up their hands. "Well, we do it, all the time."

"And it's not even an *accurate* metaphor," Mosscap went on. "You're basing that shorthand off of the human relationship to leeches, not the entire experience of being a leech. They're as vital a part of their ecosystem as anything else."

"Gods around." Dex rubbed their face with their palms.

"Would you use the term *parasite* in the same metaphorical manner?"

"Yes!" Dex exclaimed. "I would!"

Mosscap gave Dex a reproachful look. "All parasites have value, Sibling Dex. Not to their hosts, perhaps, but you could say the same about a predator and a prey animal. They all *give back*—not to the individual but to the ecosystem at large. Wasps are tremendously important pollinators. Birds and fish eat bloodsucks."

"This is making my head hurt," Dex said. "And also, none of this has anything to do with what I'm saying. I'm talking about the relationship between *me* and *other people*, not a fish and a bloodsuck."

"It's your metaphor," Mosscap said.

"Well, I'm never going to use it again." Dex picked up a stick and poked at the fire irritably.

Mosscap let the matter go, and it picked up a stick, too. "You're not alone in this, you know," it said, nudging bark off of glowing wood. "'Purpose' is one of the most common answers I get to my question." It lowered its gaze and sighed. "I'm beginning to worry that you were right, you know."

"About what?"

"About my question. You said when we first met that you thought it was impossible to answer."

"I still do," Dex said.

Mosscap looked seriously at them. "Then why do you come with me?"

"I'm not with you for the *question*," Dex scoffed.

The robot took that in as it played with the fire. "When I first volunteered to make contact, we all thought this was a very good question. We wanted to know if you'd done all right in the time since robots left your society. We knew you'd *improved*, certainly. You were on the brink of collapse when we left, and obviously that hasn't happened. Your villages have a glow at night—we can see them, if we're in the Borderlands. And the satellites, of course. Those wouldn't stay up without your help. We knew you were still *here*. We knew things were better. I never saw it for myself, but I know the previous generations watched the rivers clear up. They saw the trees grow back. My kind witnessed the world heal itself, but we didn't know how well *you* had healed. Nobody was sure what I'd find out here, least of all me. So, you see, it was a very sensible introductory question. What is it that you need?"

"You thought it might be something basic," Dex said. "Like . . . we need food. Or living space. Better technology. Something like that."

"Possibly, yes. But I've been nowhere with you where those needs aren't provided for. And when people interpret my question beyond the things you require to stay alive and healthy, it gets . . ."

"Complicated?"

Mosscap nodded, looking exhausted. "Every answer I've received falls into one of two categories. Every single one." The robot gestured emphatically with its metal fingers. "The first category is extremely specific things. 'I need my bicycle fixed so I can deliver these goods to another village.' 'We need to prepare better for the next time the river floods.' 'I need to find my dog.' Things like that. Either a very personal, individual need or a broader need within the community, but all in all, specific and isolated."

"Okay. And the second category?"

"The second category is esoteric. Philosophical. I get answers such as 'purpose,' or 'adventure,' or 'companionship.' A broad requirement the person has in regards to feeling satisfaction with their life. Some people lack whatever it is and are searching for it, but others already *have* it. They interpret the question as me asking what aspects of their lives they would not want to do without, not as an *unmet* need. And I hadn't considered this, at the start. Must a need be *unmet* if it is to satisfy my question?"

Dex exhaled and shook their head. "You tell me, Mosscap," they said. "I have no fucking idea."

"Neither do I, and that's just it. I thought this was the most bothersome thing on my mind until I spoke with your father the other night and he asked me what *I* need." Mosscap dropped the stick and turned to face them. "Sibling Dex, *I don't know*. I don't know at *all*. So, what am I supposed to do now? How am I to ask my question of others when I can't answer it for myself?"

Dex listened to this complaint, and as they processed it, a slow, wry, not-at-all-funny smile spread across their face. "How am I supposed to tell people they're good enough as they are when I don't think I am?" they said.

Mosscap responded with a single heavy nod. "You see," it said. "You understand. I wish you didn't, because I know it means you're as tangled up as I am, but . . . I'm grateful that you do."

"Is that why you didn't want to go to the City?" Dex asked. "Because you're not sure about your question?"

"No," the robot said after a moment.

"Is it because there's too much going on there?" Dex asked. "We can cancel stuff, no problem. I'd love to, honestly—"

"No, that's not it," Mosscap said. "I didn't—I *don't* want to go to the City. I don't want to go to the City, because the City is the end."

Mosscap didn't need to explain what it meant; Dex under-

stood. The end of their travels. The end of their companionship, maybe. They hadn't discussed what they wanted to do
after the City, but therein lay the problem. It was a question
mark, an empty space. It wasn't the only thing that had made
Dex about-face on the road, but it was the one they hadn't
known how to voice. Not until now.

"We don't have to split up," Dex said softly. "We don't
have to go anywhere we don't want to go, do anything we
don't want to do." Their brow furrowed. "You are the weird-
est, most inexplicable thing that's ever happened to me. You
make me crazy, most days. You say so much shit I don't understand." Their voice cracked, and grew almost inaudibly
quiet. "But whatever it is we're doing, it's the first thing in a
long time I've been sure about." They swallowed. "Most days,
you're the only thing that makes sense."

Mosscap did nothing but nod several times, in fervent
agreement. "So, what do we do?" it said. "Do we go to the
City? Do we go back to the wilds? Do we . . ." It waved its
hands emptily.

"I don't know." Dex's fingers found their pendant, and
they held the symbol of their god hard. "You know, *I* never
answered your question."

"Yes, you have. I ask you all the time what it is that you
need."

"Yeah, but you ask about everyday stuff. I never answered
it the first time you asked. Remember?" Dex would never
forget. "You walked out of the woods, and you said, 'What
do you need, and how can I help?'"

Mosscap smiled at this. "I remember, yes."

"Well, I didn't know then," Dex said, "and I still don't. But what I do know is . . . you help. You're helping me figure it out. Just by being here. You help."

"Then we have the same answer," Mosscap said. "I don't know either. But you are my best help, Sibling Dex." It looked at the fire built of the last of the driftwood, dying more quickly than the ones that had come before. "What if that is enough, for now? What if we're both trying to answer something much too big before we've answered the small thing we should have started with? What if it's enough to just be . . ."

Us, Dex knew Mosscap meant, though the robot didn't finish. "Then we tackle the rest when we're ready," they said. "However long that takes."

Mosscap started to say more, but its attention was captured by something else. "Look!" it cried, pointing toward the sea.

Dex looked. The last of the day's light had faded, rendering the water an inky void. There was no dividing line between ocean and sky any longer, no horizon separating here from there. Motan's stripes still hung in their comforting curve, and stars were waking by the handful, but at first, all Dex saw below these cosmic constants was emptiness.

Their eyes adjusted, and as they did, color and shape appeared. A gentle wave broke, and would have been invisible, were it not for the blue glow that blossomed in the crest, a vibrant splash winking in and out, quick as breath.

Dex and Mosscap each leaned forward, eyes fixed on the shore. Another wave came, right on cue, and with it, another burst of blue.

"I've heard of this," Mosscap said in a hush, "but I've never seen it for myself."

"Same," Dex said. They stood up. "Come on."

The two hurried down to the water. The sand beneath Dex's bare feet became wetter with every step, squishing up around their soles. The edge of a wave ran over their toes, caressing them with a liquid hello. Dex looked down and saw a blue swirl outlining their feet like ink in the process of being spilled.

"It's bacteria, right?" Dex said. "Or plankton, or something?"

"Phytoplankton, yes," Mosscap said. "Tiny little not-quite-plants." The robot bent itself in half, bringing its face close to the water. "And aren't they beautiful." It reached out its hand, making contact with things too small to be seen alone.

Dex crouched down and did as Mosscap was doing, tracing their fingers on the surface and summoning light in their wake. As they did so, a more spirited wave snuck in and splashed its way up Dex's trousers. "*Agh,*" Dex said, taking a few hurried steps in retreat.

Mosscap looked over. Its eyes glowed in the dark, a different shade of blue. "Should we go back?" it asked.

"Not a chance," Dex said. They did what they should've done at the start and stripped their clothes off, piece by piece.

They left their garments in a heap on the sand a safe distance from the water, then turned and ran full tilt into the waves, whooping like a little kid. They gasped as the water crashed into their naked body, cool and enveloping, spraying salt in their mouth and filling the world with light.

Mosscap ran after them, laughing in harmony. There was nothing more that could be said in words. There was only shouting, cheering, cries of delight as the two of them jumped and played and marveled at the spectacle that would've existed whether anyone was there to witness it or not.

ACKNOWLEDGMENTS

What a difference a year makes.

I finished *A Psalm for the Wild-Built* just before lockdown started; *A Prayer for the Crown-Shy* was handed in three months before I was eligible for my first jab. To say that getting these books done was a challenge is a massive understatement, and I couldn't have done it without help.

Thanks to Lee Harris, Irene Gallo, Caroline Perny, and the entire team at Tordotcom for being such a powerhouse of support. Thanks to my agent, Seth Fishman, for always having my back and making sense of the messy details. Thanks to Feifei Ruan for the cover art that continues to make me swoon.

Thanks to Susana Polo for being there for whatever bullshit I'm currently on. Thanks to Greg LeClair for existing. Thanks to Rollin Bishop, Kate Cox, and Alex Raymond for the story that got us all through it, and for helping me remember how to write. Thanks to the Waymoot for being such wonderful, wonderful humans. Thanks to my family and my friends for loving me even when I'm all over the place. Thanks to my wife, Berglaug, for being so indescribably easy to love back.

ABOUT THE AUTHOR

BECKY CHAMBERS is a science fiction author based in Northern California. She is best known for her Hugo Award–winning Wayfarers series. Her books have also been nominated for the Arthur C. Clarke Award, the Locus Award, and the Women's Prize for Fiction, among others.

Chambers has a background in performing arts, and grew up in a family heavily involved in space science. She spends her free time playing video and tabletop games, keeping bees, and looking through her telescope. Having hopped around the world a bit, she's now back in her home state, where she lives with her wife. She hopes to see Earth from orbit one day.